Diving
for
Pearls

JAMIE O'CONNELL

doubleday
IRELAND

TRANSWORLD IRELAND
Penguin Random House Ireland,
Morrison Chambers, 32 Nassau Street, Dublin 2, Ireland
www.transworldireland.ie

Transworld Ireland is part of the Penguin Random House group of companies
whose addresses can be found at global.penguinrandomhouse.com

Penguin
Random House
UK

First published in the UK and Ireland in 2021
by Doubleday Ireland
an imprint of Transworld Publishers

A CIP catalogue record for this book
is available from the British Library.

ISBN 9781781620557 (tpb)

Typeset in 12.6/16.27 pt Dante MT by Jouve (UK), Milton Keynes
Printed and bound in Great Britain by Clays Ltd, Elcograf S.p.A.

The authorized representative in the EEA is Penguin Random House Ireland,
Morrison Chambers, 32 Nassau Street, Dublin D02 YH68.

Penguin Random House is committed to a sustainable
future for our business, our readers and our planet. This book
is made from Forest Stewardship Council® certified paper.

To John Hallissey

'Perhaps she would not have thought that evil
was a state so rare, so extraordinary, so disorienting,
and to which it was so restful to emigrate, if she had
been able to discern in herself, as in everyone else, that
indifference to the suffering one causes which,
whatever other names one gives it, is the most terrible
and lasting form assumed by cruelty.'

Marcel Proust, *In Search of Lost Time*

Prologue

White. Two purring engines. Six round windows on each side. It flies, a sleek machine slicing through currents and gusts. A movie star inches down his Ray-Bans and looks out at the cloudless sky. 'Beautiful,' he says.

'It only rains every couple of years,' his companion replies, fixing his white robes. 'Keep your eyes on the horizon. You cannot miss it.'

For some minutes, all the star sees are straight lines cutting across sand. Where do all those endless motorways go? His neck aches from the journey. A flight attendant asks if he'd like something to drink. 'My usual,' he replies, stretching out across the soft leather. Celery and cucumber juice with a dash of lemon in a Riedel glass.

'Thirty minutes to landing,' the captain's voice announces over the intercom.

'Can I get you a hot towel?' The attendant returns. 'Would you like the masseuse?'

The star laughs, benevolent as a king, shaking his head and thanking the young woman anyway. He goes to the bathroom and checks his appearance in the mirror, splashing his face with water from the gold taps. A light tan hides the fatigue of flying. Drops make the whites of his eyes gleam, the irises like emeralds. And those teeth. The famous smile. He picks up the mouthwash.

The weight under his feet shifts. The plane begins its descent. He opens the door and makes his way back to his recliner, waiting for the skyline to appear.

Some miles below, Hiyam Husayin floats past rows of white yachts, out into Dubai Marina. Arms outstretched, she appears dazzled by the brilliance of the city. Lining the docks are beautiful skyscrapers, finished with white and blue-grey Carrara marble and studded everywhere with sparkling glass and steel. The window panes, sheets of tinted blue glass, are tinged green as they reflect the sun's gold rays.

Above the marina, a monumental bridge supports a motorway. The sound of cars echoes down over the crystalline water: Ferraris, Porsches, Jaguars and Lamborghinis. Suited men on phones flag RTAs to Media City, tourists seek Atlantis on The Palm, and women jog with their personal trainers. None of them seems to have noticed the woman floating below.

At the marina's edge there are many people – men, women and children – walking about, eating outside cafés, all dressed in a variety of sandals, flip-flops, shorts, burqas and string vests. Someone points out into the water and others follow his gaze. A young woman screams. Meanwhile Hiyam continues to bob, her clothes floating outwards. Children run away and hide behind their mothers as her blood furls and pools.

A line appears on the horizon, a tapering needle that quivers, over twice the height of other towers that nestle around it. Beyond them, desert.

'It's nearly as high as we are.' The film star smiles. He

attempts to appear calm. Will those ropes be strong enough to hold him? One knot slips and . . . it doesn't bear thinking about.

'Too late to say no now.' The other man laughs a little. 'Don't worry. We have taken every precaution.' He touches his keffiyeh and seems satisfied.

The needle grows closer, the base fleshing out – a series of rising cylinders that stagger into the final point. It gleams in the morning sun, elegant, an architectural poem, uncluttered, balanced. A jewel at the centre of a crown.

'Impressive,' the film star says.

'Higher than your Empire State.'

The film star gives his signature smile – the flash of white teeth – but doesn't say a word.

Outside the city, a television presenter grabs a handful of sand and talks into a camera. His suit is immaculate, possibly Tom Ford. He speaks in a series of clichés and tosses the handful aside.

'Fantasy became reality. In the space of just twenty years, Dubai turned from desert into a jaw-dropping oasis of stone, marble, concrete, glass and raw excitement. And now this – a crowning moment. An international mega-star is to conquer the world's tallest building.'

And with that, the camera rises up above him, panning over the city.

Somewhere in the distance, there is the sound of police cars. Crowds are forming on the walkway of the marina, gazing at the body of Hiyam, raising their phones. She looks insignificant through a lens. Her bobbing elbow could be the fin of a dolphin. It wouldn't take much for her to vanish altogether.

A mother tells her maid to move her son away from the barrier – too grim a sight for a nine-year-old's eyes. But he doesn't want to go. Who is the woman floating? Why is she dead? The woman ignores his questions, promising ice cream and possibly a toy if he'll just come away from the water's edge.

'Look,' a person shouts. Not far from Hiyam's body, a bag floats upside down. Louis Vuitton, Autumn 2010 collection. Somewhere at the bottom of the marina lie MAC liquid eyeliner, sugar-free gum, Dior Demoiselle 2 sunglasses in twilight green and storm blue, an iPhone 4 with a Swarovski crystal case, a black hijab and three condoms.

Inside the airport, people gather by the glass. A girl glances at her watch. 'He's late.'

'Patience, darling. It's only ten minutes.'

'Will he wave?'

'I'm sure he will, if he sees us.'

Maybe he will see them. Perhaps the star will give them a friendly raised hand, almost a high five. A bit of his lustre will rub off, leaving them with the afterglow of having come close, even for a moment, to something extraordinary.

Downtown, preparations have begun. Film crews bring in the large cases of equipment, filling the elevators, watching as the numbers on the dial rise, 138 . . . 139 . . . 140. Ears pop and, as they step into the lobbies, they can feel the slight sway of the colossal metal frame.

One of the workmen steps up to the glass and gazes down. The sun's rays shine on the mall below and its fountains glimmer. Gleaming candy is offered for sale, as well as gleaming shoes, gleaming hats, and gleaming clothes of all sorts. People wait in lines for cream-and-red RTAs.

Billboards announce the arrival of this star. In a few days' time, he is to ascend the Burj Khalifa, the highest man-made summit. He will conquer this tower of iron and glass, taunt death and climb higher still. People will inhale at the sight of his daring in a land of great feats. But he won't slip. This is now, this is Dubai, and nothing else matters.

Aasim

Aasim Husayin touches his wrist. TAG Heuer Monaco Calibre 12 Automatic Chronograph. Sounds like a gun. The balance of circles and squares. There is no doubting it. He owns *the* most beautiful watch in the world. He lifts it close to his face, examining the white lettering. Monaco. What a word. All it suggests.

The cream curtains glow in the autumn sunlight, reflecting off the watch's steel finish. Aasim tucks his cool arm back under the blanket and gazes sideways. David is asleep on his stomach and strands of his blond hair are caught in his stubble. His clothes lie beside the bed; they have a worn, washed-in-saltwater quality Aasim finds curious.

The sounds from Pearse Street are muffled, though he makes out the occasional revving of a Dublin Bus. David's eyebrows twitch. Sleeping is such a strange thing. All those hours that could be spent reading, shopping or meeting people; there has to be some drug or treatment that would solve the problem. He lifts the strands of hair off David's face. David's eyes open. He stretches and smiles.

'Morning. You sleep OK?'

Aasim nods.

'Breakfast in a bit?' David slips his arm under Aasim's neck.

'Yes, though I must go to the library.'

'Me too. Godard awaits.'

Aasim rests his head on David's chest, stroking the hairs, sensing the solid thuds of his heart, the flow of blood from the ventricles to the atria and out of the aorta. He thinks about the sinoatrial node pulsing. Is it normal, he wonders, that these things come into his head while he's naked in bed? But maybe all RCSI students have these kinds of thoughts.

'Your toes are freezing.' David shivers as Aasim tucks his feet around his calves. Aasim strokes David's boxers, tracing the line of flesh through the fabric, wondering if he'll slip his hand inside. 'I'm glad you're back. It's a pity about the new terminal being such a mess.'

'There were people everywhere. I'm sorry about dinner.' He'd spent their 'date night' stuck in Heathrow, his heart sinking as one by one all the flights into Dublin T2 got delayed, imagining David in the apartment, checking his phone, wondering if he should cancel L'Gueuleton.

'How was your brother?' David asks.

'No different.' Aasim gazes at the empty glass on the bedside table. His lunch with Mahmoud and Mama in the Kensington restaurant had been the same as all the others. All that talking without saying anything – it was hardly worth him flying over to London.

He'd gazed across the restaurant, watching happy families at other tables. A jazz singer sang 'Strange Fruit'.

'We don't often hear from you,' Mahmoud said. He looked like he was missing a night's sleep.

'Do you want to?'

'My boys, don't fight. Look. I bought you a present.' Mama

handed Aasim a TAG Heuer bag. 'A little late for your birthday, but still.' She kissed his cheek.

Mahmoud stood up. 'I must get to my meeting.' They watched him walk towards the exit.

'Your father couldn't do without him,' she said. Aasim frowned at the mention of Baba.

'Did you see the doctor?'

'Earlier. It was only antibiotics.'

'Did you confront Baba? How did he get it? Who was the girl?'

'No. Alhamdulillah. The new projects mean he works night and day. We must make allowances.' She adjusted her hijab and Aasim regretted asking so many questions. He didn't want to add to her unhappiness. 'So, Dublin is good?'

'Yes.'

'Hiyam showed me pictures of your friend David,' Mama added. Aasim was silent, wondering what his sister might've said, but there was no escaping the heat rising in his cheeks. 'Maybe I could visit next time. I would love to see where you live and meet your friends.'

'It's cold there,' Aasim said, his tone sharper than expected. Then he smiled and added, as playfully as he could, 'The shopping here is much better.'

Aasim gets up and steps into the bathroom, picking up his toothbrush. Should he tell David about Baba cheating? Maybe in time. He doesn't want others knowing and Mama humiliated. He would love to tell her to leave Baba. But if she did, where would she go? How would she live?

David appears behind; his lips press against Aasim's hair.

Aasim smiles. He has a boyfriend. The idea still catches him unawares.

'Is that what I think it is?' David touches the outline in his boxers. Aasim spits out his toothpaste. David's arms tighten around his waist, leading him back to the bedroom.

Afterwards, Aasim listens to the cars outside on the street. He glances sideways and listens to David's soft snores. He lifts his phone, looks at David again, before opening an app and scrolling through the male profiles, glancing at the messages he's received, blocking most of the guys. He thinks about Mama and Mahmoud returning to Dubai. Though it's less than two years ago, his old life there feels faint, like someone else's. He doesn't recognize that version of himself, how naive he was or how exposed he felt back home when there were conversations about raids of clubs and arrests of gay men. Of course, he's never heard of any men actually getting flogged or worse, but they might as well be dead. There was no returning to normal life afterwards.

Hiyam hadn't seemed to care when he'd got the offer from RCSI; she pretended she was listening but her fingers moved across her phone. Zulfa was cleaning the windows . . . was it Zulfa? He could never remember the maids after they got uniforms.

'But Ireland?' Hiyam had asked.

'It's not here,' he said. Sitting beside her, he opened his laptop and searched for Dublin. He looked for malls; St Stephen's Green was close to the college.

'Think of the parties you could have,' Hiyam sighed. 'Get somewhere big and I'll come visit.'

'Baba will never let you.'

'He won't mind. It doesn't matter how I behave, as long as I don't get caught.' She pulled her phone close. She had a sly look. Baba called her Cleopatra from that old film and joked she was 'too pretty to avoid trouble'. Mama said she would one day be the most beautiful woman in the Middle East.

'Doing nothing as usual?' Mahmoud appeared.

'Aasim got university in Ireland,' Hiyam said. Her phone vibrated.

'Good . . . Zulfa, I need lunch. Quickly now.'

Zulfa scurried away. All the maids were like frightened mice when Mahmoud was around. The sound of cutlery falling echoed in from the kitchen. Mahmoud rolled his eyes. He looked back at Aasim.

'At least now you'll be doing something useful and not just spending money.'

Aasim gets out of bed, putting on an Armani T-shirt. David yawns, slipping his feet on to the floor. Leaning against the desk, Aasim watches as David puts on Jo Malone rather than the Dolce & Gabbana aftershave that he brought him back from London. Trinity students are strange; boys wear dirty canvas shoes and skinny jeans, haircuts are scruffy, and bags are made of old leather. Why do they want to look poor?

They leave David's apartment, go through the main Trinity gates and walk up Dame Street, Aasim watching the yellow-and-blue buses slip by the college. Do people think he is Arab or Brazilian? Most of the time his skin doesn't seem to matter, but there were those couple of times when drunk people told him to fuck off home, reminding him that he was different.

David leads him up South William Street, the pavements full of people eating and smoking outside cafés. Passing by Lemon, Aasim waves at two girls drinking Americanos and smoking.

'Come here to me,' JodieB calls out. 'How was London, my Arabian dream? It's been weeks and I'm still in recovery from Halloween.'

'Epic.' Vicky laughs, taking a drag of her cigarette.

Aasim blushes. The cleaner has tried to get the stains out, but a wall in his apartment needs to be repainted. That dumb first-year and her red wine hour-of-power. He hasn't replaced the bed yet either.

He remembers kissing Vicky. It'd been JodieB's goading. 'Give him a kiss. He's a great score.' The music blaring. The guys pretending to be blown by Halloween masks. The room had stunk of cigarettes and poppers.

'I'm snedged,' Vicky had said, stretched out on the duvet. Aasim had pulled out a clear bag of three pills. Picking up a glass and fishing out a cigarette, he bit a pill in two. It tasted terrible. He'd slipped the other half into Vicky's mouth.

The bed leg had broken. The gang had slipped to one side, JodieB kissing some randomer, everyone's heads hanging over the edge. The gorgeous gilt mirror from Mama was covered in powder and fingerprints, and there was that one guy banging away on the bodhrán, off his tits:

There are nine million mickies in my gee,
That's a fact,
It's a thing I can't deny with . . . with a langer in my eye . . .
That's a fact.'

'You'd never think . . .' Vicky had said to him later that

night, blinking hard, trying to remain conscious. 'You were that shy thing a year ago.'

Aasim walks away from the café and waves back at the two girls. Vicky is mad. Still, she was right in what she said. Away from Dubai he can be himself, 'out' and having fun, without Mahmoud or that hypocrite Baba spying on him. What's wrong with enjoying himself? Life is for living.

'You think you'll meet the girls later?' David asks. Aasim can sense David doesn't really like Vicky; she's tolerated as his friend. If David knew how mad the parties were, the cute guys and the amount of drugs, there'd likely be more arguments. Yet, in the seven months since they first hooked up, they've never agreed to be exclusive. But maybe that's implied?

'I've too much study this week.' Aasim's cheeks feel warm.

'Cool.' David walks fast, stepping inside George's Street Arcade. Inside Simon's Place coffee shop, they sit beneath thick wooden rafters, the large space echoing with the low murmur of voices. The smell of fresh coffee is delicious.

'No word from Hiyam?' David asks. He glances at Aasim's phone. Aasim, with a blush, puts it away.

'No. I don't know why she didn't want to come to London with Mama. Who knows? She does what she likes.' Sometimes Aasim wants to talk to Hiyam openly about his life, but he can't imagine saying the words 'I have a boyfriend' to her. However, she'd almost caught them when she flew to Dublin unannounced in early September.

The buzzer had gone off twice. Aasim opened his eyes. They stung from cigarette smoke the night before. What time was it? He glanced at his watch. Ten a.m. What fool was calling to his place at this hour on a Saturday? Probably one of the hangers-on who'd come back after the bar, looking for their phone or jacket.

Another buzz.

'I'm coming, I'm coming,' Aasim called out, sitting up. Of course, they could hardly hear him on the ground floor. He rubbed his eyes. Fuck. His head.

'Who is it?' David asked, wincing at the light pouring in around the blinds, pulling the duvet back up. That was the problem with glass-walled apartments; it was impossible to keep out light.

'I've no idea.' Aasim stepped into the main living area. Lifting the receiver, glancing at the small black-and-white screen, he saw two figures at the door below. Hiyam and her silly friend Fadiyah. Neither of them was wearing a hijab.

What were they doing here? He put down the receiver and ran back to the bedroom.

'Get up, get up.'

David looked confused. Aasim dragged the covers back. 'Fucking Hiyam is downstairs.'

'What?'

'Come on.'

The buzzer began a third time. The noise continued for longer. Aasim's phone vibrated on the bedside table.

'You'll have to go to the couch,' Aasim said. 'Here, take a pillow.' Wrapping a dressing gown around himself, he followed David to the main living area. Shit. Cans everywhere. He answered his phone.

'Hiyam.'

'Hey, handsome. We're outside your apartment.'

'You're in Dublin? No way. Give me five minutes?'

'Of course. We'll let your lovers escape.' A big laugh. 'Fadiyah and I will get a coffee.' The screen went black.

'Get a bin bag,' Aasim called to David, before scooping cans and bottles inside it. He shoved it into the airing cupboard and opened the windows. There were sweet-sour beer stains everywhere.

'Will I go?' David asked.

'No. Hiyam will see you. I know what she's like.'

Fifteen minutes later, Aasim buzzed the girls into the building. David sat on the couch in his jeans and T-shirt from the night before, blond hair dishevelled, his pillow and blanket beside him, sipping coffee. They waited for the knock on the apartment door.

Aasim opened the latch. Hiyam kissed his cheek, her blue eyes already looking over his shoulder. 'We were in London with Mama and thought we'd surprise you.'

'Did she mind you coming?'

Hiyam laughed. Aasim greeted Fadiyah.

'Had a party?' Hiyam asked, her gaze stopping on David.

'David, this is Hiyam and Fadiyah. Yes, I had a few friends here last night but David couldn't get a taxi.' Aasim knew how feeble this argument was. All it took was a glance out of the window to see the endless parade of cabs on the street below.

'Hi, David. I've seen you in Aasim's pictures.' Hiyam smiled but gave away nothing. She walked into the kitchen. 'Do you have any sparkling water?'

'There's nothing there,' Aasim replied.

'Why don't you tell me when you're having parties? Fadi-yah, you'd love to come, wouldn't you?' She glanced in the empty fridge and turned to Fadiyah. 'See? My brother doesn't eat. It's just coffee and cigarettes.'

David stood up and yawned.

'I better be off.' His voice was gruff. Aasim glanced at Hiyam, irritated that she was enjoying the awkwardness.

'Course, buddy.' He watched David put on his shoes before walking him out. The lift began to descend. Aasim turned back to his sister.

'Handsome, isn't he?' she said with that stupid laugh, nudging Fadiyah. She walked over to him and hugged him close. He could smell the candy perfume. 'We all need dis-tractions.' Giving him a kiss, she released him and started talking about their suite in the Westbury, leaving him unnerved about the beautiful heedless creature his eighteen-year-old sister was evolving into.

In the coffee shop, David reaches across the table and rubs Aasim's thigh, the way a parent might ruffle the head of a child. Aasim smiles, brought momentarily back from his thoughts of Hiyam.

'If everyone could just relax we'd all be much better off,' David says, tucking his hair behind his ears. 'I forgot to tell you. Mam rang the other day, all upset. She'd wanted Dad to put an extra door on the conservatory; she said that it'd be handy when one of them died. Visitors could see the coffin without traipsing through the house.'

Aasim laughs though it feels tinged with something else. David often redirects conversations when they get too serious. Maybe it's naivety or perhaps wilful blindness, but when he says things like, 'If everyone could just relax,' Aasim realizes how different their worlds are. 'Just relax' is not an argument that would work on Baba or Mahmoud if they found out about his life.

The coffees arrive and Aasim shakes in two sachets of sweetener, stirring in milk. He envisages the metabolic processes of aspartame, the formaldehyde forming in his intestines. But something will kill him. Something kills everyone.

The waiter serves the breakfasts. He's handsome, most likely Brazilian. Aasim watches him look at David and smiles. He wants to say, 'He's mine. You don't stand a chance.' Yet it's nice that David is fancied by other guys, especially good-looking ones. Why is it better to be admired by hot people? As Hiyam said once, 'Even the ugly have eyes.'

He sips his coffee, watching David eat a sausage. The meat makes Aasim's throat feel tight, though such a reaction seems stupid. Having sex with men is surely a bigger sin than eating pig. What is pork anyway? No different than any other flesh he's seen under a microscope. Yet, he can't quite put the meat into his mouth when it comes to the point.

'How is Eva?' Aasim asks, flagging the waiter, ordering a second coffee.

'Fine.' David says nothing more. Mentioning David's sister is an awkward business. Surfing in Liscannor over the August bank holiday, a chance for them to connect, had been a failure. Their rented bungalow had been a dump though David, Eva and the others didn't seem to notice the mismatched china, the avocado-coloured bathroom and faded floral bedding. 'What do you expect for eighty quid each?'

David had laughed at Aasim's face as he touched the peach pillowcase in their bedroom. 'It's called rustic charm.'

That was only the beginning. He'd felt Eva's eyes on him every time he took out his phone at the dining room table and didn't appreciate her half-jokes. 'You're never off that thing,' she'd kept saying. Of course, he'd got himself a Vector Pro wetsuit and a Kelly Slater surfboard which, at first, she admired. However, when he put one foot in the Atlantic, he declared there wasn't a hope in hell he would be getting in the water.

'But what about all your new gear?' she had asked.

'Whatever.'

She had shaken her head slightly and headed back into the waves.

The sting of the final morning stays with him most. He'd woken alone; David was already out of bed. He sat up and looked through the gap in the curtains. Low cloud blended with the sea in a mass of grey. He felt around under his pillow, pulling out his phone. No message from Hiyam or any of the Dublin girls. Facebook had pictures of his RCSI classmates at a house party. Damn, he'd missed it.

Those dark clouds. He inched off the mattress, slipping on his D&G sweats and Versace V-neck. Pulling back the curtains, he examined the sky. It'd likely rain before long. He shivered again.

The smell of coffee filled the hallway. He heard Eva's flip-flops tap off the lino in the kitchen. Then David's voice echoed through.

'. . . so-so. You?'

'Was Aasim all right?'

'He was sick in the night.'

'Lightweight.' A slight laugh. 'Never a dull moment with him.'

Aasim had peered through the tiny gap in the door, holding his breath. Eva wiped the main table with a certain attitude. David, in a wife beater and grey shorts, leaned against the countertop, picking at his nails, his hair falling forward.

'You know what his family are like. It's not easy for him.'

'They aren't going anywhere.'

David shrugged.

'Like, you wouldn't blame him for being the way he is. Not where he's come from,' she continued.

'You never know.'

'I don't know much,' Eva sighed. 'But I do know there's not a hope you'll get an Arab guy out of the closet.'

'Maybe.'

'There's no maybe.' The coffee-pot began to bubble and Eva took it off the flame, sitting it on the draining board and turning over two cups. 'You think Aasim might try the waves today? Such a waste.' She handed her brother a cup.

'Perhaps. He'll moan plenty but he'll get over it.'

'After all that persuading him to come in the first place.'

'He'll get used to coming on trips.'

'I'm sure he will, dragging his Louis Vuitton behind him.'

They leave Simon's Place. David says goodbye at Trinity gates. For a few moments they stand close and their fingers touch. Aasim thinks about kissing him but doesn't. The yearning remains.

Swinging his Alexander McQueen satchel over his shoulder

and walking towards Grand Canal Dock, he thinks about his morning with David, the parties with Vicky and JodieB, his family: the accumulation of different events that have made up his life. Granted, it hasn't always been easy – in fact, it is far from perfect – but he wouldn't have it any other way. Maybe one day his family will come to terms with who he is. The world is changing; Eva doesn't know shit and for now it doesn't matter either way.

It starts to drizzle; there is no getting used to the cold and rain of Dublin. He puts up his hood and selects P!nk's 'Raise Your Glass' on his phone. Its screen is still smashed, though he isn't sure if it was from Halloween night or the party before.

You know what, fuck Eva. There is much about his relationship with David that she doesn't know. The laughs they have, like that time they went for a tour of The Casino at Marino, wandering around the fake Grecian temple. The guide described the eight different woods in the parquet floor, pointing out two that were no longer in existence.

'I want extinct wood in our house,' Aasim had said.

'How the hell are we going to get extinct wood?'

'We'll make a floor and then get the tree wiped out.'

David had laughed. Properly laughed.

As Aasim walks along the outside of Trinity College, he glances up Pearse Street. It seems endless. David will already be in the library studying. P!nk, Gaga and Rihanna play in quick succession on his phone. He thinks about hailing a cab and wonders if the Gucci loafers he ordered in Brown Thomas have arrived. Finally, he reaches Grand Canal Dock.

Opening the front door of his Alto Vetro apartment, he feels his shoulders loosen. Even though he loves David's company, there is a joy in this alone feeling. When he'd first moved in, he'd sat on the couch and listened to the silence. He'd watched the silver grasses rustle on the balcony. Beyond, there were more apartments but he couldn't see in their windows. He'd stepped out and examined the glass of the sliding doors. They were mirrored too.

Then he'd sat on the couch again and, after a few minutes, he could hear faint noises in the building: a muffled television, the lift, and a lorry on the street below. Yet there were doors and locks between his space and theirs. His intercostals had relaxed for the first time in as long as he could remember.

Eighteen months later, that same calm alone feeling returns. He throws his satchel on the countertop, frowning as he notices more cigarette burns across the couch. His phone vibrates and he puts it on the coffee table, goes into the kitchen and turns on the kettle. There are weeks-old bananas in the fridge sitting next to an unopened bottle of Veuve Clicquot. The phone keeps vibrating, moving slowly across the glass surface. Aasim listens to the kettle boil.

The phone does not stop. Eventually a text message comes through. *Aasim, call me as soon as you get this.* It's Mahmoud. Aasim inhales. He hadn't given anything away in the restaurant, had he? He dials the number and Mahmoud answers after one ring.

After the call, he sits in silence. Eventually, he picks up his phone again and dials. David answers.

'Aasim . . . are you there?'

'I have to go home . . .' Aasim's throat tightens as soon as the words are out.

'What's happened?'

'It's Hiyam . . . she's dead.'

Joan

A lone magpie lands on a barrier of the M50. For the rest of the journey home, Joan Crangle imagines Trevor's plane dropping from the sky over Lebanon.

'Honestly, Mam,' he'd said as she slipped the medal into his pocket. 'If the plane goes down, there isn't much you or Saint Christopher can do about it.'

There are a few splashes of toothpaste on the mirror over the sink. She glances at the cleaning products placed beside the toilet and notices a muddy shoeprint. Trevor's size twelves. Twenty-eight years telling him to leave his trainers by the front door and him not taking a blind bit of notice.

Sometimes she wishes Siobhan never married Martin Cusack. She might have heaps of money, but for what? Stuck in the desert. Poor Milo and Rocco – they'd grow up without any sense of reality. How could they, with all the Legos and Pingu Pigs Siobhan bought them? All that plastic would end up in landfills. It'd be a long time rotting in sand.

Jack didn't take to Martin. 'There's only one sort of man that wears pinstripe,' Jack had said, 'and nothing good ever came of them.' When Siobhan brought Martin home for the first time, he gave Joan a great big bunch of lilies. After they left, Jack watched Joan trimming the stems and called him a lickarse. 'If flowers come a second time, I'll be impressed.'

She kept Jack away from the Cusacks at the wedding. He nearly had a conniption during the speeches when Martin's father made a joke about Siobhan. 'The airs on him,' Jack said after, 'and he farms pigs.'

'They aren't long forgetting it,' she replied.

With the elbow of her cardigan, Joan wipes a spatter on the mirror. 'Wrong side of the tracks.' That's what Martin's father had said in his speech, apparently as a joke, but no one was laughing. The cheek. She'd rubbed her finger along the top of a wardrobe in the Cusack house and there was dust an inch thick. So much for that girl Karina they'd coming two mornings a week.

The telephone rings. She guesses it's the man who left three roses on her doorstep three weeks ago. Pat Furlong was handsome enough two decades back. Now, things weren't looking so good with his chipped front tooth.

She had asked about it over Szechuan. He had cracked it opening a tin of tuna. But that was the way with men like him; thirty years single were bound to leave a man with a few quirks. His mother, a weapon, barely let him out of the house. It was all dry eyes at that funeral.

'Is that you, Joan?' Pat says.

'How are you?'

'I'm well. Did you see Trevor off?'

'I did. There was a bit of fuss with the new terminal. A white elephant, if ever I saw one.'

'You're still on to meet?'

'Of course. We can talk next week.' She says goodbye and hangs up. Pat is a good soul, harmless really. She'd downplayed their outing to Pearl River to Trevor, not wanting him to overthink it.

'I worry about you when I'm away,' her son had said.

'Don't be silly,' she'd replied. 'At least you won't be dragging muck over my clean tiles.'

Joan rubs her fingerprints off the phone with her cuff. She gazes at the immaculate walls and floors and thinks Dubai wouldn't be the place for Trevor. With his shock of red hair, he'd get scorched. That sweltering day in Brittas Bay – even natural yoghurt hadn't helped.

The winter before last, she'd headed out on her own to Siobhan and the boys. Tommy next door had given her a look when she'd asked if he and Maggs would keep an eye on the place, even though their own place was a kip. Bottles everywhere. 'Drink helps each cope with the shite the other speaks,' Trevor said once. She clipped his arm and tried not to laugh.

'Isn't it good they can at least look out for each other?'

Joan's mobile vibrates. She lifts her glasses off her chest and unlocks it.

Hi mam, you by the computer? Free for chats? x

Five mins, hisses mam. Joan frowns. These touchscreens – and she'd just got used to her old phone. She turns on the computer, glancing at the instructions Trevor left by the mouse: 'push the round silver button to turn on'. He must think she's a fool. And his handwriting – the vowels are all squiggles. Heaven knows what would've happened during his Leaving if she hadn't been on at him the whole time, threatening to cancel his gym membership.

The blue call-screen opens. Joan glances at the video that appears; those dreadful lines around her mouth, like a dog's arse – that's what Trevor said, winding her up. Her forehead looks like it goes halfway back her head, and the pot on the windowsill behind her isn't centred.

'Hi, Mam.' Siobhan's face appears. Joan squints, looking at her daughter's lip.

'Hi, darling. You're looking great.' The reddish dot on Siobhan's lip vanishes. No. It isn't a cold sore.

'It's very poor reception. I'll go nearer the box.' As Siobhan descends stairs, Joan hears a television in the background.

'Rocco, get those shoes off the couch,' Siobhan shouts. 'Did you finish your homework? Rocco . . . did you finish your homework?'

Joan gets flashes of bikes and prams scattered in the hallway, before Siobhan sits down at the kitchen table. Behind her, Joan makes out the sliding doors and beyond, blue skies.

'Where's Gete?' she asks.

'She's putting Milo down for a nap.'

'What time are ye now?'

'It's just before dinner.'

'And what time is Trevor landing?' She'd asked him before he left the house. But just to be sure.

'I think he's in about four or five. But you know he'll get stuck at the passport gates; the queues there are always crazy. Martin is back in Egypt, but Trev can get an RTA easy enough.'

'Will you let me know when he lands? He has that change-over in Heathrow and that place is a maze.' She knows she is being overcautious, but after all that's gone on with him in the last year, how else would she be?

'I'll get him to text when he arrives.'

'Even if it's late. I won't sleep.'

'Mam, is there any cornflakes? I'm starving.' Rocco appears, opening a kitchen cupboard. He's tall for just turning six.

'Gete will get you dinner in a few minutes. Say hello to Nan.'

'Hi, Nan.'

'Hello, young man, is that a United jer—' Before she's had time to finish, Rocco has vanished from view.

'Ignore him . . .' Siobhan says. 'Milo!'

Joan hears the little boy's laughter.

'I'm sorry, Ma'am. He won't go down.'

'Don't worry, Gete. He can say hello to Nana. Would you put on some chicken nuggets for Rocco?' The top of Milo's head appears on camera. Behind, Joan watches Gete open the fridge. Couldn't she wear something a bit nicer?

Siobhan pulls Milo on to her lap.

'Will you give Nana a kiss? Not even a wave?' Joan asks.

Milo tucks his head into Siobhan's shoulder.

'You're not shy of Nana, are you?' Joan says. She pretends to cry.

'Ah, look what you've done to Nana.' Siobhan rubs Milo's hair. But the noise of the television grows louder, and Milo wiggles off her lap and vanishes. Joan stops her fake crying.

'Will you be all right without Trevor around?' Siobhan asks.

'I'll be fine, though my stomach isn't right since the airport.'

'It's probably wheat intolerance. I'm going to this new girl. Gabriel was no good. I couldn't shift the weight.' A shriek comes from the living room.

26

'I hope now you don't—'

'Rocco, what did you do to Milo?' Siobhan gets up and vanishes. Joan watches Gete at the countertop. Siobhan's raised voice and Rocco's muffled replies. 'I'll call you back later, Mam,' she shouts.

Joan cancels the call, relieved it's over. She'd be done for murder if she had to put up with all that noise again. Siobhan is way too soft. Rocco is nearly an animal. Being locked inside isn't good for a boy of his age, but the garden isn't much use with the sun splitting the stones.

Walking out of Dubai airport that first time – the heat was something else. The blast of it, even though it was nearly three a.m. Martin had laughed at her and said, 'Wait till lunchtime tomorrow.' The smug head on him. It was no barrel of laughs to be half dead from the sun, hopping from air-conditioned apartment to air-conditioned taxi to air-conditioned mall. The boys' chests crackled like firewood. Inhaler this and nebulizer that – neither of her two had been puffing on those things when they were that age.

She'd told Maggs before she left it'd be forty-odd degrees hot. Maggs had thought it'd be a lovely dry heat, like you get in Portugal. However, you couldn't see the horizon. The Gulf was a sweating lagoon. There wasn't a hope of drying clothes on the line; everything went in the tumble dryer.

It was all about oil. It had to be. Otherwise, they might as well have been living on the moon. Siobhan said they'd only be there a couple of years and it'd be worth the bother. Of course, the two years were well up, but Ireland had gone to the dogs.

Joan glances at her watch, surprised at the time. She steps

into the kitchen and puts a chicken Kiev and two potato waffles on to a tray, emptying some beans into a saucepan. Leaning against the countertop, she listens to the oven fan. Yes. Trevor is happy at home. Hopefully it is just talk about him moving; Siobhan is a terror for putting ideas in his head. Of course, he's enjoyed the trips out before but that's very different to actually living there. There's no need for him to be uprooting himself.

Upstairs, her uniform is pressed and hangs from the wardrobe door. Joan buttons up her white top, glancing in the mirror to make sure there are no stains. Trevor is happy now, isn't he? She'd hate to think she's stopping him doing what he wants. Picking up a photograph on her dressing table, she looks at the lace on the baby's collar. It's grubby, though she knows for a fact she put all his clothes on boil washes.

Bacterial meningitis. Sam, her first angel, didn't stand a chance. Bit of a shock for her and Jack. But it seems less surprising when she thinks about those years working on the wards. The summer he'd been born, there'd already been four cases and three kids had died. Each day she prays for forgiveness, if the bacteria had been on her hands when she'd touched her firstborn.

Jack never said a word about it after the funeral, though they didn't get close again till the following Christmas. Siobhan came the September after. Maggs had her and the baby around for tea and biscuits, and said wasn't it a comfort for her that Siobhan had come to take her brother's place. Trevor was born almost two years later.

Christ. Imagine if Trevor had died last year – her second dead son. Twelve months, nearly to the day, since falling into the Liffey, pissed as a fart. The *Metro Herald* had a field day.

'Thank God your father is dead and won't see you make such a show of yourself,' she'd said in the heat of the moment. Then she'd got tearful, thinking about him drowned, floating out into Dublin Bay, and began sobbing. 'What's wrong with ya, Trev? Why can't you get it together and do something with your life?' However, he'd no answer to give so she just cried and hugged him.

Now that the dust has settled, it's the timing of the whole thing that bothers her most. After Jack's death, the fight with Lucy Quirke's boyfriend, getting kicked out of the army, and the last few years hanging about drinking too much, she can't bring herself to ask the awful question, 'It was an accident, wasn't it?'

Joan glances out of the window. The daylight is beginning to fade. November is a tough month, bleak and still plenty of winter to go. She doesn't like working night shifts, driving home through Crumlin, with young lads skipping reds, smoking weed and messing with phones.

The oven beeps downstairs. Joan puts down the photo, hoping the garlic butter from the Kiev hasn't gone into the waffles. Though it'll all get jumbled up in her stomach, she likes a neat plate. Sometimes, if she cooks a curry and uses the wooden spoon to stir the rice, it irritates her to see the white of the rice with a streak of sauce going through it.

Trevor said she'd a screw loose. But he has funny ways, disciplined all week with his food and the gym, then going mad once the weekend hits. He'd have been at the airport way too early if it wasn't for her saying three hours was plenty of time. 'You'd know you were in the army,' she teased him.

She flicks on the radio and sits at the kitchen table. The Kiev is just right, though the top left-hand corner of a waffle is too brown, while in the middle of the beans she can see a greyish one. She picks it out with her fork and rests it on the table mat.

The state of her cuticles; the sanitizer is lethal. She'll put Olay in her bag for later. Siobhan has gorgeous smooth hands, Shellac done every week. How she manages to do anything with them is beyond her. When Siobhan was young, she'd bite her nails down to the root. Joan used to slap her fingers down and tell her she'd the hands of an itinerant.

Poor Jack. He'd spoilt her. He was forever telling Joan to 'go easy on the girl' and giving Siobhan handouts behind Joan's back. She'd only find out about it when Siobhan came home with another handbag or skirt, and a brazen puss to match. It was just as well she married a man good with the handouts. She was never one to break a sweat.

Martin's parents – the things Jack would say about that lot. After they met Shirley and Richard, she'd more sympathy for Martin. She can still remember the smell of the mansion the first time they were invited to dinner. Glade PlugIns and pig shite. The farm was only a half-mile away from the house and poor Shirley spent the evening opening and closing windows, depending on the direction of the wind.

The house was all show, with a double staircase that split in the middle. Red-faced, brandy-swigging Richard spent most of the time talking about the paintings he'd bought.

There was one picture in his study that he thought was the bees' knees – a picture of a horse and three hounds standing beside a pile of dead pheasants. He told them he'd spent thirty grand on it.

As they did the tour from room to room, Joan blushed at the idea that they would have to return the dinner invite. Of course, there was nothing wrong with her own home, but there was no double staircase or bidet with gold-plated taps to impress the likes of Shirley Cusack.

Trevor wasn't able for the Cusacks' showing-off, like a five-year-old hopping from foot to foot as the tour continued. She'd warned him and Jack to put on suits and both of them were tugging at their necks as if their shirts were choking them.

Siobhan was loving it all, hanging off Martin's arm. She always had a taste for the good life, and when the champagne was cracked open she went back for three helpings. Joan tried to give her the eye but there was no stopping her throwing it back. Richard gave a toast to the happy couple and even got a few lines in about the pig farm. 'One day when Mart takes over the family business.' Martin's eyes were glued to the Axminster rug. After, when Richard asked Jack did he want to say a few words, Jack coughed slightly and replied, 'I think you said it all,' and Joan did her best not to laugh.

'Can I use the bathroom?' Joan had asked, hoping to get a break from Richard. He was still blathering about pork. However, when she got to the hallway landing, curiosity got the better of her, and instead of going to the bathroom she pretended to be lost.

The first bedroom was a spare and the next one was too.

Richard's voice echoed along the corridor. Something else about pigs. But then she came across a bedroom which must've been Martin's before he moved out. Every wall was littered with breasts. She recognized Pamela Anderson on the biggest poster, but the other girls were worse again with their tongues hanging out like dogs in heat.

In the car on the way home, as if they knew something, the clouds were grey and getting blacker the further west she looked. There was a weird feeling in her bones. Something bad would come of all this.

'What did you make of them?' Jack had asked her, his eyes on the road.

'It's your fault, you know. You spoilt her too much.'

'It won't come to a wedding.'

'How do you know?'

'I just know it in my gut.'

Joan tutted and looked out of the window. What did he know about romance?

A rake of butter in the chicken Kiev. The calories. Still, it was delicious. Joan puts down her knife and fork and listens to the headlines on the radio. The students are up in arms again. It's grim all round, the eighties all over. Next thing you know, SIPTU will be on about strikes. And now jokers from Europe are flying in to sort out the big mess. Siobhan will never be back. Bailouts and loans will have the country crippled till long after they're all dead.

Putting on her coat, Joan sets the TV to record her shows. Sure, they're no patch on the ones in the nineties; nothing could beat *Blind Date* and *Surprise Surprise*. She'd loved a cry when some sad case saw their long-lost brother or sister after fifty years. And poor Stevo down in Cork pickled from drink. Jack used to call her a sap, handing her tissues when Cilla sang that song at the end. But the tears were cleansing in a way. She always felt better after.

As she locks her front door, number seventeen opens. Maggs is wearing a skirt that'd make a Gypsy blush. There's the usual bang of cigarettes.

'How are you, love?' she says. 'Off to work?'

'I am indeed.'

'It's a miserable night, isn't it? It's getting dark so early. You'd never want to leave the house.'

'I know. I couldn't get the place warm and the heating was on half the day.'

'Trevor get off all right?' Maggs has that look. God. She's getting sympathy from an alcoholic. Maggs never joked about Trevor's embarrassment, which made the whole thing much worse. There was only one reason why now, a year later, they wouldn't joke about it.

'I'm waiting to hear if he landed safe,' Joan replies, wishing to change the subject. 'You off out?'

'Yah, it's my sister's birthday.' Maggs lifts a packet of Silk Cut out of her bag. 'The big five-oh.'

'You're back on them?'

'I was out with Sharon and Noreen last night and I couldn't say no. Tommy has been laughing at my rubber arm all day.' She coughs, clearing a lump, tapping a cigarette. The inside of her lips is the colour of beetroot.

'You need a lift as far as Thomas Street?' Joan offers.

'I've a taxi called. Let me know when Trevor lands.'

Joan wishes her a good night. 'My regards to your sister,' she says, opening the window of the Megane and pulling out of the drive. There is a Christmas jingle on the radio – no stopping it now Halloween's over. What will she get the boys? There is no way she's buying Rocco a third bike. He's only one arse and two legs.

It can't be a good thing to get everything you want. What would you do with yourself? It's like when she cleaned the house and found it hard to sit down, for fear of wrinkling the plumped cushions Siobhan had bought her. She isn't sure about their rose pattern. The roses on Jack's grave had been that sort of red, and she doesn't need reminding of it every time she sits down to watch *Chatty Man*.

Those awful breakfast rolls with greasy bacon and eggs. She would stick porridge in front of Jack but the second he was off on the sites, what could she do? All those wrappers under the driver's seat; she never met a man who liked a warm chicken baguette quite like him, all that mayo and cheese washed back with a milky coffee with two and a quarter sugars. The talks with the consultant about BMIs didn't faze him. It was an awful waste. Fifty-three and Rocco only just born.

Maybe she'll get Rocco some Lego. Trevor was mad into them around that age. Though she doesn't want them left about and Milo choking on them. It's worrying when they get to an age where they can get about but haven't a sense of danger. The time she caught him climbing on the worktops, the marble floor beneath him, she nearly lost her life. Poor Siobhan got an earful.

*

When she arrives at the hospital, she has a quick cup of tea in the canteen. She folds her coat and bag into her locker and asks the girls how the day has gone. Busy so far and getting busier if anything. She nods, rubbing sanitizer into her hands and forearms.

The evening passes but her phone doesn't vibrate. She goes to the bathroom and checks it regularly. That bloody magpie. *Touch green, never seen.* And not a blade of grass in sight.

The A&E is full of weekend drunks, kids with broken bones and addicts, all looking like they've seen ghosts. The hours creep along; *The Late Late Show* is on mute and nearly over. The orange board says there's a ten-hour wait. Ambulances come and go. Sawdust is brought to clear up the sick.

Surely, he'd have landed by now. He was going to Dubai, not Mars. She thinks about calling Siobhan, trying to figure out the hours flying and the time difference, but none of the conclusions satisfies her. It was all Siobhan's fault, buying the ticket.

It's gone midnight before Joan's phone vibrates. *Hi Mam. plane survived. No deaths 2 report. wrecked. tlk tomor x*

Trevor

Phew. I was worrying. hisses mam x

Passengers pull bags out of the overhead lockers. The plane was twenty-seven minutes late landing, shaving a clear half-hour off his holiday. Trevor Crangle's eyelids drag across his eyes. He regrets the five Carlsbergs he sculled while he watched back-to-back episodes of *Family Guy*. He rubs his eyes but that only makes them itchier. It takes a certain amount of willpower to put his hands down.

The air hostess's lips are as red as they were when he stepped on the plane. He watches as she puts on her red beret, flicking the cream silk over her shoulder, covering most of her hair. Another hostess talks to an old man, who scratches his ear for the whole chat.

Where are these girls from? Their skin means they could be from just about anywhere but Ireland, the kind of colour movie stars get after they hit the big time. Siobhan has gone that way since going to Dubai. She's always liked going on the beds but now she gets this young one to come in and spray muck all over her. She said he should get a bit of a spray, trying to get a rise out of him. Whoever saw a ginger bloke with a tan? Maybe that gay fella off the telly.

The passengers move forward. The old couple, who cling to their luggage like drug smugglers, finally get up. He reaches into the overhead bin and drags out his Nike hoodie. A medal falls out of the pocket. There's no stopping Mam.

For all her talk of Saint Christopher, at least she isn't hung up on mass or that joker of a priest who called his old man 'Jim' at the funeral. Mam goes to the anniversaries, of course, dragging him along too. It's painful saying the same boring shite over and over.

It takes four minutes to walk up the plane, through the business class seats – all wrinkled blankets, TV screens and magazines – before he stands in the walkway, stretches and yawns, then strides to the main terminal. Christ, he feels rough, and the people in front are half-dead walking. His mouth tastes like the underside of a doormat and the building is blindingly bright.

The bags aren't long coming, though that means little. There's the passport lot to deal with. No doubt he'll pick the wrong queue, where the two hundred people in front of him each have old passports, raw cheese and cobras hidden in their cases, and he'll be stuck in Dubai airport till his flight going back is ready to board.

It's a cool-looking building. All shining surfaces. The water going down the wall is a nice thing too. It probably costs an oil rig to keep it going, or some poor Pakistani fellas are filling buckets and running up and down stairs.

The Emirate passport lads are something else with the white robes. The flashy watches and Aviators the Dubai blokes are wearing – big lumps of metal with all sorts of bells and whistles. Last time, knowing no better, he spoke to one of the guys, saying he'd a fine watch, but your man stamped the passport and glanced at the next sap in the queue.

It's a sweet deal to wear robes out this neck of the woods; he's getting sweaty downstairs and wants to rearrange himself, but fuck knows what would happen if they caught him at himself. They aren't great fun, the Emirates. You wouldn't want to be pissing them off. Siobhan is full of stories of English lads getting caught on the lash or having it off with some young one, and the next thing you know they're in jail for a year. Imagine that – a year – for getting a bit of action.

He glances about, wondering if any of the uniformed men carry guns. Surely, they do. He pulls down the crotch of his jeans and feels some relief. They'd have guns all right, great fuck-off ones. He always wanted a Heckler & Koch HK416 assault rifle after seeing one in a book his old man gave him for Christmas. Mam had a conniption when she saw it and fucked the book into the wheelie bin.

Granddad Nagle had a shotgun. Mam used to get in a mood on their trips to Cork when Granddad let him hold it. When he stayed at the cottage after Nana died, they'd go shooting together. Granddad would always be roaring at him to get behind the gun. But that was part of the craic, getting a belt across the ear and being told to cop on.

Having Mikado biscuits back at the house, Trevor remembers Granddad saying, 'Well, young man, what are you going to do when you grow up? Aren't you in secondary now?'

'I want a wrecking ball.'

'You what? What would you want one of them for?'

'To flatten things.'

'Sure, what needs flattening in Ireland?'

'Newgrange. I want to flatten Newgrange.'

'Why do you want to flatten Newgrange?'

Trevor shrugged. He'd only said it for the usual reaction of Granddad calling him a right eejit but ruffling his hair and laughing at the same time.

Granddad Nagle's brains went about four years after that. It wasn't Alzheimer's but dementia, not that one was much better than the other. When he came to live with them in Dublin, his confusion seemed to get worse. Some days, when Trevor got in from school, Dad would send him up Firhouse Road, following Granddad Nagle as he did his afternoon loop with the dog, where he'd pretend to bump into him and guide him home.

Trevor glances at his watch. He stares at the passport counters. Half of the fellas are chatting. For fuck's sake. There surely aren't first-class folk hanging around, scratching their holes? Though Siobhan said most of them go through a different part of the airport. No roughing it for the guys on top.

How long is it now? Ah, this is taking the piss. This is why he could never work for the government. Though the army wouldn't have been like that; maybe, if things hadn't got fucked up, he'd have been in Lebanon the last four years instead of messing around at home with his mam at twenty-eight years of age.

It was Lucy Quirke's fault. Sometimes, it seems like the only thing women are good for is ruining men's lives, and my God had she done a job on him.

Junior Cert year, he, Ross and Eoin had agreed Lucy had the finest rack of all the Leaving Cert girls. The third button was always open; everything looked like it was about to topple out. Blonde highlights, short skirts, she could've been Geri Halliwell in the Union Jack flag.

If only Siobhan hadn't brought her home to get ready the night of Wesley Disco. When he heard Lucy leave the bathroom, he opened his door a crack and spied up the hallway. Lucy was about to turn the handle on Siobhan's door but stopped. He whipped his head back inside his room but then there was a knock and she came in. He sat on the bed, doing his best to ignore his hard-on. Her hair was all wet tendrils. The door closed behind her.

She lowered the towel and Trevor thought the eyes would fall out of his head. Then she reached down and lifted his two hands, placing them on the skin, water trickling down her front. He stood up and leaned in to kiss her but she pulled away. Then she was gone.

The lads didn't believe it happened. And many times, when he thought back on it, he wondered himself. Either way, life after that moment was a disappointment; he'd felt pairs just as good since and sometimes bigger but they'd never had quite the same effect.

Lucy Quirke. What a woman.

Trevor opens his passport and flicks to the back page and glances at his picture. His neck is much thinner. It must've been before he started the kick-boxing. What would he say to that young fella, if he could see him? Well, beyond telling Lucy to sling her hook.

Trevor smiles. Whatever about telling the young lad back then, he could do with telling himself the exact same thing right now. Isn't it terrible to know something is bad for you and you keep doing it anyway? No matter how many times he told himself he was done with her, some picture of her online with a guy would make him feel rotten. Or she'd ring him at three a.m., a bit drunk and in the mood, and he'd have the ride of his life, only for her to vanish again. Worse still, she'd text him some Sundays when she was bored or hungover and she'd say things like 'she just wanted a nice guy for once', but then Monday morning she'd leave his messages unread.

Fuck. It's miserable to think the best moment of his life happened before eighteen. Look at him now, working in a crap gym, barely over minimum wage. He's a right sap. At least Siobhan is mad to get him out to Dubai; even being in the airport gets him excited. With so much money floating around, there has to be some sort of opening. As much as he has serious reservations about the place from previous trips, he'd be a fool to sit at home on his high horse if there's actually an opportunity out here to make something of himself.

Siobhan had said all the women out here were mad to get instructors. 'They'd love you and the red hair. They go for anything a bit different.'

'Maybe we could open a health and beauty place,' Siobhan had said another time. 'You could do the gym and stuff, and I'd do the make-up and nails. We'd be a dream team. We can look out for each other.' Yet, they never talked about it again after that. She'd got some other mad idea about going back to college and becoming a vet. That only lasted a week.

Hey darlin, you arrived yet? You find the RTAs all right? Sio x
 Landed fine. Massif passport queues. Tlk sn. Trevor wonders

about the cost of the text. It's mad to think how the text found its way from where he is, in the middle of the desert, all the way to Ireland and back out again to Siobhan's phone, in a second.

He glances down and frowns, seeing the faint creases ironed into his jeans. Will Mam ever listen to him? He looks like a Jehovah's Witness. She needs her head checked when it comes to cleaning.

'Will I get a cooker for the shed?' she asked him once. 'Wouldn't it be better than having meat and steam stinking out the place?'

'Not cook in the kitchen? You're tapped. I swear to God.'

The time she washed out his wallet was even worse, her lining the pennies and receipts beside his bed, the condom stuck right in the middle of them. But in all fairness, it's just her way, to fuss over them all. She's even good to Uncle Stevo, the waste of space that he is.

'He'll only piss it away,' Trevor said as Mam counted out notes. It was hard to see her put under such strain by the whole situation.

'That's his choice. This is mine,' she replied, sealing an envelope.

Trevor's phone vibrates again.

Msg when you leave airport. Don't forget duty free. Gete has your bed made. xx

Good aul Gete. She's the only Ethiopian he's ever encountered. Aren't they all supposed to be bean poles? When he was over that time before, he asked her if she had a fella but she didn't seem to know what he was on about. Christ only knows what it's like where she came from. Half of them are married at thirteen.

Gete has great skin, nothing like Lucy Quirke's freckly arms, like dirt floating on milk. The lads call the women he pulls 'Miss Worlds', as he always goes for ladies with a bit of flavour. He likes seeing different shades of nipple, types of hair and feel of skin. Sleeping with a foreign girl is like discovering a new world. After eight pints, he'd describe himself as a 'connoisseur of the fairer sex'. Maybe, after a decade, he's just looking for an alternative to 'the curse of the Quirke' and something is yet to stick.

The lad in the white robes calls the old crone in front of Trevor. She looks surprised and Trevor realizes she hasn't even got her passport open. The dope. He could punch a wall at this stage. Finally, the passport man waves at him. Trevor says howareya but there's no response. He glances down, rubs one shoe off his calf. The man clears his throat. Trevor takes back the passport.

Liquor time. Go on my son. Trevor picks a bottle of Morgan Spiced, Gordon's gin, a couple of bottles of Pinot Grigio and Hennessy. He realizes again how dry his eyes are and glances at his watch. Almost four thirty.

Martin likes Hennessy. Trevor puts it down and gets Absolut instead. At Siobhan's engagement party, when he'd been using the jacks, Martin came in and used the urinal right next to him and there were ten others empty. That wasn't right. As Granddad Nagle would say, 'I'm sure he'd help out if they were busy.'

To think they were married six years now. It was the baby

that clinched it. How could she have stuck it out with him otherwise? The stories that were going around about him and various young ones in Dublin couldn't all be lies.

Duty free my arse. Though the dirhams make everything look like it costs a bomb. Half the time, he doesn't know what currency Siobhan is quoting. But she likes to sex things up a bit, make the expensive things dearer and say cheap things cost fuck all.

Trevor hands his card over to the cashier. He hopes Prime-Fitness has lodged his pay-cheque. Andy can be a bit of an arsehole when he wants to be. Taking money for uniforms and everything. 'Brown Apple,' that's what the girls call him, because 'he was rotten before he'd ripened'.

Course, everyone in the gym has nicknames. The lads called him 'Ariel' after the Liffey fiasco. It didn't help that the Little Mermaid happened to have red hair too. He laughed it off and called them all a bunch of bollixes. No need to give them further ammunition.

'You're some dope,' Dave-the-rave laughed in the canteen. 'The bleedin river in November.'

'A lucky fuck, more like,' Marianne on reception said. 'It's a wonder you weren't found wrapped around a boat propeller.'

'All brawn, no brains,' Brown Apple added. He'd just come into the canteen. Course, that killed the conversation dead. It was the only time Trevor was ever glad to see him. His stomach went into knots every time the stupid subject came up. Between Mammy and the counsellor, then Siobhan landing in from Dubai that week, he'd heard enough about it.

★

He walks through the arrivals area, looking for the sign for the RTAs. The doors slide open, and the heat is overwhelming as he steps into the night. It doesn't feel so much like a gas that he has slipped into but a hot liquid that gets under his clothes. He takes off his jacket, stuffing it into his hand luggage. It's only a moment and already the first beads of sweat begin to form.

A man, possibly Indian though more likely Pakistani, in a white shirt and red tie, takes his case and lifts it towards the car. He goes to take Trevor's hand luggage but Trevor stops him, knowing the large bag is the bones of 20kg. He sits into the cream taxi, feeling the air-conditioning hit his damp forehead. He smiles; in a half-hour he'll be knocking on the door.

'To Garden View Villas, boss. Beyond JBR.' It feels weird calling him 'boss', patronizing the fella when he's anything but 'boss', but it was what everyone said when he was over previously.

The man nods a couple of times.

Trevor glances up. There are no stars; the only light comes from the colossal square fingers that jut out of the ground. Dubai looks like a computer game, too clean to be real. He likes looking at the tops of the buildings, all different shapes as if they're wearing hats. The one on the left looks like the thing Lucy wore when she turned up at Siobhan's engagement party. Though it didn't look great when Siobhan put her foot through it.

'Fuck off,' she'd shouted. 'What's your problem? Can't you just leave him alone?'

'Siobhan, it's none of your bloody business.' Trevor had

squeezed himself between the two women. 'Go back into the party and stop making a show of yourself.'

'Of course it's my business. I introduced ye.' She shook her head. 'What's wrong with you, Trev? Why are you such a pushover?'

The driver weaves in and out of traffic. Trevor thinks about when Mam sat in the back seat, blessing herself and saying a rosary as they sped along Sheikh Zayed Road – eighteen lanes and everyone doing what they liked. Though Siobhan got around in her 4x4 not a bother.

The car travels along the main stretch, the buildings rising fifty storeys, if not more. There are no pavements or outdoor shops. If it wasn't for the cars, you'd think the place was a ghost town.

The Burj Khalifa appears to the left. Trevor leans back, trying to see the top of it. It makes the buildings around shrink into nothing as it climbs, growing slimmer, a strange metal mountain. The Hollywood fella will be hanging off the side of it in a few days. Showing off. The dope.

On the right are twin buildings based on the Chrysler in New York, their curved metal tops lit up with bands of white light. There are two of them, of course. Trevor feels his eyes closing. He'd forgotten the length of Sheikh Zayed Road. He looks forward to falling on to the smooth and wrinkle-free sheets. Good aul Gete.

Fuck he's tired. He almost feels drunk when he is like this, like there's Vaseline coating his eyes. He glances at his phone, rereading the message from Mam. And the missed calls too.

Talk about overprotective. Ever since the Liffey. As if he's made of glass.

If only he could remember it better. He gave Siobhan an earful when she tried to say he might've done it on purpose. Come on, like. He wasn't mad.

The end of the night was a blank. He remembers staggering along the banks of the river, no taxi stopping, and looking at the water, thinking about his life. Back in the bar there was a half-finished pint on the counter, Lucy at the far end wearing the face off some fella.

An ache from somewhere, everywhere. Army over. No woman. He wasn't eighteen any more – twenty-fuckin-seven in fact – he was a bigger embarrassment than Stevo. How had his life become so pathetic?

Still no. He couldn't have done it. There was a big difference between deliberately fucking yourself in a river and just being a bit careless with your life, drinking and getting into scrapes because things weren't turning out the way you hoped, no matter what the stupid doctors had tried to suggest.

Thirty minutes later, the RTA slips into the estate of luxury villas. The dry roadside is replaced with lush green lawns, manicured shrubs, expensive road lights, and rows of 4x4s and black town cars. Trevor calls out the number and, after a series of turns, the RTA stops outside the home.

'Thanks, boss. Keep the change.' The taxi costs eighty dirhams. Fifteen euro or so. How do these fellas make any money? The driver lifts out his case and Trevor thanks him again. Again, the heat makes him feel submerged.

Hours and hours travelling. Maybe that explains him being a bit frayed around the edges. Siobhan can always tell when he's hungry or tired. She says it's something in his gaze that lets her know he's zoned out. 'Sometimes I don't know what's wrong with you. Other times, a sandwich would cure you.'

It'll be good to see the boys. If only Rocco didn't look so like his father. Thank God that dope is away. Trevor knocks and a light appears upstairs. From the other side of the door, he can hear Siobhan's voice and keys rattling in the lock.

Gete

Milo is crying. Gete Senai sits up, feeling dizzy. The cheese on toast gave her that dream where her teeth crack and fall into her palms and she tries frantically to push them back in.

Five minutes past seven. If only Milo would be a good boy and go back to sleep, she might get another hour. Siobhan calls.

'Coming, Ma'am.' Gete puts her feet into her flip-flops, rubbing her eyes. She feels an ache in her shoulder.

She passes Siobhan's bedroom. 'He's in here, Gete.' Milo is curled up in Siobhan's arms in the king-size bed. Without make-up Siobhan looks very different; it's like there're no eyes and lips.

Gete hears Milo's sobs.

'He misses Daddy,' Siobhan says. 'Come on now, my big man. You and Rocco are the men of the house when Daddy is away.' Milo wiggles in further. Siobhan shakes her head.

'Should I take him, Ma'am?'

'We'll give him five minutes . . . God, I'm tired. Did you hear Trevor last night? I couldn't sleep till he got here and then we had a cuppa.' Siobhan glances at her watch. 'I'll be a zombie.'

'I'll take him, Ma'am. You rest.'

'Thanks, Gete. You're a star.'

Gete reaches down. Milo clings to Siobhan but is half

49

asleep. The ache in Gete's shoulder returns. Siobhan slips under the covers, pulling down an eye mask. 'Try get another hour yourself.'

Sitting in the wicker chair in Milo's bedroom, Gete strokes his head while he sleeps on her breast. Baby Milo. Milky skin and beautiful soft red hair. When she'd called him Meelo that first day, Siobhan laughed.

'You're a scream. We'll get on, I'm sure. It's very relaxed here at Chez Cusack. And take no notice of Martin. It's all the hours he works.'

'Yes, Ma'am.'

'You're happy with the room? The air-conditioning could be better at that end of the house. But I'm sure you're more used to the heat back home.' Siobhan fanned herself with Gete's application.

'It's very good,' Gete replied. Her bedroom and bathroom were off the pantry, next to where the washing machine and tumble dryer were kept. The single bed was comfortable and the slim wardrobe would easily hold her small rucksack of clothes.

'While you're here you can have this, if it's of any use to you. Rocco got an iPad for Christmas and he's no interest in this now.' Siobhan held out a small laptop. 'Does your family use Skype?'

Gete strokes Milo's head. He is a good boy. They all are till they get to the age of five or six. Then white boys don't pay any attention no more. Not even to their fathers. She'd heard Rocco use bad words to Martin, even punching and kicking him when he lost his temper. But Martin laughed and said,

'That's the spirit.' In Ethiopia, a boy would be punished for that sort of unchristian behaviour.

Milo snores lightly, soft like a small piglet. His fingers play with her bra strap and she can feel a slight wet patch where he drools on her T-shirt. He painted her a picture once. 'We paint one for Mummy too?' she asked.

Afterwards, Gete hid the picture. These Dubai Ma'ams are jealous. She's heard stories. Yet Siobhan has been kind, even if she says bad words. Gete cleans the picture of the Virgin in the sitting room, but she never sees Siobhan around Jebel Ali for any of the services.

Gete hears a man's sneeze down the hallway. Her body tenses. She hopes Ma'am's brother won't be so underdressed like before. She'd only been three weeks with Ma'am when he'd first visited and she made sure to sleep with her clothes on at night. On the beach or by the pool was OK, but when he was in the kitchen as naked as this it was very distressing. If something more happened, if he came to her room in some little underwear, what could she do? The police would never believe her over a white man.

Slowly, she inches Milo off and places him back into bed. He stirs slightly, but doesn't wake as she covers him with his Bob the Builder sheets and steps lightly out of the room. She shivers; the air-conditioning has a faint hum. From Siobhan's room she can hear the sound of relaxed breathing. Glancing in, she sees Ma'am's head has fallen to one side, her phone on the sheets. Moving quickly, past the room with the man in it, not daring to look through the crack in the frame, she slips back downstairs through the kitchen to the safety of her own bed.

★

Gete wakes again. Siobhan is calling. It's eight thirty.

'There you are,' Siobhan says as she appears at her bedroom door. 'Milo is needing his Coco Pops. Lord, I'm half dead.'

'You want your tea, Ma'am?'

'Thank you, Gete. And a slice of toast. You're a pet.' Siobhan grabs her phone. From down the hall Milo's squeals erupt. 'Trevor's winding him up.' Siobhan shakes her head.

As Gete goes downstairs, Milo appears with a large box in his hand.

'Unky Trevor got me,' he says. Gete thinks about the three bikes and scooter he already has. Milo tries to come down the steps with the oversized box.

'Careful. I'll bring it for you.' From the living room, Gete hears cartoons. 'Hello, Rocco,' she calls. But there's no reply.

She brings Rocco a bowl of Crunchy Nut Corn Flakes. Trevor's present is lying by the door, half unwrapped. Rocco has spilt orange juice on his Superman pyjamas and on the rug. She gets kitchen paper.

'Morning, Gete.' Trevor is wearing a small pair of sports shorts and flip-flops. He has more muscles than she remembers. As he stands in front of the fridge he yawns and stretches, the freckles on his back moving around like fish on a wave. 'You don't know if there's any cottage cheese knockin about?'

'No, sir. I don't think.' Gete looks down and goes back to the sitting room. After cleaning the juice, she sits Milo into a high chair and encourages him to eat his cereal, trying not to look at Trevor as he eats peanut butter on toast, the red hair on his chest like scrubland.

'Morning.' Siobhan enters the kitchen in a silk dressing gown and bare feet. Her blonde-highlighted hair is in a messy ponytail. Gete wonders why Siobhan doesn't leave her hair that beautiful red colour. There is no one with hair like that in Ethiopia. Of course, she'd seen Western girls on television with yellow hair when she'd visited her aunt's in Addis Ababa. But red hair, she couldn't believe her eyes when she first saw it. It had to be paint or pigment.

'You OK?' Trevor asks Siobhan.

'I'm exhausted.' She rubs her eyes. They look small without make-up. It's easy for white people to look old. 'Thank God for Gete with the boys. Some of the girls that come over are useless. You should hear the stories.'

Gete scoops up some of the brown milk and encourages Milo to open his mouth. He obeys her but his gaze remains focused on the small Taz teddy he is holding. He pulls its cord and the toy shakes.

'. . . honestly, most of them don't know a thing when they hop off the plane. They've been lifted out of the back arse of nowhere.' Siobhan scratches her scalp. 'This airconditioning. My psoriasis has gone berserk. Don't worry about my toast, Gete. I'll buy a smoothie later. The trainer is booked at nine. Will you keep an eye on the boys? You're coming, aren't you, Trev?'

'Gimme twenty minutes. I'll sort my gym bag.'

'Oh, Gete, would you pack the boys' swim gear and get some snacks together while we're out. We're heading to Wild Wadi after.'

Gete holds Milo at the front door and he waves as the 4x4 slips out of the driveway. Trevor pulls a silly face as they drive off and Milo giggles.

Behind, she can hear the explosions of a computer game.

'Rocco, you've had enough of that now. You have to study for school,' she calls. He doesn't reply. 'Come now. If you want to go to the water park, you need to complete your homework.'

'I'm playing.'

'I'll have to tell Ma'am. She will not be happy.' What is wrong with these boys? Do they not realize how lucky they are? Back home in the village, many miles away from Addis Ababa, school is only one room with a chalkboard and not enough benches, so children sit on the floor, nothing like the air-conditioned classrooms in Dubai with iPads and projectors.

'Rocco?'

His gaze remains on the television. Gete lifts Milo upstairs.

'Come now, please behave,' she says. 'Will you brush your teeth, like a good boy?'

As she looks through Milo's wardrobe, she wonders which of the seven full drawers of T-shirts and shorts she will dress him in. Siobhan always changes his clothes. 'Christ Almighty, Gete, you can't put him in *that*,' she said, taking off a brand-new Coca-Cola T-shirt that Milo had been given in Dubai Mall. 'Throw it out.' But Gete took it, certain it would fit one of her cousins in Addis Ababa.

Afterwards, Milo plays on the kitchen floor with Rocco's iPad and Gete searches the fridge for snacks, putting Cheestrings, Ribena Toothkind and organic rice cakes into the foil bag. There are Buttons and packets of Doritos in the

54

top cupboard, but the school complained and Siobhan told her not to pack them. Now, it seems, the only person who eats the chocolate and crisps is Siobhan, though Gete takes the occasional packet when she is home alone.

'Rocco. You need to shower and get dressed. Mummy will be home soon.'

No response.

'You won't be able to go to the water park.'

Gete hears a game controller land on the couch and feet patter up the stairs. She sighs. Her father would know what to do with a boy like him. All those treats would be taken away and he'd be better for it. 'Spare the rod and spoil the child.'

She hasn't prayed today so, as she cuts crusts off bread, she says a few lines in her head. She wonders what her family are doing. Her brother Lemuel will be up by now.

She glances at the clock. It is almost eleven thirty, ten thirty at home. Her Indonesian friends can never talk to their families when they want with the time zones. At least Aunt Candace can go to an internet café. Lemuel writes letters from the village once a month, which carry their father's advice along with verses from the Old Testament. On the plane to Dubai, she found a piece of paper slipped into one of the small pockets of her rucksack with the Ten Commandments written. Underneath was her father's name.

The front door opens.

'You see why I signed with Pavel,' Siobhan's voice echoes into the kitchen. Gete hears the bags slip to the floor.

'He's a tank,' Trevor replies.

'Boys, are ye nearly ready?' Siobhan shouts out. 'It's almost water park time! Did you get the snacks ready?'

'I did, Ma'am.'

'And Rocco's homework?'

'I . . .'

'You need to be firm with him.' Siobhan sighs.

'D'you want me to have a word?' Trevor asks.

'He doesn't listen to anyone.'

'I've no problem doing it, if you want.'

'Since when did you get so worried about school?' She gives Trevor a look.

'Since way too late. That's when.'

Siobhan grabs her stomach, pinching it.

'Jesus, I'm starving. I don't know why I can't shift this weight.'

'Shower time.' Trevor leaps up the stairs, two at a time.

'Will you go see what Rocco is up to?' Siobhan asks. Gete tenses, not wanting to go to the first floor. She creeps step by step until she sees the guest bedroom door is closed.

'Rocco, are you ready for the park? Have you packed your swimming trunks?' Gete walks into his bedroom, stepping over the WWE wrestlers on the floor. Rocco lies across the bed, playing with his game console. She picks up his school-bag and finds a half-eaten sandwich. The bag smells of rotting apples. Hooking it over her shoulder, she searches inside a dresser, lifting out a swimming costume and goggles. 'Come now, Rocco, Ma'am wants to go soon. Put down that toy.'

Milo's feet patter on the floor.

'Get out of my room!' Rocco shouts.

'Be good to your brother.'

'He breaks everything.'

Milo laughs and runs out of sight. Rocco slides off the bed and grabs his trainers. Gete smiles; with his face concentrated like that he looks like a little frog, small-nosed and bug-eyed. There is a tap on the bedroom door.

'You don't know where the big towels are, Gete?' Trevor asks.

'In the big cupboard in the main bathroom.'

'Thanks . . . oh, look.' He steps towards her, hand raised, about to touch something on her head. 'You have *up doc* in your hair.'

'What's *up doc*?'

'You're a hoot, Gete.' Trevor laughs and tries to explain something about a television cartoon, but she's no idea what he means.

An hour later, the Jeep pulls out of the driveway. The house is silent. Gete lifts the first basket of ironing from the cupboard and puts it on the bed in her room. She picks up a white blouse belonging to Siobhan. The collar and armpits are stained yellowy-brown. It is strange that she coats herself in tanning cream to become dark. To have pale skin and red hair and to try and look sun-scorched and yellow like all the other women makes no sense.

Gete turns on the radio. She recognizes a song from that MTV channel. The girl in the video is very immodest. In church, the pastor said how bad the world was, girls dressing and showing so much of their bodies, promoting sin.

There'd been certain sorts of girls who would hang on the street outside Aunt Candace's house, showing their bodies and making money. Their laughs and fights could be heard through the grille in the big room. Candace turned up the television when they bargained prices with the men in shirts. 'Be sure to go to church when you arrive in Dubai. Find yourself a Christian community,' she said as she poured the tea.

'May God bless you, sister,' Lemuel had said, glancing at the window. He held her hand. It was the first time since their visit to the employment agency that he had spoken about Dubai without frowning.

Gete irons around the buttons of the blouse, making sure every crease is removed before she carefully folds it like the girls do in the shops. She recognizes the labels from the advertisements in Addis Ababa and the Dubai malls. Parts of Addis Ababa in recent years are beginning to look like Dubai; tall glass and metal blocks that gleam in the sun, where newly wealthy people live as well as foreigners. Some people are getting very rich, but not most.

Some of Siobhan's clothes cost hundreds of euro, thousands of birr, months and years of wages. She's not sure if she is a fool to work for low wages or if Siobhan is a bigger one for spending so much and getting so little. One burnt mark on Siobhan's blouse and all that money would be lost.

When she first came to work for her, Siobhan sighed, showing Gete how to fill the iron with water. 'You get what you pay for, I suppose.' But she was happy later when the pile of sheets was done. 'The girl before you – three hours and she'd only four shirts ironed. I had to let her go after a week. She was worse than useless.'

Gete turns up the radio as the headlines are read. News from America and Europe is told. Nothing from Ethiopia. There's talk of a film star coming to visit Dubai. He is to climb the Burj Khalifa – the building she first saw from the window of the plane. She saw it tower over all those other buildings, gleaming like a giant pipe out of the ground.

'. . . A young Emirate woman has been found in JBR Marina. Her family have been notified. Police are investigating the cause of death. No names have yet been released . . .' the newscaster says.

Gete pauses. Nothing more is said about the girl other than that she is Emirate. There will be consequences. She overheard Siobhan talking on the phone once:

'We traded it in. We had to . . . yeah, a 4x4. We had to, Mam. You saw the locals speeding down Sheikh Zayed Road. They don't give a shit . . . I know, don't even talk to me . . . and like, if one of them hit you, there's no point in even fighting it. The police will say it's your fault. I'm just glad now that the boys are high up off the road and away from those lunatics.'

The law favours Emirates, then whites, then everyone else. The news isn't really real. If the girl's family are local and powerful, who knows what will happen.

The sky is turning gold. Gete folds the ironing board and flicks on the light in the kitchen. She puts away the toys that are scattered across the floor, wondering if she should make the boys dinner or if they'll get takeaway, then cooks a small portion of pasta and reheats some bolognese sauce from the previous night on the hob.

She eats in her room, turning on the small television. The little computer takes a while to start and she checks to see if her family have sent a message.

Gete's shoulder aches again. It's long hours but it could be worse. Martin does not pester her the way many men do their maids, and Siobhan is never jealous like some women are. She could be with one of those families who were cruel and didn't pay her. The lady who met her at the airport still has her passport.

The front door opens and voices echo through. Gete closes the computer and goes into the hall.

'Thanks, Gete.' Siobhan hands her the boys' rucksacks, her eyes squinting. Milo is asleep in Trevor's arms. 'I'm getting one of my heads. That sun . . .'

'You sound like Mam,' Trevor replies. *I've one of my heads . . .'* He vanishes upstairs.

'I'm going to lie down. Will you make Rocco and Trevor some dinner?' Siobhan says, rubbing her temples.

'Yes, Ma'am.' She watches as Siobhan flicks her hoodie forward and creeps upstairs like an old lady.

Ten fifteen. Gete picks up the bottles of Heineken that Trevor left beside the couch. The blue screensaver on the television lights the room. She tries not to think about Trevor when she collected Rocco from the sitting room at nine. Dressed in shorts and a vest, Trevor had burped and both he and Rocco laughed. He'd seen her expression and tried to keep a straight face. Red-cheeked, he looked about the same age as Rocco. In many ways, he is just a big boy.

'Go on, up to bed with you,' he had said to Rocco, pausing the game. 'It'll still be here in the morning.'

Rocco sulked at first but followed Gete upstairs.

'You won't have a drink, Gete?' Trevor called out. 'You've been going all day. You must be shattered.'

'No, sir. Thank you.'

The floors are swept and Gete gives the kitchen sink a rinse before turning off the light. She slips back to her room and closes the door, putting a bag against it, just in case, remembering her father's warnings.

The house is quiet but there are moments she's not quite sure she likes it. The feeling of being alone takes hold. It's almost a relief that she's without time to think.

'Say your prayers. God will watch over you,' her father had said. 'There are laws to protect you too.'

She kneels beside the bed, asking God to care for her parents, Lemuel, Aunt Candace and the rest of the family. At least she had not been forced to convert, as some employers demanded. Only six months now till she will get to fly home for one glorious month.

'You must complete your contract,' the agent said when she agreed to come here. 'Or else there are costs.'

She agreed and paid nine thousand birr. Lemuel had stretched backwards in his chair, his nostrils flaring as she counted out the notes on the desk. Even though it was his idea for her to become a maid, he couldn't understand why she should have to pay to work and exclaimed that he wished he'd never suggested it. However, he kept his word and was silent throughout the meeting.

'At least it is a proper agency. How else am I going to improve my prospects?' she said as they stepped back on to the street. 'We must trust, brother.'

'Trust who?'

Gete didn't answer.

Tahir

Tahir Nasiri imagines he will one day tell his grandchildren about the people he drives up and down Sheikh Zayed Road – his big adventure to Dubai. But how will he ever make a story out of it? So much of each day is the same as the previous.

He glances at his watch. Five thirty. The sound of the others' breathing. It takes time to get used to the noise of seven men, the creaking of bunks, the gas, the snoring. Muhammad, sleeping in the bunk below, snores the worst. It sounds like a table being dragged across a wooden floor. Sometimes, if Tahir shakes a bit, rattles the bunk, Muhammad turns and the noise stops. He has complained to the agents about the snoring; he told them it was dangerous on the road without sleep. The RTA man nodded but nothing came of it.

Anam never snores. After the wedding, he had watched her sleep. She was neat, even unconscious, still and silent. He had touched her shoulder to make sure she was warm. Outside he could hear young men shouting. Karachi was never quiet.

He longs to undress her, lift back off those layers of fabric. *The next time I am home, you won't be allowed out of bed*, he wrote. *What if someone opens your letters?* she replied, but she included a picture, her hair shiny around her face, her beautiful eyes like Mahira Khan.

Eighteen months now. Before marriage, going without

seemed less difficult. But he got used to the warm body next to his and now it is hard to be satisfied alone. He does release himself – the shameful thing – but it is always with his left hand in the dark of night. He makes sure to shower before prayers.

Ibrahim had caught him once when they were boys. Baba would not allow locks on the bedroom door and Tahir didn't have a chance to hide himself. Ibrahim didn't say a word. All men do it, he said. It means nothing. Ibrahim did what he liked. Even asleep, he was selfish with the blanket. Especially after he smoked hashish.

Tahir lifts back the bed sheet and creeps down the ladder. His foot slips on a rung where Muhammad has left a T-shirt to dry. There are clothes hanging about the room. Mama would not like it. Bad for your lungs, your bones, she said, to sleep with damp clothes. What wasn't bad for his health? Something in life would kill him – it was the will of Allah. But he would like to live before he dies, not spend every day driving Sheikh Zayed Road. More time with Anam, not just the yearly visit.

No. He doesn't want to die just yet. God let him live. The motorbike. 'Inshallah,' Ibrahim had said. The boys gazed out at the six lanes of traffic before Tahir ran out. He was two days unconscious. When he woke, Mama had called him her 'miracle boy'. Ibrahim had bruises on his back and legs from the beating.

Tahir puts on his sandals and steps out of the cabin, inching the door closed. A couple of men stand under a camp light. One is smoking. He nods at them and steps around the wet patches of mud, using the network of planks. Closer to the bathroom the smell grows stronger. Men are no good left to themselves. They don't see dirt the way women do.

The water is cold but Tahir likes the feeling as it cuts through the heaviness of the night, the continual sweating from sleeping in a box in the desert. The humidity makes it hard to breathe; there's always a pressure on his chest, an extra demand with each intake of air. Every morning, just under his forehead, it feels as if there is something tar-like preventing his brain cells from communicating. Nothing but the cold water hitting his face seems to cure it.

He washes his body, the bar of soap causing his palms to wrinkle. One of his hands is more tanned than the other, with a few darker patches. Driving in full sunlight. There is a payment for everything. No matter what he does, how he works, there is always a consequence.

He tries to avoid the loose hairs that circle around the basin of the shower. That is the problem with bathrooms – they are as clean as the dirtiest person using them. Pigs, that's what Anam said when she smelt the builders on the roadside in Kabul, sweat and hashish, burping in that foul way.

All the men will be awake shortly, shouting, squeezing past one another, trying to be first in line for water and the toilet, fighting over who will get the taps that still work and the showers with the strongest flow, leaving a trail of muck from their sandals across the concrete. Tahir works his scalp harder with his fingers, dipping his head under the cool jets of water. Not long now.

At least while driving the car there are only a couple of voices to contend with. It's the jumble that he hates, the clutter of words caused by groups. If there are only a couple of people in the taxi he can listen to how they speak. Are they happy? How are they dressed? Are they going somewhere they shouldn't?

Baba is a storyteller. All his tales from travelling to India and Afghanistan, before the troubles. The Russians. Brutal order. 'If we can't rule ourselves, others will do it.' Baba reads the Afghani headlines these days, pulling at his eyebrows. The endless trickle of people dying – ten here, twenty there. A lot of blood to get nowhere.

The bathroom door opens. Tahir hears voices and wraps a towel around his waist. He shaves in front of the main mirror, looking at his exposed chest. Unlike most of the men, there are just a few strands of hair around his nipples and a line down from his belly button. He was jealous of Ibrahim when the line of hair appeared on his upper lip. 'I am a man now,' Ibrahim said at fifteen, showing his chest hair by opening extra buttons on his shirt. When Tahir got his beard, Ibrahim said he was 'still a baby, just a hairy one'.

Tahir rinses off the soap. Already, behind him, the men are beginning to queue. A scruffy bunch, he thinks, shadows of beards, a smell of sweat, some hoarse laughter. Soon they will all be clean-shaven and dressed in white shirts, the remains of their beards scattered across the sinks, spatters of toothpaste on the mirrors.

After getting dressed, Tahir prays, searching for the cleanest bit of floor for his prayer rug. There isn't much time and the door opens and closes, distracting him. Muhammad sometimes joins him but he breathes heavily and smells of damp clothes. The agent has warned about his hygiene but it hasn't made a difference. 'What can they do? How can things get worse?' Muhammad laughed. He missed his son's wedding driving taxis.

Tahir glances at his watch. Only twenty minutes for breakfast. He will catch up on his prayers in the evening. He walks along the planks to the kitchen area, making sure that his trousers and shirt do not touch anything. There is a queue inside the kitchen for the rows of hobs. He eats some porridge, and the man next to him complains he lost a fare of seventy dirhams because he never pressed the meter. 'At least we're not on the sites,' Tahir says.

'I know, Alhamdulillah,' the man replies. 'The best they can hope for is blood money.'

Twelve hours to think. Or not to think. Not thinking is better. The day goes faster. To be somewhere between imagination and reality, dreaming about little Fatima and Alayna. Two girls at once. 'Twice the gift from God,' he said to Anam. Alayna will find it easier to marry with those Mahira Khan eyes like Anam. Fatima likes reading; maybe she will become like Najma Hanif and run for parliament.

The same horizon and gleaming skyscrapers. New buildings inching taller every hour. Cranes swinging, lifting concrete high. Men in hard hats behind barriers. Robots. They are all like robots. Maybe one day they'll all be replaced by robots. And probably for the best. It isn't good for the mind to be always doing the same thing. Straight lines look curved if you stare at them for too long.

'Good morning, boss. To Media City.' A white man sits in the back seat and they slip away from the Botanica Tower.

He smells of perfume, his suit immaculate. In his hair there is pomade and it's slicked to the side. There is a piece of jewellery slipped on to his blue tie. Buildings or oil, Tahir thinks.

Baba blames himself for how things have turned out. It was the second shop that did it. The wrong neighbourhood. Protection money was demanded but not paid. Smashed windows. Two fires. 'This neighbourhood has a disease,' Baba said. But it was too late. The disease had spread. The banks took away the shops. 'Greed lessens what is gathered,' Baba whispered, his eyes glassy as he gazed out of the small apartment window.

'Yes, over here. Thanks, boss.' The man hands him a twenty-dirham note. 'No, keep the change.' He lifts his phone again and continues talking as he steps on to the pavement.

Five dirhams. A start. It all helps. A toy for Alayna. She has always liked 'things', real toys that can be touched and played with, while Fatima goes for curious things, like climbing in boxes, rather than playing with the tea set Uncle Ibrahim had bought. 'Tea, Baba?' Alayna would place the little wooden cup to his lips, no bigger than an eggcup. She will make a good wife.

Poor Ibrahim. It would be good if he could marry again. It is easy to forget that the headlines are real; the background news of shootings and kidnappings becomes a white noise. Till a bullet had hit Parveen. Twenty-three. A spray of a machine gun and it was all over. Ibrahim hardly leaves the house now. Which man on what bike had taken the shot? Was it about the protection money?

*

'Hi, boss, to Dubai Mall, please. Rocco, put down that thing. Get in. Come on.' A blonde woman wearing a floaty green dress gets in. She smells like sweets. Tahir glances at her exposed shoulders; her arms are covered with freckles. The young boy drags himself across to the far side of the back seat. He is holding an electronic game console. She lifts a toddler on to her lap. He is drinking a juice. 'Will you open the boot?'

Tahir gets out of the car, and helps a red-headed man put a pram and three baby bags into the boot. The man looks like he could carry the car on his back. His T-shirt is too small, like an action star, his chest and arms stretching the white fabric.

'Thanks.' The man closes the boot with such force the car shakes. Tahir says nothing.

Inside the car, the woman speaks. The ginger man must not be local. Too pale. They have the same small teeth.

'Dubai Mall, boss,' the woman says, leaning forward. 'Will you take him?' She puts the little boy on the ginger man's lap, strapping herself in and pulling her sunglasses off her hair. There is big metal writing on the side of them. She sighs. 'At least that ordeal is over. Honestly, leaving the house – it's like preparing for war. Do you know if Gete packed the fruit boxes?'

'I dunno.'

'We'll pick something up at the mall. How's Mam getting on with that fella, what's his name?'

'Pat? Fuckin hell. Teeth like broken china.' He laughs.

'Watch the language. Seriously, Trev.' She smiles but her nostrils flare. 'I mean it. It's no joke out here.'

Tahir glances in the mirror. These things happen, small offences in the back of his car. He could report them. Like he could report the couples who fall bleary-eyed into the RTA at three a.m. The ones whose hands aren't always visible. Let Allah judge them. It is better to keep quiet. Hours complaining are hours not driving. The drunk ones are the best tippers. A lot of things in life can be forgiven with a tip.

'No word from Martin?' the ginger man says.

'He's in meetings most of the day. Poor Rocco.' The blonde woman touches the boy's head, before straightening her sunglasses. 'Be careful, lovey, it'll get all over Mummy's dress.' She puts the little boy's juice box back upright. He reaches out and picks at a flower on her top with an index finger. She catches Tahir's eye in the mirror and strokes her shoulder; he gazes back to the road. 'Would you turn up the air-conditioning, boss?'

Tahir does what she says. He glances at the older boy, who is absorbed with his game console. His cheeks are round and fleshy, almost pink. White children are like this, fleshy from all the rich food they eat.

The call to prayer sounds throughout the city. Tahir glances at the clock on the car's dashboard. He recites a few lines in his mind. Hopefully Allah will forgive him. It is the best he can do. Tonight he'll make up for it.

Cars queue in front, following the curved road into Dubai Mall. He watches the ripples of heat rise off the bonnets, the smooth lines becoming shaky.

'Come on now, Milo, we're nearly there.'

Tahir glances in the mirror. The little boy is wiggling around in his seat.

'Please, pet, only five more minutes. Yes, five minutes. We'll get you ice cream. Yes. Would you like ice cream? Look at that fat belly.' The little boy laughs as the woman tickles his stomach.

'Can I've ice cream too?' the older boy says.

'Of course. Promise me now, you'll put that thing away when we get inside.'

They glide up the curved road, opening out on Dubai Mall; a row of red and black flags flutter along the roadside. The mall, impressive because it is massive, reminds him of a factory on the outskirts of Kabul. It seems like an odd place for people to shop, though it looks better at night when the glass gleams from the spotlights, especially the entrance where the arches glitter like precious stones.

He stops outside.

'Sixty-seven dirhams, Ma'am.'

The woman hands him a hundred.

'No change?'

'No, that's all I have.' Her eyebrows rise a little. 'Twenty back will do.'

'Very good, Ma'am.' He gives her a note, thinking about the tip. The car doors open and the woman complains about the heat. It floods into the car, taking all the breathable air with it. He gets out and helps the man with the pram.

'. . . they never have change. It's ridiculous.' The woman tries to sit the boy into the pram. He fights against her, arching his back, and she does her best to push him down. 'Behave for Mammy now. You want ice cream?'

Already there is a customer waiting to get in. She hands him her bags. Hilfiger. Ralph Lauren. Sephora. He puts them in the boot while she watches. The car door closes and he drives off. A different sweet smell.

'JBR, boss.'

New passenger. Bur Dubai. Financial Centre. Dubai Mall. Al Manara Park. Mall of the Emirates. Media City. The Palm. Jumeirah Lakes Towers and Metro. Jebel Ali. Drop client at destination.

New passenger. Jebel Ali. Jumeirah Lakes Towers and Metro. The Palm. Media City. Mall of the Emirates. Al Manara Park. Dubai Mall. Financial Centre. Bur Dubai. Drop client at destination.

New passenger. Bur Dubai. Jebel Ali. Jumeirah Lakes Towers and Metro . . .

How many times can a person repeat the same thing back and forth before they become like those dogs that chase their own tails? Where is the meaning in it all? But as Anam said the day he left, sometimes in life you have to pick the lesser evil. Then she began crying.

Tahir breathes deeply, trying not to let these thoughts take over. They do about once a shift, at a point long enough into the day that he starts to feel tired, but not close enough to the end of the twelve hours that he can think about returning to his bunk. There is no cure for the feeling deep in his stomach. Is this all there is? What is the point of existence?

If he were alone, perhaps he would do something foolish in these moments. However, there are Anam, Fatima, Alayna, Baba, Mama and Ibrahim to think of. He must keep going. The next generation will have it better.

'Would you put on the news?' the woman passenger asks.

'Yes, Ma'am.' He glances at the woman, wishing he could

thank her for allowing him to turn on the radio. Anything to distract him.

The newscaster sounds American as he reads the headlines. Europe is having trouble. Bailouts. The rich doing what they can to keep rich. Cholera outbreak in Haiti. The drowned Emirate girl.

'Turn that up,' the woman says. They both listen to the details. 'Isn't it strange they haven't released a name yet?'

'Yes, Ma'am.' Tahir is quiet. A few times today, he has overheard passengers talking in low voices about the death of the girl. Sometimes, the best way to get accurate news in Dubai is through general gossip rather than through any official channel.

'She would hardly have been out by herself. A local girl out alone at night. It's very odd,' an older lady with a posh accent had said.

'They say she was last seen at the York hotel. Yeah, I know, buddy,' a young man had snorted, chatting on his phone the whole time while Tahir took him to Media City. Tahir had felt his stomach tighten as the man mentioned the York hotel, wondering if the police would come asking questions of the taxi drivers. He collected customers there nearly every night.

The York hotel. Drunk men. Cheap women. Good tips if he didn't say a word. If the Emirate girl had been there, what would her father think? Imagine, if one day in the future he were to find out Alayna had visited such a place. It would break his heart. If word ever got out, what honest, respectable, God-fearing man would ever want to marry such a woman?

'One of the mothers from my school . . . yes, she lives in the Sadaf block, really near the marina, she was saying the police told passers-by if they took pictures, they'd be arrested,' a young woman gossiped on the phone, while stroking the arm of her sleeping daughter.

Tahir inhaled, anxiety creeping into his chest, as if there were something he wasn't quite remembering. The days were so long. Time on these roads became jumbled. He would ask the other drivers later if they knew anything at all.

The sun is turning red. Tahir drops his last passenger at the Crowne Plaza. His stomach groans. His back is sore. He'll pray extra tomorrow. For now, at least, he can go back to his lodgings and try not to think about work, though the others in the cabin will want to talk about the difficult passengers they'd met that day. Or complain about the ones who didn't tip.

He queues to use the hot ring. Burnt rice stuck to the countertops. The walls covered in spatters. Tarnished and blackened saucepans. Sticky residue underfoot. Pigs. Tahir glances over his shoulder. Men sit on benches, scooping up slop with torn bread. A sea of bloodshot eyes. Muhammad sits at the far wall with the other six men from his room and waves over. Tahir nods back.

Beads of sweat form on Tahir's brow as he cooks the small piece of fish and rice. He blinks a number of times but his eyes remain dry. He stretches, reaching his hands towards the ceiling. What time is it? Food. Prayers. Bed. Then it all begins again.

'Masaa el kheer,' Muhammad says, as Tahir puts his metal

plate on the bench. The other men slip along the row. Muhammad's *Gulf News* lies open. 'How was your day?'

'Poor,' Tahir says. It is always 'poor'. It is not wise to tell desperate men about tips he's made. He takes a mouthful of his food. 'And your day?'

'The same. These people . . .' Muhammad says, lifting the paper. There is a picture of a woman in a red sari, her hair on show.

'Has she been pardoned?'

'The pope asks that she not die. Filth. The mullahs say they will kill her if she is.' Muhammad turns the page.

There is a face on the other side. Tahir frowns. He has seen this woman before.

'They have named her now, the girl from the marina,' Muhammad says. 'Hiyam Husayin.'

'Do they know what happened?'

'They do not say any more. It's shameful, a Muslim girl out alone like this late at night.' Muhammad tuts.

Tahir stands, putting his spoon on to the plate.

'Not finishing your dinner?'

'No. Prayers. You want?' Tahir pushes the plate towards him. Muhammad smiles. He hasn't noticed Tahir's colour. Tahir walks towards the exit, over the planks, back to the Portakabin. Others call him over but he ignores them. His neck feels all twisted. His legs feel like they are working on their own.

No one is in their bunk yet. He lifts his Nokia 3310 out from under his pillow. There are a couple of dirhams of credit left. He texts Anam. The two mouthfuls of fish rise up to his throat.

Anam, text back. Please. Text back. Tahir opens his jacket and pulls out the rolls of dirhams he has saved. How much would a plane ticket cost? Would he be allowed to go? He could tell them Baba was sick, dying. If they had any compassion, they might give him his passport. Otherwise . . .

No. There is no point in thinking of what could happen. He must leave.

Siobhan

The doors slide shut behind Siobhan Cusack. 'Can you feel the air-conditioning? Isn't it lovely, Milo?' A minute outside and sweat is already dissolving her Benefit foundation. Thank God for Mitchum deodorant. Those awful wet triangles on her maxi-dresses.

'You can take off the glasses, Dymph,' Trevor says, nudging her and laughing. 'Too cool for school . . .'

'Go away and find a T-shirt that fits.' Siobhan puts her glasses on her head, glancing at one of the mirrored walls of Dubai Mall and fixing her hair and dress straps, resisting the urge to look at her waistline.

Dymphna. Dymph Na. Siobhan checks her teeth, sliding her tongue over her incisors. What was Mam thinking, giving her that middle name? It was grand for Aunty Dymphna, born in about 1820. It sounds like an insect. Saint Dymphna. Patron saint of parasites. At least 'Trevor' is no better.

'Can we go to Game, Mam?' Rocco asks.

'Of course we can, pet. We can go everywhere. Watch where you're going.' Siobhan puts her hand out as Rocco trips on a mat. His eyes remain focused on the screen.

Trevor looks around, slightly dazed. Wait till he sees the new Hilfiger store. Hopefully they still have that gorgeous bomber. He'll look great in it if the jacket fits over his biceps – his baggy jeans look like skinnies. Hopefully he isn't on steroids and has read those articles she posted about wrestlers who'd died of heart attacks. And that one about shrinking balls. If that didn't stop him.

Stupid handbag. A thousand dirhams and the catch made in China. Her Shellac ruined. How do other women do it, keep themselves together while caring for children?

Trevor swings Milo on to his shoulders. The little boy laughs, holding on to Trevor's head, nearly taking his eyes out. Trevor pretends to nearly drop him a few times, and Milo squeals and says, 'Again, again.' They gallop forward. Siobhan directs Rocco's shoulder and they follow behind. Her phone vibrates. Martin? No. Gete. Do they want dinner made? *No, pet. Thanks.*

Leaving the entrance to the mall, they wander into the first shopping atrium. Milo is straight to the indoor fish tank, which reaches over three floors. Sharks and stingrays swim past. He puts his face close to the glass, fogging it up.

Other toddlers run around; squeals echo through the mall. None of them are dressed as nice as Milo. That gorgeous Ralph Lauren hoodie. Navy suits those blue eyes.

'It's the biggest fish tank in the world,' she says.

'It's impressive all right.' Trevor scratches his shoulder, his T-shirt lifting and showing his abs.

'Imagine cleaning the glass.'

'Mam would have a field day,' he laughs.

'So, tell me this, any woman on the cards?' Siobhan watches the slow procession of shoppers through the mall.

'Nothing serious.' Trevor glances down.

'What about Pamela?'

'Long gone.'

'Carolina.'

'Headed home. Her visa.'

He was always a terror for the foreign girls. Between the hook-ups and run-ins with Lucy, he went through a string of them. 'A change is better than a rest,' he once said. There wasn't much 'rest' happening when he got his hands on a Latina. The noise from his room at two a.m. on a Friday night. The foreign girls sounded different. Their 'ohs' and 'ahs'. She'd bet with herself about the race of the girl who'd be sitting downstairs the next morning, waiting for a taxi, and nine times out of ten she was right. It was a miracle Mam didn't put him out on his ear, though Daddy never minded, proud that his son could bag some of the most beautiful women in Dublin. Though would he have minded now, after a decade of him messing around?

Maybe it was the tragedy of the whole thing that kept Mam from doing anything. He hadn't been like it as a boy, a slim little redhead with a cheeky mouth but wouldn't say boo to a mouse. Then Lucy Quirke, Lucy fucking Quirke, bringing the drama. Trevor getting into scrapes and, worst of all, oblivious to every nice girl who came his way.

If only he'd stayed in the army. He was barely in the door and there was that stupid fight on Harcourt Street with Lucy's arsehole boyfriend. A glass bottle thrown and both of them arrested.

'D'you think I'd let him smack her about?' Trevor had said when she collected him from the Garda station.

'There was no fear of her. The claws were out,' Siobhan had replied.

'What if that'd been you or Mam getting hit?'

'Mam was OK about you coming over?' Siobhan asks.

'You know what she's like. Worrying away. She's heading to Cork in the week, down to see you-know-who.' Trevor pulls Milo away from the aquarium. 'We'll come back later.'

'How is Stevo?' Siobhan asks.

'Wasting space.'

'Ah, now . . .' Poor Stevo. He is family after all.

Crazy. That whole world feels like a lifetime ago. Nothing was worse than those Dublin years before Dubai, Martin's business getting worse by the day despite the apparent 'economic boom' and Rocco only a toddler. Buying clothes on eBay to at least look the part, and Martin still with a sour puss as he looked at the receipts. Worse still, paying the mortgage on the pile-of-shite apartment in HSQ. 'At least it'll always be rentable,' Martin said.

Martin's father was a prick through it all, that smug face on him while Martin tried to keep his business afloat, thinking he'd get Martin on the farm yet. She can still see the water in Martin's eyes, the only time she's ever seen him in tears, after they drove home with no money offered to bail them out. 'I hate that man,' was all that Martin said, though he said it six or seven times. 'We'll manage,' she replied. 'Team Cusack.' There was no doubt in her mind that this was only a setback. The Dubai job came along a few months later, and they were able to give two fingers to Richard and all his plans.

Of course, she was the one who had to break the news to Richard and Shirley. Information by that point went from Richard to Shirley to herself, then finally to Martin, and back again. 'Don't kill the messenger,' was the last thing she said on the phone. 'You talk to your son.' But Richard never called.

Siobhan looks down at her watch, her fingers gliding over the Chanel logo. Gorgeous. The faces on the girls when she pulled it out at Rebecca's barbecue. Somewhere between surprise and jealousy. More jealousy. Course, they didn't know it was fake. Ten grand. You couldn't justify it. Even if you had the money. After being so short on cash in Dublin, she can never quite lose the run of herself.

Now and again, she wonders is it right that she and Martin are making so much money when the poor migrants aren't even on minimum wage. But as Martin said, if it wasn't them making money, it'd be someone else, and where else could they give the boys such opportunity?

He was right. What country wasn't built on some form of cheap labour? Famine roads. Victorian England. Most of Europe's cities. If they tried to avoid it, they'd end up on the Aran Islands eating spuds and knitting jumpers.

'In here, Rocco.' She walks into the Diesel store.

'I want to go to Game.'

'In a while. I promise . . . I promise . . . look, we'll definitely get you something. Come on. You too, Milo. We'll find you something nice in the Disney store.'

Now that is a beautiful top; the studs are gorgeous.

'It's very low,' Trevor says.

'Oh, they're nice.' She looks at the pair of torn jeans he is holding.

'A1, Siobhan.' Trevor looks at the price tag and frowns. 'Fuck. I'll hang on for TK Maxx.'

'I'll get them.'

'Don't be daft.' Trevor puts them on the nearest rail. A South-Asian girl slips by, picks them up and returns them to the right stand.

'Oh, it's in grey too.' Siobhan looks at the rail. 'A lovely cotton.' She takes the two tops to the counter and lifts out her card. There are some gorgeous wallets behind the glass – Martin would like them. Black or brown?

Trevor says black. 'It'll go with all his suits.'

She'll have to check out the dresses in Monsoon for the Christmas party. Zara and Karen Millen would be worth a look too. Trevor remains quiet as she calls out the shop names. He asks her how many there are in the mall. 'Over a thousand.'

'A long day so,' he says with a strained smile on his face.

So many gorgeous things. She wishes she could buy every-thing. Even with Martin's six-figure salary, they haven't saved a penny. Rocco's schooling costs an arm and a leg – nearly forty thousand dirhams a year. Lord knows what will happen when Milo joins him and that figure doubles. So much for six-figure salaries and no income tax. It all sounds amazing but everything is relative. Big bills follow big wages.

'We'll go for lunch in a while. Then we'll go watch the fountains, won't we, Milo?' The little boy nods and smiles.

Even though he's seen them loads, he always gets a fright from the popping of the jets.

'Who is your man with the face everywhere?' Trevor asks, glancing at a huge poster that hangs from the middle of the atrium.

'The Sheikh. Martin read his book. He said it's brilliant.'

'Tell that to the Pakistani fellas.' Trevor picks up a Hollister hoodie.

'That's gorgeous. You should get it.'

Trevor looks in the mirror, shifting from side to side. He smiles and they take it to the cash desk. He hands his credit card to the South-Asian girl.

'What's that?' Siobhan glances down at his wallet. A photograph sticks out.

'Nothing.'

'Really?' She knows who the girl is. If only she'd never been friends with Lucy in school, all of this might've been avoided. She'd been pretty brutal once with Trev and said he was just a 'filler man' in between the guys that Lucy had actually wanted to date, but at that point this hot-and-cold crap had been going on over five years. A good woman would've sorted him out. Look at what she'd done for Martin. But how the hell would Trevor ever have a chance with the shadow of that big-titted wagon still fogging his brain?

Poor Beata. She'd been a keeper. But he dropped her too. 'I'm wrecked,' he said afterwards. 'I haven't the energy for a woman.'

'Well, go to bed early and have less intercourse,' Mam replied. One of the rare moments she was annoyed with him.

*

Trevor takes his card back from the assistant and lifts the Hollister bag.

'Whereabouts are you from?' he asks.

'The Philippines.' The girl looks like one of those giggly women you see in those Japanese cartoons Rocco likes.

'Trevor . . . Trevor. The boys need food. Don't you, Milo? Will we get a McDonald's? Some chicken nuggets? Nom nom.' Milo laughs as she tickles his stomach. 'Are you hungry, Rocco? What do you want? Yes, then we'll go to Game. Straight away after. No other shops.'

'Siobhan.' Rebecca waves across from the entrance of the food hall. Siobhan puts down her cheeseburger. There's a streak of ketchup down her dress from Milo's sticky paws. Typical.

'I'm good.' She kisses Rebecca's cheek. There's a smell of lavender. 'This is my brother Trevor.'

Of course, Rebecca gives him a kiss. A flash of the veneers. Her hand touching his arm.

'Where's Mike?'

'In work. You know him.'

'Sit yourself down,' Trevor says. 'Have you time for coffee?' He pulls over a seat before she answers.

'That'd be lovely. A skinny latte, thanks,' Rebecca replies. 'And how are you, Rocco? You must come over and play with George soon. Sound good?' She takes Milo from Siobhan and gives him a cuddle. By some miracle, Milo keeps his hands off her cardigan. He has his eyes on her pearls. As they continue to talk, Siobhan watches his fingers creep upwards.

'Careful, pumpkin,' Rebecca says, pulling his fingers free. 'Look at the cute freckles on your nose,' she says to Siobhan.

'Don't talk to me. Even with factor fifty,' Siobhan replies. So much for Benefit working.

'I'd love a few freckles. They're adorable.' And her English-y skin like Kate Winslet.

'There you go.' Trevor puts down the Costa coffee cup. Rebecca thanks him. A big smile. The two are as bad as each other.

'So, you know each other well?' Trevor says.

'Everyone knows everyone out here,' Siobhan replies.

'We'll have to hang out while Trevor's around.' Rebecca sits up a little. 'Maybe brunch on Friday? Have you heard of Dubai brunches?' Rebecca touches his shoulder.

Siobhan frowns. You never knew what to make of the 'Jumeirah Janes'. She said to Martin how fake they all seemed, swanning around with their personal trainers and hairdressers, bitching about their maids. Martin only laughed at her.

'Aren't you one of them yourself?' he'd said.

'Ah, come on. Hardly,' Siobhan replied. When they'd moved to Dubai without Mam or any family around, it'd been lonely and overwhelming, and she'd threatened Martin she'd fly home if she didn't get help. At the start, when Martin was away, she'd tried being friends with their first maid but that didn't work. The poor thing thought she had done something wrong and got all in a panic.

Milo yanks at Siobhan's maxi-dress.

'OK, OK. The Disney store. Sorry, Rebecca, but I promised him.' Siobhan stands up.

★

'Rebecca is lovely, isn't she?' Trevor says, throwing Milo back on to his shoulders.

'Jesus, Trev, you'll make him sick.'

'It's great that you've friends like her. You weren't sure at the start.'

'She took a shine to you.'

'That was harmless. Do you meet her often?'

'Yeah, at coffee with the girls.'

'It can't be easy with Martin off as much as he is.'

Siobhan doesn't answer. Sometimes it seems like it's the only cloud in an otherwise blue sky. She should really give him a call. Though it's hard to know what to say beyond the 'How are you getting on?' Before, they could chat and she wouldn't have to think about where the next sentence was coming from. That was one good thing about them being broke in Dublin. It kept them close. 'One day, beautiful,' Martin always said after a few drinks, 'I'll have the money of a banker and we'll be living like rock stars.'

The Disney store. Milo runs around like he's on speed. Rocco kicks his plastic bag from Game.

'Stop that,' Siobhan says. 'If you break it, I won't be buying you another one.' Rocco frowns and begins picking a scab on the back of his hand. 'Milo . . . Milo, I said just one thing now. No. Not that. That won't even fit in the car.' A giant Mickey Mouse of all things. *It's the Mickey Mouse Clubhouse, come inside, it's fun inside.* That cartoon. Worse than the Teletubbies.

What's Trevor doing, hovering by the shop entrance? Is he actually enjoying himself? His mood swings, exactly like Granddad Nagle, liking his own space to a point of antisocialism.

Milo pulls at her dress.

'OK, lovie. You can have that. And the chocolate too . . . well, only if you behave for Mammy. Good boy.' Siobhan puts the chocolate dinosaur and Mickey Mouse plastic scooter on the countertop.

'Doesn't he already have one of them?' Trevor asks.

'Not the Mickey one, do you, darling?' Siobhan hands over the card. 'Now, one more place to go . . . only one, I promise. It's for Daddy.'

'My feet are hurting,' Rocco says.

'It's just over here,' Siobhan replies, pointing to the suit shop. Trevor has gone quiet. She wonders if he thinks she spoils the boys. Milo is dragging his scooter. Her three men. A bunch of mopes. She steps inside the shop.

'I want to swap this.' Siobhan puts the bag on the counter and a new shirt beside it.

The shop assistant is useless but no surprises there. Trevor stands beside her, looking at his feet. He's always had a soft spot for the underdog. A typical Irishman. No backbone. Being direct is the only way you get anything sorted on this side of the world. Everyone is on the make, even the shop assistants. She'd fallen for a few of their sob stories early on, before being conned out of one thing or another. The place is a nest of snakes.

Her phone rings. Martin. She finds herself a little breath-less. It always surprises her, the slight anxiety that occurs when his name appears on the screen.

'Hi, love.'

'How are the boys?' he says. His voice is to the point.

'Good. Trevor arrived safe and sound, and we're out seeing the sights. I got you something lovely too. From Diesel.'

'Ah, OK. Look . . .' He pauses, as if unsure of what he's going to say, and Siobhan continues, 'Will I put on Milo? He's wanted to speak to you all day.'

'Not right now. I've a meeting in ten.' A pause. 'Now, don't get mad but I'm going to be delayed here a bit longer.'

Siobhan turns away and walks towards the changing rooms.

'Really? Trev is only here for the week. You promised me.'

'Something came up, like I really have to stay here for a few days and see how it pans out. What do you want me to do about it?' His voice grows impatient.

'But—'

'They're calling me in. Ring you later.'

'Love y—' But he's already gone. She sighs. Do all marriages go like this after a certain point? It's like she can no longer get his attention, 'yeahs', 'ems' and 'ohs' replacing proper conversation.

'How's Blue Eyes?' Trevor asks.

'Fine.' The look on Trevor's face. First time she brought Martin home, he joked that he'd the blond hair and blue eyes of a Russian spy. Daddy laughed. Mam slapped his shoulder and called him a gurrier but she was smiling too.

At least Martin is in Egypt; women are hardly prowling around there the way they do in Dubai. All the porn on his laptop is bad enough. 'I need it to wind down after work,' he said. 'It's only a bit of fun. Come here to me, beautiful. Enough with that face.'

'Look, forget about the shirt.' Siobhan pulls the bag back from the shop assistant. 'Is there anything else you want to look at?'

'Nah.' Four hours and Trevor still has just the one bag. If only he'd let her buy him a few bits. She'd love to spoil him rotten, send him back home with a smile on his face.

Mam was more worried than ever. 'He hasn't that spark he had before. There's no fight in him. I almost preferred it when he was messing around,' she said.

They walk out of the suit shop. Of course, there are still another few hundred places they could check out. But the boys' faces. 'I know where we'll go,' Siobhan says.

'They don't show this place in the guidebook. It's like we're in India or something,' Trevor says. Slipping down the narrow streets of Birr Dubai, past stands of cheap watches and souvenirs, Siobhan catches him just before he steps out in front of a speeding motorbike. Walking past a glittering mosque of purple and mint-green mosaic, Trevor asks her to stop.

'Would you get my picture? Can we go inside?'

'I wouldn't if I were you.' She glances in the entrance but it's hard to see. 'You don't wanna be annoying them out here . . . Rocco, get in off the road.'

She takes Trevor's picture, Milo tucked into his chest. Rocco is pointing at something off camera. He really shouldn't point. What did Mam used to say? 'Monkeys point, Trevor, rude little monkeys.'

'Is there anything you're looking for here?' Trevor asks.

'If there was a nice watch for Martin. He's always talking about getting a Hublot.' Maybe it's worth splashing out. It might keep him happy for another few months.

They wander down narrower and narrower streets. Men call out to them from inside shops. 'Scarves for the lady?'

'What do you have?' Trevor asks one of them.

'Anything, everything you want, sir.'

Trevor laughs.

'These lads would sell their grannies if they'd get a few quid.' He yanks his head sideways so a keffiyeh isn't wrapped around his head.

'You should get one,' Siobhan says. 'With a pair of Ray-Bans you'd nearly pass for an Arab.' She's relieved. He seems to be more himself. In the mall he was hard work, like a caged bull.

'Hi, Ma'am, you like watches? Chanel? Gucci? Armani? Versace?' An Indian-looking lad in his thirties, wearing lots of gold with stonewashed denim, comes out of an abandoned shop. Indian? No. Lebanese.

'Yes.' Siobhan glances at Trevor. He nods. They go into what appears to be a small abandoned shopping mall. Climbing a broken escalator, its steps embedded with dirt and torn packaging, they step inside a small shopfront, through broken boxes and torn plastic bags.

'It's like *28 Days Later*,' Trevor says. But his eyes brighten as the man pushes against a partition and it slides back. Behind is a room with shelves of designer glasses, bags and watches.

The neon light flickers. Siobhan glances around, touching a fake Louis Vuitton satchel.

'These are no good, boss. You have better quality.'

Trevor is looking at his feet again. He doesn't understand. If you don't push, you don't get.

'OK, Ma'am.' The man presses against another fake wall and in behind is a smaller room. Siobhan smiles.

'That's more like it. Don't touch anything, Milo.'

Trevor browses along the shelves, hands by his side. The man watches them.

'You have any Police sunglasses?' he asks.

Siobhan frowns as an RTA slips around her. Who does he think he is, James Bond? Typical, Sheikh Zayed Road in rush hour. Everyone driving with the pedal down and only three feet between her and the next car. Just as well they'd gone home and collected the 4x4.

In the passenger seat, Trevor watches the Burj Khalifa dwarfing the skyscrapers around it. It is beautiful. Even though she sees it almost daily, there's something magic about its shape. The tallest building of them all, it is also the most elegant. Simple. Slender. Martin always raved about it when they went home to Ireland. 'These Arab guys have vision,' he said. Of course, no one back home understood what he was going on about.

'Imagine, he'll be climbing that Wednesday. They say the film crews are already setting up,' Siobhan says.

'It's some building.'

'The point at the top. It always reminds me of the Pyramids.'

91

'How many slaves built them?'

Siobhan glances in her mirror. The boys are crashed out in the back.

'What can we do? It's not our fault.'

'I suppose.'

'Sometimes you just have to get on with things, Trev,' she adds. 'When you've a few quid in the bank you can worry about principles.' She says the words but feels odd quoting Martin. 'I'll take you to Karama another day. There's great fakes there too. You'll have to go to Bu Qtair restaurant too. Literally, about as anti-Dubai as you can get. A few plastic tables and chairs outside a shack. The food is unreal, though. I know you're not mad on fish, but if you tasted these prawns. Divine isn't even the word.'

'Crackin,' Trevor replies. Imagine, once again, he's come all the way to Dubai for a taste of the good life, and the only places he wants to go are the back-street dives, hunting down alleys that are the Middle Eastern equivalent of Moore Street. 'All dese bananas for a euro.'

She can't understand it. On the phone they've talked about him moving, getting his own personal training business underway, and he seemed excited, but now he's here she's not sure he even likes Dubai.

At that moment, Siobhan remembers something she was told by one of Rocco's teachers.

'They used to dive for pearls here. Dubai was known for it, wild pearls . . . imagine. It was like a gold rush before all the oil.'

'Oh.' Trevor turns towards her.

'Yeah, they'd have to go down like a hundred feet without

92

air. The chances of them drowning and then actually finding a pearl. It was crazy. But like, if they found one . . . it was
like winning the Lotto. You were made.'

'Or dead.'

'Well, yeah. Kind of romantic though, don't you think?
"All or nothing."'

'They don't do it any more?'

'They're all farmed now.'

Trevor sighs. She's surprised, as she was sure he'd like that
story. Nothing seems to please him sometimes. What exactly
does he want? He likes designer clothes but it seems to be
more about his own body than the label. He even wears the
extra-small T-shirts that Mam buys him in Penneys (Mam
knew to get the extra-smalls). As he sometimes says, 'Ten-
dollar T-shirt, million-dollar muscles.'

No wonder he and Martin have nothing to say to each
other. Martin is all about the flash. He wouldn't be seen dead
in a Penneys T-shirt. No matter how rich they are, he pretends to be richer. And why not? 'You have to fake it to make
it,' he said once.

'The way you were haggling with your man inside the shop.
I didn't know where to look.' Trevor glances over his shoulder. The Burj Khalifa is somewhere behind them. The
straight road appears to go nowhere but desert.

'There's no point in just giving them money.'

'Six hundred dirhams. It was for nothing,' Trevor says,
scratching at the glass on his fake Rolex. Siobhan wonders
will he keep wearing it beyond the next few days. Once
the rush of the purchase is over, will he glance down and

think he looks like a right knob-end and just put it in a drawer?'

'They won't respect you unless you knock them down. Didn't I get the money off in the end?'

'In all fairness, you did.'

'What are those cars with the sand on them?' Trevor asks. 'The ones in the car park.'

'That's people who legged it. If you get in trouble out here, you head straight to the airport. You don't hang around for the police to take your passport.'

'They'd leave a new Merc, just like that?'

'Not much good to you in prison.'

'Fuck.'

'At least it's safe here. I can let the boys go with Gete and not worry. You remember that time when I was on the camogie team in school? That fella flashing at us girls through the fence? Dirty fuck. If he did that here, they'd chop his cock off.'

'I suppose.' Trevor looks at a huge billboard that lines the side of the road. *Whoever said winning isn't everything doesn't know Dubai.* Beside it is a picture of the Sheikh.

Siobhan is silent. She glances in the mirror at the boys. Rocco is dotey asleep. If only he could be the same awake. Martin should be giving him a bit of discipline. Why does she always have to be bad cop?

'Are things good now, since . . .' The second she's said the words, Siobhan realizes it's not the right moment.

'What?'

'Nothing. I'm delighted you've come.'

It is only day two after all. No need to ask too many

questions. It's great to just have him here – a grown-up to talk to. She could talk to the girls in the other villas, but it isn't the same. Sometimes, when Milo is off with Gete and Rocco is off in school, the house becomes something strange. Too silent. There is no one to call. The girls back home are all at work. Martin can barely talk for more than a minute. There's the internet, of course, but how many times can she press refresh on her profile?

It could be different if Trev landed a job in a gym here. He'd get to hang out with the boys – give them a bit of male attention when Martin isn't around, play football and talk about guy stuff. Not that she'd want him giving Rocco advice on women any time soon, or ever, for that matter.

'Did many come out for Daddy's anniversary mass?' Siobhan asks, the road endless, though the first shadows of the Media City skyscrapers appear in the distance.

'Just me and Mam. Five years – can you believe it?'

'I don't like missing it.'

'That's life.'

'Poor Daddy. He was too young.'

'He was mad about you.'

Siobhan doesn't reply. Maybe Trevor didn't notice how things ended. She'd always been Daddy's favourite, 'fathers and their daughters' and all that, but when Martin came on the scene something changed. The things he'd say behind Martin's back. There was an almighty bust-up the week before their engagement:

'That's new, is it?' Daddy had peered out the living room window at Martin's new car.

'Yes,' she replied.

'How many seats?'

'Two.'

Daddy laughed. She knew what he was thinking. She waited for him to ask what size engine it was and how much the insurance would cost, relishing the thought that he'd have more reasons to dislike Martin. Course, he didn't know that Rocco was on the way and they wanted to tie the knot before he was born.

'It's gorgeous,' she said. 'You should see the looks we get.'

'Yeah. "Look at the dopes." ' Daddy laughed.

'Daddy.' She gave him a look. 'That's my future husband. Get with the fucking programme.'

She and Daddy were never the same after that. He did the motions, said the right things at the wedding reception, but it was the lack of bad jokes that let her know he wasn't happy.

She'd hoped that in time he'd see Martin for what he really was, that yeah, he did talk a fair amount of shite, but that was only because Richard made him feel so bad about things. Martin worked himself to death for her and the kids, was a handsome devil, spoilt them all rotten, and could make her laugh till tears came to her eyes. But Daddy never got to see any of that. The heart attack finished him off within the year, and when people at the funeral told her 'you were his favourite' instead of offering her any comfort, it hurt like hell.

Trevor strains forward, gazing across the road at the Al Kazim Towers, turning the knob for the radio. The DJ is talking about a dead girl. Trevor turns the volume low.

'I think I might head out later. I've an awful thirst on me,' he says. She must've unnerved him with her earlier question. That fateful night in the Liffey.

'A thirst? I'll book you into the GUM clinic, will I?' Sometimes all she could do was joke about his behaviour. She could feel it coming on all day. He'd get in a humour – she calls it a 'humour' because she can't think what else to call it when he disconnects and goes beyond her reach. He'd vanish off out, and the next thing he'd be back home at the end of the night, royally pissed, with some girl in tow.

The most upsetting thing was Siobhan could sense, in amongst all the laughs and bravado with the lads, Trevor wasn't even enjoying the nights. It was like he couldn't stop. She knows that feeling herself, the rush of going out, the looking forward to something, how it can make feeling bad go away for a short time. That seemed grand at nineteen, but almost a decade later it feels more tragic than fun.

'You've an awful mind.' Trevor laughs. He glances at the boys in the back.

'You're a terrible example to them.'

'I suppose.' He looks back at the horizon.

Lydia

Lydia Sushkova thinks she would've been as famous as Maria Maksakova if she'd had a better voice. All the girls said she was more beautiful. Bianca even said she had the best body in Dubai. Poor Bianca with legs like an antique chair.

The RTA stops across the road from the Westin hotel. Lydia steps out of the car and into the marble lobby with Eric (probably not his real name), ignoring the Pakistani doorman standing at the front desk, dressed like a toy monkey with crashing cymbals. The lobby is refreshing. Even the two minutes on the street have made her brow damp.

Her clients are stupid. Fake name at the bar then phone bills lying open in their apartments. Or tags on their luggage in hotels. She doesn't give her real name either, calling herself Anna Karenina. Most of the time they don't even notice.

Mama says being good-looking is bad. 'It gives you ideas. Makes you lazy. One day you'll be old with nothing.' But she is jealous. She was beautiful, worked hard, and ended up old and poor anyway.

Eric has a bald patch. He is about the same height as she is, but her heels mean she can see the light on his scalp. Though his blue-and-white striped shirt is not tucked in, the outline of his love handles comes through the fabric. He has no wedding ring and there is no tan line. Not that it matters.

Many of them don't bother to remove their rings, their wives back in Europe and America.

Men are pigs. Sweaty hairy monkeys. Lydia smiles and tries not to look at the tuft of fair grey hair that crawls out from underneath his shirt. He has a weak chin, a sad face, like melted wax.

Eric was confident in the York. 'I have a big cock,' he whispered on the dance floor. She laughed.

'All men say such things.'

'I do. You'd even pay me for it.'

She could feel something against her dress. His breath smelt of mint and alcohol.

'There is nothing for free in life,' she said. 'A thousand dirhams an hour. Three thousand the night.'

'We'll start with a thousand,' he said. He took out two notes – five hundreds – and tucked them into the strap of her dress. 'Not many girls can take me for long.'

'You are a cocky man.' She laughed and allowed him to slip his arm around her waist. 'You are staying close?'

'By the Westin. Let's get out of here.'

'Sure . . . I am Anna.' She looked over at Bianca. Bianca danced with an Asian businessman. His thigh was high between her legs. Bianca waved.

In the lift, Lydia straightens her dress. Yes. She is still beautiful. She is always the first to find a customer in a club. Poor Bianca. The Asian girls never do as well, always left with the men who have not so much money.

Lydia fixes her hair in the lift mirror. Not a line on her face; there are some years before her time is done. Eric glances at his watch. A Montegrappa. His right hand rests on her back but doesn't travel lower. A gentleman. Maybe. Some men can be very attentive even though money had been paid.

Is he as big as he says? He is very confident for a fat bald man. He has nice green eyes – the only part that doesn't look old. He cannot dress; his shirt is Dolce & Gabbana but his jeans are too baggy and make him look short. A wife would have fixed that.

Before, she might've hoped that something could've happened with a man like this. But dating clients did not work. They always knew where she came from and jealousy would eat them up in time. She could never be trusted, and when they lost their temper they would call her a whore.

Floor fifty-six. Eric stands back while Lydia walks out into the hallway. Marble. A plant on a mahogany table. Another mirror. She follows him to the furthest apartment. Stuck under the door are a number of takeaway leaflets.

'You live here alone?'

He nods. Inside, a marble hallway opens out into a large dining room of French furniture. It looks odd to see old-style furniture in a new apartment. Beyond, the full-length windows look east towards The Palm, the fronds spread out like diamond fingers. Beside them, the twin Chrysler buildings are lit with blue fluorescent lights.

'Drink?' Eric asks. She shakes her head, glancing down at her fake Dior watch from Birr Dubai. He laughs. 'Time is ticking, is it?'

'These minutes are not cheap.'

'This way.' He leads her towards the bedroom. She is

docile, compliant. He will make a good regular client. In time, he might even buy her nice jewellery, like some of the other men have.

In the end, it is not about sex with men, even if they do talk filthy things to their friends in bars and clubs. 'Make them feel important,' is what Svetlana said before her first time back in Moscow. 'Moan with pleasure at each touch. Pretend to come. Afterwards, listen to them while their emotions are open. Men fall in love in the moments after fucking.'

Eric kisses her, searching for her tongue with his. His hands slide down her back, grabbing her rear. She feels him pushing against her thigh. The expected formula begins: kissing, wanking, sucking, licking, and fucking. 'Deep breaths,' he whispers as he enters. She tries to relax, but it's difficult when she knows it will hurt after a certain number of inches. She thinks about his bald patch, the scratching of his body hair on her breasts and stomach, but there is no ignoring the stretching feeling.

Afterwards, he disposes of the condom on the floor.

'Too much?'

'You did not lie.' She smiles. She wipes her stomach with a tissue. 'I do not come for many men.'

'You did not fake it?'

Lydia smiles, then glances at her watch.

'My time is finished?'

She nods. It's been over an hour.

'I'll get myself a taxi. Can I shower first?' She picks up her underwear and walks towards the mirror. There is an ache low down in her abdomen.

★

Outside, she flags an RTA.

'Buddha Bar, boss.' The taxi driver looks a couple of times in the mirror. She must appear mythical to him. Not many blonde women of 175 centimetres where he is from. There is a bad smell of sweat. He has probably come from a remote mountain.

'Long day, boss?'

He nods. Her phone vibrates. She reads the message.

You are free another time? Mr Big Cock is greedy.

Of course. X X.

Kiss-kiss – men like these sorts of things. Their egos. They like to think they are good enough lovers to seduce a prostitute.

After paying her fare and getting out of the RTA, Lydia kisses the bouncer outside Buddha Bar.

'Hello, Nicolas. Good night?'

'It is quiet. Some English at the bar. A nice Rolex at the back. Svetlana is with him.'

'That means nothing.' They both laugh. She is more beautiful than any of the other women. She is first to leave bars. Of course, some day she won't be. But that isn't today. Or tomorrow.

There is a red-haired man at the bar. Very muscled. A personal trainer. Personal trainers never have money the way some businessmen do. She stands at the counter and taps her nails on its polished surface. A barman asks if she would like a drink.

'Not now. Thank you.'

House music plays. A large golden Buddha looks down on scattered groups at various tables. Low-key lighting. Shiny black stools. Gold cushions and curtains. Gentle chatter. It's easy to spot the other working girls. Their skirts are shorter.

They look around the room, not at their friends. They smile when men look over.

At the back, there is a man looking at her. Lots of jewellery. Lebanese. All show, no money. Not generous with their cash. The English group have taken a corner table. A bottle of Grey Goose is in front of them. The English talk too loud and never want to pay. It's the Arab men who have real money. It is possible to get three times the fee she would get from a white customer.

However, Mr Blue Eyes pays well. A strange accent. He always pays more if there are other women involved.

'I did not know you Irishmen were so cheeky,' she had said, when he took out a bottle of amyl nitrite and asked if she would use her finger to find the spot.

Last Thursday, he had a girl with him.

'You mind if a third joins us?' he asked.

'You pay, you get,' Lydia replied. She smiled at the girl. 'You are Brazilian?'

The girl looked confused.

'Turkish. My name is Hiba.'

'How are you? You want a drink?' The red-haired man stops in front of her. She can smell Le Male by Jean Paul Gaultier. Through his white shirt she can see his nipples. Diesel jeans. Very good.

'I am well. Thank you.'

'Good night?'

Lydia doesn't respond.

'Are you sure you don't want a drink? You're Russian, right? You can't say no to vodka and call yourself Russian.'

'I'll have a Grey Goose.' One hundred and twenty dirhams. That will scare him away. But the ginger man orders one for himself too and hands over his card. Flashing his holiday money.

'I'm Terrance.' He hesitates as he says it. As if his name matters.

'Anna.' She shakes his hand.

'You're here with friends?'

'No.'

'You're out alone?'

She nods.

'Oh . . . *Oh* . . .' He pauses, looking down for a second, and she wonders if he is going to walk away. He frowns, then turns back to her.

'I've never, ya know, gone down that route. I've always been able to, you know, easy enough.' His cheeks are growing red. Lydia nods, not quite sure of what he is saying. She wonders if he is getting aroused at the idea of what she does.

'How'd you get doing that sort of thing? Like, you could be a model. *FHM* or anything.'

'I have modelled.'

'I knew it. Russian women are lookers.' He laughs and his muscled torso tightens, the veins bulging. 'You remind me of a girl I knew back home. Lucy was her name.' He leans from foot to foot, apparently nervous.

'Very good.' There's an awkward pause. He is looking at her neck.

'That's a nice necklace.'

She touches the single pearl on the gold chain.

'Thank you.'

'Is it a real one?'

'A real what?'

'A real . . . it doesn't matter.' He pauses. She stares at him. 'So, have you been in this . . . line of work long?'

'Not long.'

'Do you mind it? Like, sorry now, if it's nosy for me to ask.'

'It's fine.' She can feel her impatience increase; she turns away and reaches for her purse. These amateur time-wasters.

'Look, stay. At least for your drink. I'm on my holidays and this place' – he glances around – 'is no craic.'

'Maybe come on a Thursday when it is busy.' She keeps moving.

'Stop. Wait up a second . . . OK. OK. Like is it expensive?'

She lets go of her purse and looks at him again.

'One thousand an hour. Three for the night.'

'Christ. I'll have to go into the business myself.' He laughs. He glances left and right.

'You want an hour? Or more?'

'Ah . . .' She can see his brain deliberating. He really is new to this. 'Well, like, if you don't mind.'

'Cash up front.'

'OK. But like, I don't have a place. I'm with family. Not my wife or anything like that, my sister and her kids.'

'That's fine. I do.' Men are no good at lying.

'So, when does the clock start?' The man then washes back his drink and returns it hard on the counter.

'Clock. What clock?'

'Don't worry about it. Go easy on me now, Anna. I'm all new to this thing.'

'You are virgin?'

Terrance laughs. It appears his confidence is returning.

'Nah. I haven't been one of those in a long time. You're in for a treat.'

'Why? Are you a big man?'

'You'll remember this night, all right.' He's trying to make jokes, it appears, but they aren't funny. Lydia lets the cool vodka slip down her throat, enjoying the warmth in her stomach. 'Will we get out of here?'

'Of course.'

She smiles at Nicolas as she passes through the entrance, following the red-haired man. Nicolas calls out goodnight but in an unfamiliar way, like he would to any customer.

'This is for yourself,' the red-haired man says, handing her a wad of money, with all the manner of a father giving his daughter something to spend. Lydia slips it inside her coat pocket.

'I will flag cab,' she says. 'You have change?'

He nods. When the RTA comes, he opens the door for her, touching her back lightly as she gets in and she tells the driver where to go. When he sits down, she feels the heat of his leg against hers, the immense amount of muscle hard against her thigh. It is a wonder his jeans do not rip.

She wonders if he is already aroused. Some of the new clients do not get to intercourse before losing control. Others are the opposite and do not get hard at all. Sex is strange on the mind. Drunkenness. Hangover. Guilt. Tiredness. Heartache. All is exposed.

When sex is a failure, they tell her it's never happened before, that they've never come so quick. She tells them that she enjoyed their company anyway. She can't tell them it doesn't matter whether they perform or not, that it's about the money. Of course, some blame her, saying her looks made it hard for them to keep in control. Others call her a whore. Mostly, the failures want her to leave.

The red-haired man ... what was his name again? Terrance. Yes. He taps her thigh, giving her another wink. She hopes that Bianca and Svetlana have cleaned the living area.

The red-haired man looks around her room, glancing at a picture of a man for a second, then turns back.

'Your brother?'

'Yes. Igor.'

'He looks like you. A handsome bunch . . .'

'He is in Russia.'

There is a pause.

'So . . .' There is something in the way he holds his shoulders that seems boy-like. Lydia moves forward. He places his hands on her hips like they are slow dancing in a club. His lips are thin, his tongue sharp. She's learnt to adapt to the different types of kissers, the darting tongues, the wetness, the stale taste of cigarettes. It is worth adapting; for every thousand she makes, she saves four hundred. She will be old one day. But not poor.

Well, she tries to save four hundred. But there is a beautiful Gucci halterneck that is on sale, that turquoise Hermès scarf, the Louis Vuitton weekend luggage and the Louboutin Mary-Janes. There are the facials, the microdermabrasions, the spray tans, the manicures and pedicures. There is the gym trainer, the hairdresser and the taxis. 'We'll all be dead before we're old,' Bianca says. She saves nothing at all.

Sex with this man isn't bad. His body is solid. He has a regular-sized penis. Though his six-pack looks like a turtle-shell, as if it's from injections.

'You ready? You close?' he asks.

She nods.

'Are you?'

'Yes. So . . . so close.'

'Yes. Me too.' She moans at the right moment. He pulls the right sort of face and groans. A few harder thrusts before his weight comes down on her.

'You're some woman.'

'I'm glad you are happy.'

He stays inside her for a number of moments, looking at her face closely. He is like a saint having a vision, like the ones in Mama's prayer book.

'Can we do that again?' he says as he lies next to her.

'As often as you want. It's a thou—'

'Thousand dirham.' He laughs. He gets the hint from her stiff body. 'Good stuff. I better be getting back to the sister and the kids.' He rises off the bed and puts on his River Island boxers. 'Nice meeting you, Anna. You have a number?'

'Of course.' She calls it out. 'Nice to meet you . . .'

'Terrance. No. Stay there. Don't be stressing yourself. I'll find my own way out.' His cheeks grow red again and he can't quite look at her as he puts on his shoes. She understands what has happened. The haze of his orgasm has faded; that fleeting 'in love' feeling has morphed into embarrassment.

She watches as he leaves the room, lifting her ear to make sure the apartment door clicks shut. After a moment, she checks the main room to see that he's definitely gone before turning on the shower.

The water trickles down over her torso. Lydia turns, letting the jets hit her shoulders. The red-haired man is like the other Irish, just normal size below. When they drink wine together, she, Bianca and Svetlana often discuss dimensions:

'Russians. They are biggest,' Bianca said.

'No, Canadians,' Svetlana said. 'Or Brazilians. Though they are not very pretty. Too curved.'

'Tell us, Lydia, what do you think?' Bianca added. 'Who was your best? Who was your first?'

Lydia pours the Clinique body wash into her palms and smoothes it lightly over her arms, not wanting her tan to fade. She thinks back to five years ago. Edward. English. Awful sex in a bad hotel. He left money beside the bed the next morning. It was easy.

What would Igor say about her new 'profession'? Hosting in Odessa made no money and the modelling work dried up as soon as she was twenty. What was there left to do in life? Continue hosting in Moscow till she was too old for that? Watch people eat and have a good time while she worked? There is no joy in a party if you are on the wrong side of the glass, looking in on it.

Perhaps Igor wouldn't say anything. He might just cut her off. It was Veronika's doing, of course, slowly pushing her out. There was something in the way he talked that changed after he started dating that woman; his voice didn't sound like himself when he made excuses for cancelling her visits.

'You're going to see Veronika, aren't you?' Lydia would laugh. 'She has you hooked.' But it was not funny after his tenth apology. She'd always won fights over men but she couldn't win this battle.

Why do men always marry the girls who are good-looking but not the best-looking? Veronika and her ugly wedding dress, which maybe wasn't ugly. Her hawk face would've looked stupid surrounded by frills. The type of face that won't age. All bones.

After the wedding, Igor was a ghost. Mama was unhappy. 'He is selfish, that boy. No gratitude for my sacrifices. And you, Lydia, when are you home? Working all weekend, like a fallen woman. Why do you not find a man?'

'Igor got married and you complain. I don't marry and you still complain. Why don't you shut up?'

Mama muttered to herself. Lydia could make out a scattering of words: 'ingratitude', 'selfishness', 'heartless'. The same words that she said every day. She couldn't blame Igor for taking his chance with Veronika. The steel wire that ran through her would mean they'd make something of their lives.

What was outside Mama's window?

Poverty.

Poor: the worst word in the world. She would never be poor again. The square apartments. The rubbish on the streets, the rubble, the pipes and electric factories. The hopelessness. Wild dogs. The metal bars on windows. The dark corridors. Boys selling the copper. Bad teeth, baseball caps. Used needles.

'You are a model?' a man had asked her as she served him wine; Odessa was busy and he had to repeat the question over the noise of clinking cutlery.

'I was. Not so much now.'

'I may have work for you. I've a client in Dubai. Have you been? Here is my card.'

It seemed only natural that during her two months in Dubai they would fuck. She lived with him on The Palm and enjoyed her time; it was only sex after all. Though she knew it would end – how all these flings with photographers ended. A new girl would appear. The lens would shift.

'There is no need to apologize,' she said, after she found the used condoms in the bin. 'I will be fine.'

'What will you do?'

'Carry on, of course.'

'What do you want?'

'I don't know. I'm too tired.'

As the RTA drove back to Dubai airport, she thought about Mama, about how cold Moscow would be. She touched the Fendi handbag he'd bought her, thinking about the twenty thousand dirhams in her purse. What was there back home? She had nothing to lose.

'Boss, I've changed my mind. Turn around.'

Aasim

'You're sure you want to go here?' Khaled asks.

'I'm not going home,' Aasim replies. Another vodka soda lime is needed.

Khaled seems nervous, glancing over his shoulder at the queue of Arabic and Caucasian men, though the Arabic men are most likely Lebanese. Few locals come to this night; they wouldn't risk being spotted in a club full of mostly men when they can fly to London and go to Heaven or one of the clubs in Vauxhall.

Khaled strokes the backs of his arms, his low V-necked T-shirt like a second skin. How does he fit in so much gym and a full-time job? He and Khaled have known each other since school, but they've only become friends since Aasim spotted Khaled's tell-tale birthmark on a headless torso pic on Grindr. *Khaled?* He'd typed, feeling his nerves rise, but after some confusion, they'd ended up chatting as if everything was normal. Now, they hang out whenever he's home from Dublin.

'Your parents OK with that?'

'I'm twenty years old, for f—' Aasim stops, realizing he's on the street and he's not in Europe.

Khaled is silent.

'He's cute.' Aasim leans sideways, looking at the tall blond guy two places in front.

'German?'

Aasim nods. He clenches his teeth, his nostrils flaring. It distracts from the hot feeling behind his eyes.

'You OK?'

'I'm fine.'

Poor Khaled; he hadn't wanted to go out. However, when he threatened to go out anyway, there was nothing Khaled could do. The queue inches forward. Ahead, the men are patted down before walking through a metal detector. One guy is wearing boots outside his jeans. Aasim glances at Khaled.

'O. V. E. R.' He slowly says the letters. Khaled smiles. Though the smile vanishes almost immediately.

Aasim frowns. Is he one of 'those' people now? The type that people tiptoe around. 'Didn't you hear about his sister?' That awful invisible barrier that he'd slipped through, no longer in the regular category but somebody to be treated with caution. Conversations edited for fear of causing upset.

Hiyam is dead. Hiyam. Is. Dead.

No. Hiyam isn't dead.

But she is dead.

What a headfuck. How can she be dead? He lifts out his phone and scans through her texts, some only weeks old. Technology is weird. It's hard to die completely. All these electronic ghosts:

Saw the new Louis V in Emirates. You want me to send it over to you? They'll do the monogram. Bisous
Mahmoud!!!!! I swear if he tells Mama . . .
Did you hear the Only Girl. Rihanna is AMAZE!

Eugh. Three hours with Nana!!! Why won't she just die already? Bored.com.

And yet, she is dead. On Saturday, Mama and Nana had bathed Hiyam's body five times, binding it with cloth. It was all so quick. When it was someone old, someone who was going to die, the burial within the day felt comprehensible, but to go from Mahmoud's call on Friday morning about Hiyam's death, to a funeral in Dubai Saturday afternoon . . . it made Aasim's head spin.

'Her hair was matted with blood,' Nana said, shaking her head, and Aasim had felt a phantom pain run through his torso. Mama had begun to pray and Baba held Mama's shoulders. There was a shuddering in her body, but no sound came from her.

Later, after the small funeral at the mosque, Hiyam's body had been laid on its side in the grave, facing west to Mecca. Mahmoud had been one of the four carrying the casket and Aasim had wanted to shout, 'It shouldn't be you doing that. She didn't even like you.' He said nothing.

'We created you from it, and return you into it, and from it we will raise you a second time.' They'd recited the Quranic verse. Baba supervised while soil filled the grave.

'Aasim.' Khaled nudges him as the queue moves forward.

'Gross.' Aasim scans over his shoulder at the men. He straightens his shirt. Alexander McQueen. Autumn 2010. Eugh. He hates the sound of his laugh. It sounds tinny.

'Where did you tell your parents you were going?'

'To yours.'

'What if they see us?' The risky bit is queuing on the street, wondering who could be in the passing cars.

'Here?' Aasim lifts his arms. A security guard pats him down. He makes a face as the guard rubs his legs. Khaled laughs. They step through the metal detector and, on the other side, another guard quickly runs another device over their bodies.

'This is ridiculous,' Aasim says as they walk towards the main entrance.

'Come to Jordan. The boys loved you.'

'When this is over. Fuuuuck. I can't bear it here.'

'The worst bit is done now.' Khaled puts his hand on Aasim's shoulder. The music echoes from inside. It's 'Bad Romance'. The beat is infectious as Lady Gaga calls out for love.

'Best. Song. Ever.' Khaled nudges him. Aasim smiles as the door opens and the music becomes louder. Inside, the curved wooden walls are embedded with various blue lights.

'What do you want?' Khaled shouts.

'Vodka . . .

'. . . soda, lime.'

'Make it a double.' Aasim slips through the crowd of mostly men, past the numerous bouncers, not so much there to prevent fights but to make sure no one is getting too 'friendly'. A tap on the shoulder and the two know to step apart.

There's a queue for the toilets. Aasim tries to stop the feeling. For three days it's been lodged there, waiting. It feels like nausea, yet he knows he won't be sick.

Hiyam. Fuck. Fuck. Fuck. He pinches his thigh to distract himself from the image of her face in his mind. Seeing her body wrapped in cloth; she was smaller than he remembered. How could a body be smaller, just because someone had died?

A bathroom door opens. Aasim skips the queue. People shout as he slams the door. 'Who the hell do you think you are?'

He leans against the side and closes his eyes, thinking back to RCSI term two. Slicing into a torso. The professor directing them to peel back layers of sinew and muscle. The woman's breasts had looked pale but pert as they were dissected, a way they never looked when she'd been vertical. Afterwards, they'd examined the fine veins, the delicate nerves. Finally, the brain. All the white folds of tissue. Hard to believe there'd been a person in all that meat.

How deep was the wound on Hiyam's head? Baba had only allowed for a surface examination of her body, saying anything else was a desecration. The report simply said there'd been a hard bang to the back of her skull and she fell forward into the water. What was she doing down at the marina? Who was she with?

Sunday, yesterday, he'd heard Baba on the phone. The study door had been ajar and he listened to Baba's angry exclamations.

'Who are you? No. I want the Chief, the man in charge of the investigation. I'm her father. Yes, Mr Husayin to you . . .' There was a long pause. 'Faizan, is that you? How are you? Thank you. Yes, it is a terrible time for our family. My wife, she—'

Aasim's attention had been taken by a maid walking

across the hall tiles. He gave her a look and waved her away. She scuttled down to the kitchen. Aasim turned back to the study door.

'Where? Oh, Faizan . . .' Baba let out a huge sigh. 'Very sensitive. Yes. You must understand that, this must not . . . Good. If you could speak to . . . yes. He'll know what to do. And if there is any update, I want to know immediately. I mean, immediately. I don't want to have to make calls. There have already been rumours. You understand? Good. Thank you, my friend.'

At that moment Aasim slipped away from the door and made his way to his room. Baba was doing what Baba did best, controlling everyone and everything.

Vodka. He needs that fucking vodka. Anything to numb the weird tightness in his chest.

'The queues.' Khaled appears, handing him the glass. Khaled sighs, blinks hard, then glances at his watch. 'I'm up at eight.'

'Eugh. Work. O. V . . .' Aasim begins.

'. . . E. R.'

'I need to dance. No. I need a line of coke, that's what I fucking need.' Aasim glances out at the crowd. The dance floor is packed tight. What can he do to stop this trembling feeling, this chaotic jumble of thoughts that keep rising up?

'Keep it down . . .' Khaled glances over at the nearest bouncer. 'How is David? Has he been in touch?'

'He's texted a bit . . . They wanted to read all of my messages. Can you believe it?' Aasim's voice rises higher.

'Who? Mahmoud?'

'Him and Baba.'

'Shit.'

'I know. I need to get back to Ireland. I hate Dubai. I'm so fucking sick of it.' If it wasn't for Mama, he'd never come back again. Never, ever. Hiyam was the only one who'd understood, or half understood, or maybe just attempted to understand.

Every time he lands in this fucking place, it feels like his life is no longer his own. Even Mama, who he loves more than anything, won't get it. He thinks of Mama's sad face as she told him about Baba and the girl. He doesn't want her to know this about his own secret life, and for her to look at him with those same sad disillusioned eyes.

'Hi, Aasim.'

Aasim turns around. It's The American. His first.

'How've you been?' Aasim replies, trying to sound normal. The American reaches in for a hug. The scent of Abercrombie aftershave is overwhelming. His apartment smelt like one of their shops.

'Long time no hear, buddy. How's med school?'

'Yes. It's good. Khaled, this is Tony.'

They shake hands. Already, Aasim can sense his clothes have taken on The American's smell, drowning out his Armani.

'Are you back on vacation? We have to meet again.'

'I'm here for two weeks,' Aasim says. 'Just a short trip.' He glances at Khaled but Khaled is trying to get the barman's attention.

'You have my number still? We should definitely hang out. The new place needs a christening.' He laughs. Great teeth. Hot, though probably not as hot as he was in his twenties. Still, the body.

'I might be around later,' Aasim says. 'It depends if I can get away.'

The American pats his arm. 'I'll wait for your message.'

Aasim feels his cock pushing hard against his jeans. He drinks back most of the vodka, watching The American walk away. What is that? Drink six? Seven? A bottle of poppers and an hour with that body. Sounds tempting, if only to distract from the chaos of his mind.

What is it, almost three years since that first hook-up? They'd glanced at each other in JBR Costa. The American wore a black wife beater and grey sweatpants, through which Aasim could see the outline of his underwear.

An hour later, after they finished their coffees, Aasim asked if he lived close. The American nodded. They walked through the landscaped gardens; a few maids watched as white children laughed and ran in and out of the water sprinklers on the grass. Entering a steel apartment block, Aasim avoided eye contact with the Indian doorman. His forehead felt hot and he could hear the beat of his heart, though he couldn't ignore the feeling of arousal.

He drank wine for the first time. They inched closer on the couch. Five glasses in, he leaned over, and The American laughed and told him to ease up on the tongue. Aasim followed him on to the balcony, watching the lights in the surrounding skyscrapers. He wondered if they could be observed, though The American had turned his off.

They began kissing again. When he left the apartment some time later, thick-headed and uncertain, a shot of terror ran through him. What if they'd been seen?

'Where'd Tony go?' Khaled asks.

'Back to his friends.'

Khaled glances down at the phone in Aasim's hand.

'Don't do it, man. Not today. It's too soon after everything. You don't know what you're doing.'

'I need to blow off steam.'

'What about David?'

'He's on the other side of the world.' Aasim takes the drink from Khaled's hand. 'Do you have to go into work tomorrow?'

'Yes. There's a load of bugs with the app.'

Aasim pushes out his lower lip.

'If only I'd rich parents like yours.' Khaled smiles, though this annoys Aasim.

'You don't. They fucking own you.'

'They own me anyway. You know they want me to marry?'

'What did you say?'

'Nothing. I keep making excuses.'

'What time is it?'

'One thirty.'

'Fuck. I need to get out of Dubai,' Aasim says again.

Khaled appears to listen but the sentences are coming out all disconnected.

'. . . I said to them, "I told you in London I hadn't spoken to Hiyam in ages," but Mahmoud kept calling me a liar and saying I had to know something because Hiyam and I were always up to no good. Mama started crying and Baba told him to back off.' Aasim lifts his drink and takes a large gulp, his hands shaking. 'They are all freaked out because they thought she was with Fadiyah but she wasn't.' The words tumble out.

'What?' Khaled's face changes.

'That wasn't even the weirdest bit. Baba said something about the York, that gross hotel, and I was like, what the hell are you on about? But he wouldn't tell me.' Aasim swallows back the rest of his drink. Even in his alcohol-induced haze, he knows he's said too much. 'Let's get another.'

'You've not had enough?'

'I'm fine.' Fuck. Alcohol is a bitch. It feels kind of good for a while, then the sick feeling returns again.

'You wanna go back to mine?'

'I've got to go home. If I'm not back in the morning . . .'

'I'll drive you.'

'I'll get a taxi. You've got work and it's in the wrong direction.'

'It's not a problem. Honestly.'

'No. I'll get an RTA.'

It's warm on the street. The noise of the bar stays in Aasim's ears. He tries not to think about the tightness that is filling his chest. He's always been a lousy drunk, unless his mood is good to begin with. And how often is that the case?

'You go get your car,' he says.

'I'm seeing you to an RTA.' Khaled puts his arm out on to the road. A cream-and-red car pulls up.

'Thanks for coming out.' Aasim hugs him.

'My pleasure, bro. Well, not my pleasure. You know what I mean. Take care of yourself and I'll call tomorrow.' Khaled pats his back. Aasim, for a moment, wants to continue holding him, be kissed by him. Anything.

'Towards Al Manara Park, boss,' Khaled tells the driver.

'Thank you, Khaled. I appreciate it. I mean it. I really do.'

'Any time, buddy.'

Khaled closes the passenger door. Aasim puts on his safety belt as the car drives off. Once Khaled is out of sight, Aasim leans forward.

'I've changed my mind, boss. I'm not going to Al Manara. Keep going to Jumeirah.'

Aasim pays ninety dirhams. The RTA pulls away from the marina. He glances at the series of cranes that hover over the various unfinished skyscrapers. The block by Al Sufouh Road will be beautiful when it's finished. 'An architect's playground', that's what Baba called it. A line no doubt taken from one of the brochures.

It has to be somewhere nearby; the police said it was close to the mall. Of course, they'll have washed away the blood, if there was any, on the quay.

He walks along the curved concrete waterfront, past the white boats and folded tables and chairs. The water laps, two splashes a second. Consistent. Lost time. Wasted time. Here. Then gone. Here. Then gone.

Dubai. There is no place like it. Perfect really. Somebody's paradise.

'Some women can't fit in, and they're either adored for it or they're destroyed. I worry for Hiyam.' When had Nana said that? Somewhere deep in the past, a fight at a birthday party perhaps? Or Eid? There were so many times she could've said it.

Walking under a bridge, listening to the cars slip by overhead, he glances at the children's play area built in its shadow. Maybe Hiyam sat on one of those swings minutes before she died. Someone pushed her and she kicked up her legs. She might've been laughing. But who? And what had it to do with the York?

What then? A knock to the head? A weapon? An accident? Did she hit her head falling in? Or did she fall in because she hit her head? A hijab had been fished out of the water. Surely, she wasn't wearing it? She would never have got into a hotel bar.

Building sites are scattered between the silver skyscrapers. Those tall cranes – what are they like? In school, his English teacher would've asked him to come up with a poetic comparison, but ideas escape him now. The artificial light makes it all look fake, opposite to the way the natural light makes the trees outside Trinity College seem drab but in some way more real.

Bang. Aasim inhales as an image flashes before his eyes – a stone hitting Hiyam's skull and she falls forward. Bang. A piece of scaffolding has come loose and swung around, knocking her into the water. Bang. A concrete block falls from a site. What a sad joke if that was it. Nobody hit her. No conspiracy. Nothing. How uncreative. He can almost hear Hiyam rage against her own death. 'On a building site? At least alcohol poisoning or a coke overdose. Paleeese!'

Aasim frowns, unhappy that it seems the only memories of her that return are her being brash and spoilt. Will this be all he'll recall in ten years' time? What about the good things she did? Like at age fourteen when she shaved her head for Locks of Love without telling Mama or Baba. Spur of the moment. Just did it.

'What will people say?' Baba's voice had grown loud.

'They won't even see, not with the hijab,' she'd shouted back. Baba threw the sandals he was carrying to the floor.

'Shameful, a woman without hair.'

'Why?'

'Who would marry you looking like that?'

'Maybe I don't want to get married.'

Then Baba had hit her. Nothing hard, a slap on the cheek. Aasim winces at the thought of this, her holding her face, their father leaving the room.

How can he stop these tears? *Hiyam. Please. Die any time you want, just not before me.* Aasim squashes his face into his elbow. The alcohol has his head spinning. The waves continue to splash against the marina. Hot water seeps into the sleeve of his jacket.

His phone vibrates. His arm drops and he inhales.

It's The American.

Aasim steps out of the RTA, one street away from home, and walks along the sandy verge, flicking through his messages. The American's text: *Fun times. You didn't need to run off so quick ;)* Winky-face. Who the hell uses winky-face any more?

No message from David. What time is it in Dublin? Minus three, four hours? One a.m. David is probably asleep. He's always in bed, hardly ever wanting to go out. They aren't right for each other, are they? David. Fucking David. Hard to get him motivated to do anything. An old man stuck in his routine of studying in Trinity library with 'weed breaks' down in Lahinch.

Hiyam. Hiyam. Hiyam. He needs to scream. Right now. Or throw up. Or slice himself to ribbons. Keep digging till he finds the bit that hurts and cuts it out. He is going mad. Actually mad. Not the neurotic kind of mad, but the kind of person that throws themselves against padded walls.

Why did he fuck The American? Why? Aasim sniffs his T-shirt. It stinks of Abercrombie. His lips are chapped from that stupid fucker's stubble. Crap sex. Fuck-all foreplay.

What would David say if he knew? Aasim kicks a large rock off the verge into the road. It hurts his toes. The gloss finish on his Dior loafer is damaged. Throw them out. Buy more. Stupid fucking shoes. Stupid fucking clothes. Stupid fucking life.

What is God's reason for all this? Is there any point in praying when he's damned? He can't promise he'll behave differently because he knows he won't. He tried in the past. Nature . . . sin, or whatever it was, always won in the end.

Home. Aasim stands at the entrance, looking at the rounded arches and verandas that make up the front. He swipes the small side gate with his keys and the lock clicks open. Glancing to the far right, he thinks about Mahmoud sleeping. Or lying still, waiting in the dark.

Nana was right. 'The only company for snakes is other snakes.' She'd been talking about a boy who bullied him in school. Mahmoud is no different. To think, one day he'll be head of the family. Where will that leave him? An outcast. Hiyam is gone. Mahmoud will have only one more mistake to fix.

A red Ferrari is parked under the shaded entrance. Mahmoud's pride and joy. Aasim thinks about lifting out his keys and dragging them along the paint.

The blue lights of the pool cast ripples up the stone columns. What a waste. A pool that no one uses. A 'Hi, we're disgustingly rich, even richer than you,' to the neighbours. And those palm trees would be dead without the desalinated water pumped around them every day. The grass would be burnt in an afternoon.

Aasim slips into a shadowy part of the garden and puts his key into the maids' door. Up the servants' stairs, then fifteen steps across the main hallway will have him in his room. Mouthwash and a shower will hide any incriminating scents. He closes the maids' door slowly, passing by the washing machines and dryers, the mounds of bedding and shoes, black bin liners and shelves of cleaning products. Cheap lights. Pine doors. Ugly plastic floors.

He looks through the crack in the door at the top of the servants' stairs, into the family hallway. Across from him, an oil painting of a racehorse gleams in the half-light from the garden. There's complete silence, just a smell of scented

126

candles. Closing the door, Aasim creeps out on to the gleaming marble floor.

'Good morning.' Mahmoud stands at the top of the
curving staircase. He taps his watch. That ugly Rolex. His
shadow travels across the tiles, almost hitting the far wall.
Aasim goes to walk past but Mahmoud steps out from the
balustrade.

'Where were you?'

'That's not your business.'

'Everything to do with this family is my business.'

Their parents' bedroom door opens. Baba steps out, his
white robe wrapped around him. His grey hair is matted,
leaning to one side.

'Where were you till this hour?' he asks.

'Out with Khaled.'

'Out? On the week your sister is dead? Shame on you.'

Aasim looks at the ceiling.

'Aasim, is that you?' A light appears from the bedroom
and Mama walks into the hallway. The darkness around her
eyes is as black as ink.

'That smell. You've been drinking?' Baba says.

'Shame. The shame you bring on us.' Mahmoud shakes
his head.

'I'm going to bed.'

'No, you are not. Explain to us. Where have you been?'

'With Khaled.'

'But where?'

'Around.'

Mahmoud steps forward, grabbing Aasim's chin and turning it towards the light.

'Your lips. Your chin. They're all pink.'

'They're not. Let go of me. Let fucking go of me.'

'What did you say?' Mahmoud rams him hard against the balustrade, yanking Aasim's head out over the railing. Coins fall out of Aasim's pockets to the marble floor below. Aasim tries desperately to cling on to the balustrade, his feet slipping. 'Shame on you, using such words in front of Mama.'

'Stop it. Stop it,' Mama shouts. 'If he falls . . .'

'Mahmoud. Control yourself.' Baba pulls at his brother's arm. Mahmoud pauses. Slowly, he lets Aasim's feet rest on the floor. 'Good. We've already one mess on our hands.'

'You disgust me,' Mahmoud says to Aasim.

Silence. Each remains still. Have they woken the maids? Were they all listening from their rooms?

'I'm going to bed,' Aasim says, rubbing his neck. He moves past Mahmoud. As he goes towards his door, Baba speaks.

'They arrested a man. A taxi driver.'

'What for?'

'He was the driver who took her from the York . . .' Baba continues. 'That immoral place. I would not believe it possible but they have it on camera.'

'Immoral place. Immoral?' Aasim shakes his head, looks at Mama, then Baba. 'You're such a hypocrite.'

'What did you say to me?' Baba's face contorts. 'Thank Allah that your mother is here so I don't break your neck. Get to bed. Go on. I don't want to see your face again.'

'I'm going home,' Aasim shouts back, walking towards his room.

'This is your home.'

Aasim slams his bedroom door and turns the lock, leaning his head against the wood, his mind spinning. The voices continue for a while and he slips down to the tiles. Eventually he hears two doors click shut. Even so, he doesn't move for a long time.

Siobhan

The spinning wheel of death. Come on. Come on. Will the
connection ever click in? These stupid walls. She's told Martin enough times about getting a stronger router.

Explosions echo up the stairs. What game is Rocco playing? World War III? Siobhan, wet hair falling around her
shoulders, towel under her armpits, walks to the bedroom
door and shouts to him to turn down the TV. The volume
doesn't change. She glances over the balustrade, watching
Gete as she crosses the hallway below.

'Rocco, have you got your bag ready?' Gete calls into the
living room.

'Yes,' Rocco shouts.

'Come now. You can play games later. Do you want me to
tell Ma'am?'

'Five minutes.'

'Come now, please.'

'*Five minutes.*'

'OK. OK. Five minutes. And then you come brush your
teeth.'

Siobhan frowns, ready to make her way downstairs.
Behind her, Martin's voice calls out from the laptop. She
turns around, pulling the bedroom door shut. The explosions become muffled.

'I'm here, I'm here,' she says. Sitting herself on to the duvet, she straightens the screen. 'How are you, love?'

'You've your hands full.'

'Up to my eyes.'

The buttons on his crisp white shirt are open. That tanned smooth chest. She never thought she'd be attracted to a boyish-looking man, preferring her guys rough round the edges. But Tunisia with her Vodafone gang had been what changed all that. Martin, who was there with his own mates, got her and her girls passes to nearly every club night they wanted and all the free cocktails they could drink. When he finally leaned in and kissed her in Bonaparte, she thought he deserved a snog for all his efforts, but then the kiss turned out to be surprisingly good and, for once, she was happy to have no stubble-rash.

'A late one last night?' Siobhan asks. Maybe the screen is pixelated but Martin's eyes don't have their usual blue spark.

'The things I do to get contracts,' he laughs. 'So, what are your plans today?'

'Today is the day. The climbing of the Burj.'

'Are the boys excited?'

'I think so. Milo has no idea what's going on, but Rocco will love it.'

'How's your brother?'

'He's great. Getting on well, I think . . .' Siobhan looks at the door. 'We'll check out some gyms in the next couple of days and see if they have openings.'

'Oh.' Martin's eyebrows rise.

'It'd be just great to have him out here.' A certain annoyance rises as she observes his lack of reaction.

'It's great. Don't mind me. I'm just tired.'

'What's the meeting for?'

'It's this concierge group. The details are taking forever.'

'Oh.' She asks no further questions. He doesn't need reminding of the failed concierge business back in Dublin.

'Anto called last night, asking about visiting again. He, Louise and Clara want to come early spring.'

'Oh, great.' Siobhan does her best to appear happy, though as the years have passed she's found Anto more and more unbearable. She thought Louise might calm him down but he still nudges Martin when they're out in bars, pointing at women with huge racks, as if they both were still nineteen. The stupid deep voice Martin puts on around him – 'Hey, bro . . . what's up, bro' – as if they were both in a music video. All she wants to do is shout, 'Stop trying so hard.' But Martin can't help himself; he wants people to like him to a point that is almost pathological. Anto has been clever enough never to treat him as an equal.

'Is the big man around?' Martin asks.

'Stuck to the computer. Will I get him?'

'No. Leave him. I was the same at his age.'

'Not mucking out the pigs?'

'Not for want of the old man trying.'

Another pause. She tries to think of things to say. There's something artificial in the way they talk online which bothers her, like there is something that they're not speaking about, but she can't quite put her finger on it. Perhaps Martin can sense something too. A grin comes across his face. He sits up, his arm vanishing, as if fixing his trousers.

'Flash us – go on. Drop the towel a bit.'

'Jesus, Mart,' she laughs. 'The boys could wander in.'

'Go on.'

Siobhan glances at the window, thinking of the neighbours, but she can only see endless blue sky. Her hand loosens. The towel slips. One nipple is exposed and for a second she thinks of Charlotte from *Sex and the City*. Fleet Week. Yes. That was it.

A whistle from the laptop. She laughs. The towel jumps up.

'That's enough now.'

'Ahhhh.'

'Now where did your hand go?' she teases. Martin glances left, at something off camera.

'Shit, I better go, babes.'

'All OK?' Siobhan wonders what distracted him. Not a . . . No. She needs to be less paranoid. Ever since the spring when he'd sent her a message on WhatsApp that was clearly not for her, she has had to fight herself checking up on him. He'd said it was only flirting with one of the account managers from an industry party, trying to keep her sweet. And in his defence, she always knew he could be a bit of a flirt. Who doesn't like a bit of attention?

'Nothing. Just the time.' He starts buttoning the rest of his shirt.

'Love you.'

'Love you too . . . go team!' She smiles as he says it, finding comfort in their silly mock business speak. She warned him that if she ever heard the word 'synergy' again, he'd have a GHD aimed at his head.

The mirror doesn't lie. Martin was only humouring her. He tries to make her feel good about herself, though there's no denying she is not as attractive as she once was. How has Louise done it? How has Rebecca done it? Snapped back into shape after children, no stretch marks, as if their bodies were part rubber.

Martin was just being kind. That was all. Even though she scolds him for his cheekiness – there's something about it that reminds her of his father, boorish and vulgar – it's nice to feel desired. Course, he can take a joke too far, like the time she asked him what did he want for his thirtieth birthday and he said a threesome. 'How can you say that? We have children.' Then he said he was only joking.

The mirror. The repulsiveness of her body. She pinches her love handles. Seven years. She recalls a picture taken in Tunisia, the first photograph of her and Martin together. Part of a group shot, she is wearing that turquoise bikini. He looks handsome, his fair hair bleached by the sun.

'The blue of your eyes. Just gorgeous,' she said to him on the last night of the holiday, after four Long Island iced teas. The heat made her face feel shiny but he didn't seem to be sweating at all.

'I like them too,' he replied. Then a smirk. 'Would you believe, I'm completely blind without them.'

Smartarse. He could charm the knickers off a nun.

Her Tunisia body. Her slim tanned arms draped over his shoulder, her breasts, as if they knew a camera was on them, squeezing together. That was the body that had hooked him. Tits and ribs. It had been so easy then; she could smoke herself thin, drink coffee, go on a sunbed. Then there was that weird mole, the irritable bowel and the bad chests in winter. And after the pregnancies, it was not even an issue of losing weight; her body had changed. She'd never have that lean look again, not unless a surgeon went at her hips with a chisel.

What if he only stayed with her because of the boys? All it took was for him to grow bored and she'd be back in Dublin, a single parent on welfare, wondering what to do with her FÁS certificate as a manicurist. She could never go back to the phone shop. But what else could she do? She'd never really been that certain what she wanted from her life, till Martin and the boys came along, giving it some shape and purpose.

Fucking Richard. No wonder Martin is so soft on the boys. The way that man tries to control him. What is so important about keeping the pig farm going? Half of Cavan stinks from it. What's wrong with wanting more? Money is nothing if it's rotting in a bank while you're living in shit. Literal. Pig. Shit.

She smiles at this image. Awful though it is, these nasty thoughts seem to steady the butterflies in her stomach.

Yes. The emerald top suits her. Siobhan picks a bobble off the dresser and ties her hair back, pulling loose a few strands around her face. Grabbing her fake Hermès, she opens the bedroom door.

'Rocco. Get ready for Gete,' she calls down the stairs. No answer. She starts walking down, stopping at the sitting room door. 'Come on now. Turn that thing off.'

His eyes remain fixed on the computer screen. She taps her fingers on the wall.

'Turn that thing off now. Ah, ah, ah. No lip from you now.'

'But Gete said.'

'I don't care what Gete said. The PlayStation will be there later. You want to go see the Burj Khalifa? Come on now.'

Trevor comes in from the hallway.

'Listen to Mammy, Rocco. Or there'll be skin and hair flying. Come on now.'

'Unky Trevor.' Milo grabs at his legs.

'Up here now, wee man.' Trevor lifts him.

'Rocco, turn that thing off. Or you won't be playing it any more till the weekend.' She knows these words must sound hollow to him, as she always gives in and lets him use it.

'I'm saving it. I don't wanna lose my place.'

'Good. Now run up to Gete. She has your clothes ready. How are you, Trev? How did the night go in the end?'

'I wasn't out that late. Only a couple of drinks.'

'And who was she?'

He goes bright red. She knows him too well.

'Nobody.' His tone is defensive. He walks off with Milo to the kitchen.

There are thousands of people in the car park of Dubai Mall. Forty minutes and they've barely moved. Cars ahead and cars behind.

'Isn't it a beaut?' Trevor says, watching the Ferrari in front, while his fingers mess with the radio. Siobhan's fingers tap on the steering wheel.

'You OK back there?' she asks.

Rocco nods.

'Milo is gone sleepies.'

'Are friends in your class coming along today too?'

'George is, and I think Mark and Emma.'

'George? You hear that, Trev?'

Trevor goes red in the face.

'You want me to text Rebecca and see what she's doing?'

'Do what you like.'

'You've no interest now. You're all sorted after last night,' Siobhan says, teasing him, though he doesn't laugh, just blushes bright red again and looks out of the window.

'Fuck, it's hot,' he says finally.

'What has the sun got?' Siobhan looks in the mirror, back at Rocco and Milo, suddenly awake again. 'The sun has got . . .'

'The sun is got his hat on. Hip hip hurray!' Milo sings, and they all join in.

'I can't see anything, Mam . . . Mam . . . Mam . . . I can't see anything.' Rocco pulls on her dress. People keep standing in front of them and she can't see anything either. Trevor has put Milo on his shoulders, not that Milo will even know what's going on. Christ, the heat is ridiculous. Did Gete put sun lotion on the boys?

'Come here. Give me your hand. We'll move towards the front.'

Hairy legs. Bags. Flip-flops. Grumbling adults. A baby crying. Damn, it's hot. She takes her sunglasses off her head, shielding her eyes from the reflections from the skyscrapers all around the giant pool. In front, beyond the turquoise water and beautiful bridge, the Burj Khalifa rises, dwarfing everything around it, till it becomes a glistening point. She gets out her camera, though it's frustrating to try and get a picture, as it's pretty much impossible to get the whole of the Burj in one shot.

'Stay close, Rocco,' Siobhan calls. 'I said to hold my hand.'

A helicopter appears in the sky. Woop. Woop. Woop. Canary yellow, it hovers close to the rising point of the Burj.

'Is he on that, Mammy?'

'The film star? I don't know, love. Maybe he is. We'll see. Did you bring your binoculars?'

Crowds of people are coming outside. The space by the fountains is getting more packed by the minute. Is there any health and safety? She watches as Milo digs his elbows out, trying to keep people from pushing in closer. Behind Siobhan, a woman with a pram keeps trying to move forward, cutting into her ankles. Siobhan gives her a glare.

'Look, Rocco, look!' Siobhan shakes his shoulder. 'You see, there. No, higher. Near the helicopter. He's climbing out of the window.'

The crowd roars, the space growing tighter and tighter, as if the extra inch gained on the ground will give them a better view of the film star half a mile up.

'Look at him swinging around. You'd think he was on the ground,' Siobhan says. Though the climbing figure is a mere dot, she didn't expect to feel so breathless.

'I wanna see through the bonokulars,' Rocco says. Siobhan hands him the glasses.

'Can you see now? There he is. He's like Spider-Man. Look, look, over there. Can't you see him? There. Look. To the right. Just above the one . . . two . . . three . . . fourth ridge. He's running and everything.'

Rocco shrieks as his binoculars finally focus on the climbing figure.

'You'll be like that one day, won't you, Rocco, a big action star,' Siobhan continues. He looks at her, his eyes wide, and she's happy to see him full of childish glee.

'What do you think, Milo?' Trevor pushes in behind Siobhan, much to the woman with the pram's annoyance.

'Look at the height of him. Seriously, the height. What is that? A mile?'

'Half a mile, I think.'

The helicopter keeps circling the building and Rocco asks her what's that for, and she says it's got the camera on it. Then the film star vanishes back inside. Then a million questions.

'What's that thing hanging off the building?' Rocco is still bubbling with excitement. A long piece of scaffolding is tipping off the side of the building which looks precarious.

'That's the crane. That's for cameras,' Trevor says.

'I'm gonna be a film star when I grow up,' Rocco says.

'You don't want to be a footballer any more?'

Rocco frowns, deliberating the options. He shakes his head. 'No. I wanna do what he's doing. So cool.'

They wait another ten minutes. The helicopter remains above but no more sign of the film star.

'Maybe that's it,' Siobhan says. 'Will we go get an ice cream?'

But no one is moving. All of a sudden, there is the sound of smashing glass. The film star jumps out of the window and starts hurtling to the ground. Screams and roars burst from the crowd.

'Jesus.' Siobhan winces, hardly able to look, though Trevor and Rocco remain fixed on the sight of the falling man. The man slows down, the rope stopping him from going any further. Carefully, he is pulled back inside the building.

'Why is the string getting shorter?' Rocco asks.

'Because they have a machine to bring him back inside after he has done the stunts,' Trevor replies.

'I bet you're glad you came to Dubai now,' Siobhan says.

'What power would you rather?' Siobhan asks Rocco. 'To fly or to be invisible.'

'I'd wanna fly.' Rocco jumps.

'Invisible,' she says. 'That way I'd be able to catch you when you're being bold.' She tickles Rocco. 'Will we go for a look in the mall? We can get food, see if I can get some new tops for Milo.'

'But what if the man does more climbing?' Rocco asks, looking at the skyscraper.

'He's only a little dot. You can barely see anything. Come on, I'll take you to the movie to see it when it's finished.'

'When's that?'

'Next year.'

'But that's ages and ages.'

'Can we get ice cream, Mam?'

'You had a dessert an hour ago,' Siobhan replies. She can see from the look on the three faces that the lads have had enough of shopping.

'You did say six?' Trevor asks. 'The fountains start soon?' Siobhan nods.

'They are really cool,' Rocco says. 'They're the biggest in the world, ever.'

'Blow.' Siobhan holds out a tissue and Milo leans in. He giggles as she squeezes slightly and pulls away.

Back outside at the water. The film star is gone and so is the helicopter, and it's getting dark except for the lights. The Burj Khalifa glitters like the Eiffel Tower, while a light at the top flashes to keep planes away.

'Can't we go closer?' Rocco reaches the railings. They look into the colossal pool, which curves like a river between the skyscrapers before vanishing around a smooth bend.

'You'll get crushed, sweetheart. Poor Milo will get a fright from the fountains . . .' Siobhan flicks the neck of her top. It's still sweltering.

'Silly Milo. Baby. Scared of stupid water.'

'Don't be like that. You were frightened too when you first saw them.'

'I wasn't.'

'Yes, you were. You bawled and Daddy had to bring you inside for ice cream.'

'Can we get chocolate?'

'In a little while. You know what Teacher was saying – fewer sweeties. You're getting a jelly belly.'

'Belly shmelly.' Rocco picks his nose and wipes it under the railing. Siobhan tells him to stop it. She sounds like Mammy telling him off, though it's only because he's getting tired.

'Look, Milo, you see the lights?' Siobhan tickles his belly. The music begins. It's Celine Dion.

Pop, pop, pop. The fountains burst into the air. The crowd cheers. She blushes slightly at the words of the song, reminded of when she'd seen *Titanic* five nights in a row with all the other Leaving Cert girls.

Whoosh! Those jets fly into the air, making rainbows. 'Can you see them, Rocco, going right up into the sky.' They are all going off, fanning this way and that, dancing in flowing patterns left and right.

She remembers being here on their wedding anniversary, just her and Martin. He'd put his arm around her shoulder (they weren't sure whether around the waist was allowed in public) and she'd watched the water dance, loving the feeling of the weight of his arm, his protection, and she'd longed for him to reach in and put his lips on hers. Knowing that could not happen made the desire so much stronger. It'd been as if they were dating for the first time again – the joy of the glittering water and the rainbow of lights, the optimism of their life in Dubai, had made the moment perfect in ways she couldn't have imagined. The hairs on her arms had tingled with pleasure. It made her eyes glassy, not due to sadness but because of a rediscovered joy. 'Kiss me, just kiss me,' she'd wanted to say to him, as she glanced at the profile of his face. 'Kiss me and love me and let's enjoy our beautiful life here.'

'Can we go on the bridge, Mam?' Rocco asks, glancing over at the Venetian-inspired canal.

'It's too late now, babycakes. We'll never get a space. Look, it's full.' Siobhan blinks a few times. The tears have come again but they don't feel so sweet.

'But I wanna.'

'You'll miss the fountains. Come on now . . . look!' She doesn't want him to see her wet eyes.

Pop. Pop. Pop! The fountains rise higher than ever.

'What was that? Ten storeys?' Trevor asks. He squeezes Siobhan's hand. 'You silly goose.' The crowd continues to gasp and cheer until the music ends and the lights and the fountains stop. There are a few scattered claps and that's it.

'These boys need their bed,' Siobhan says, the rush of excitement passing. In a moment, everything is normal again. Rocco begins to moan.

'Fifty minutes, Gete. Literally fifty minutes and we were still trying to get out of the car park. You would think it was New Year's or something. Don't worry about bathing Milo tonight. He's zonked. We'll give him a scrub in the morning.'

Gete takes snoring Milo from her and goes upstairs. Rocco has slipped away, no doubt to the sitting room. She thought she heard the television but he's probably put it on mute. She glances through the kitchen door.

'Half an hour, then bedtime. That OK? I don't want tears when it's time to go to bed, now. You promise?'

Rocco nods, his gaze fixed on the screen.

'You want a cup of tea, Trev?'

'Something stronger?' He gives her a smile. She doesn't feel like alcohol. In fact, she's absolutely burnt out but she realizes this might be the moment that happens every once in a while when they have a few drinks and a proper chat.

'Gin and tonic,' she says, sitting down at the table. 'There's ice in the freezer.' Pulling out her phone, she checks again for a message from Martin, but no word since this morning. Scrolling down through her homepage, she looks at the various pictures that people have posted from Dubai Mall. The *Daily Mail* has some pictures from the Burj Khalifa. It's funny to think she was there – there's something so anticlimactic now after so much anticipation. It'd been the same in the months after their wedding, a sinking feeling of 'Is that all there is?'

'Here.' Trevor hands her a drink. She takes a sip, spluttering a little.

'Did you put in half the bottle?'

'It'll put hairs on your chest.'

'So, Mam and Pat seem to have hit it off?' Siobhan asks. They talk for a while about stupid things: friends getting married and who's having children. The first drinks are gone. Already her cheeks are warm. Of course, it'll take till drink three or four for the proper conversation to start. Sometimes she worries how unhealthy it is that, sober, he talks so little about the things that matter. It can't be good, holding stuff in.

Falling into the Liffey. She'd love to ask him the truth about last year. When she got the call that he'd nearly drowned, it wasn't tears that had formed, but a strange hollow feeling.

'The river?' she'd said to Mam. 'An accident . . . ?' The words lingered between them.

Recovering herself, Mam had said, 'Of course an accident. What else?'

The hollow shaky feeling had stayed with her all the way home on the plane, her nerves on edge with every rattle of turbulence, then her leg tapping in the taxi from Dublin airport to St James's. What would she have done without Gete minding her boys back in Dubai? Martin was off in Leba non or somewhere, and couldn't return for at least two days.

'Don't worry, Ma'am,' Gete had said. 'You go to your brother.' She really had been a wonder.

In the hospital, Mam was at reception with a doctor, asking question after question – she knew all the medical terminology. She hugged her for what felt like twenty minutes.

'I'm so glad you came home, my darling, you're so good,' she'd sobbed.

'Of course, Mam. We have to look out for each other.' She squeezed back as hard as she could, her own eyes dripping with tears.

Mam led her down the ward, past drips, those ugly one-legged tables that swung over beds, and the rows of blue curtains, mostly closed. Trevor's curtains were half pulled around so she didn't see his face till the last moment.

Pale-lipped. That was it. They'd given him sedatives and she could hear his faint snores. A series of conflicting emotions arose; she was unsure whether she wanted to hug him, slap him, shout at him, or say a prayer. In the end she found she couldn't move at all, scared to blink because she knew it would make her eyes sting. Mam stood wet-eyed beside her, whispering again and again, 'Thank God your father is dead.'

'You think if a gym makes an offer, you'll come over? Once you were settled then, you could look at setting up your own thing,' Siobhan says, sipping from her third gin. She knows she shouldn't keep pushing him – it's the one way to put him off – but she can't help herself.

Trevor pours back the last of his drink.

'I don't know. Fuck it, I haven't a clue what I'm doing.' He leans forward and scratches his head in his hands.

'It'd be great for Rocco to have you around. You could stay here till you got sorted. Whatever suits you.'

'I know . . .'

'Are you all right? You've been quiet all day.'

'Just tired.'

'You weren't that late last night.'

'It's just the flight catching up with me.' His face is pained. For a brief second, his eyes appear glassy but then he inhales deeply and straightens up, goes to make a new drink.

'You'd have a whole new set of women to keep you occupied,' she jokes.

'I've had enough women for a lifetime.' He gives a shake of the head. Siobhan wonders what went down last night. Whatever happened, there's a bang of regret off him.

'I don't want to be some sad forty-year-old cruising young ones on Harcourt Street,' he says finally.

'Then move out here and get a career for yourself.' She tries to catch his eye.

'Like Martin?'

'It wouldn't take long. You could be out this side of Christmas.'

'Of course, money-wise. But . . .' He takes a large mouthful of his gin. Siobhan is silent.

'Why won't you talk to me?' she'd asked after Trevor had come home from hospital.

'Why do you think? It's fucking mortifying. I'm all over

the *Metro Herald*.' He'd shaken his head and said what a tool he was. The look in his eyes. A slight fear. Then he'd turned on his side, facing the wall.

Now, a year later, there is still no way to ask him directly. He'll only deflect the question and change the subject. Not that she blames him. Who wants reminding about the worst things that have happened in their lives? Taking a large swig of her drink, she says, 'Seriously, are you happy, Trev, back home?'

'As anyone, I suppose.' He then grins. 'The drinks are kicking in. You've gone maudlin.'

'No. Seriously though.'

'What does that even mean?' He sits up in his chair, as if preparing for a second attack of questions. His cheeks are flushed too. Siobhan glances over at the countertop. The bottle of Gordon's is over halfway gone.

'Well, as long as you are.' There's no getting more out of him. Like Daddy, once he sticks his heels in, that's it.

'You know who I saw online the other week in my news feed. Gary, you know, from national school,' he says.

'That shithead.'

'Yeah. Married a wan as ugly as himself.'

'You remember the time when you were in fourth class? Out by the gates.'

He flushes and nods. Some memories survive intact, even after two decades.

They'd been waiting outside the school for Mam, but for some reason she hadn't appeared. Sometimes she got stuck at the hospital and Daddy wouldn't be finished till five or six at the earliest. They began walking. Twenty minutes later, Siobhan was moaning.

'We need a phone box,' she complained. Cars were speeding along Dundrum Road.

'Don't you have any money?'

She shook her head. 'What about the pound Mam said to keep for emergencies?'

'I spent it.' Trevor pulled out a bunch of stickers from his pocket. On each was a picture of a soccer player. 'I keep getting Eric Cantona.'

'Fuck sake, Trev,' Siobhan replied, her attention caught by the sight of Gary walking up the street with his brother, Neil, who was in the first year of Terenure College. He'd the same rotten sticky-out ears as his brother. Siobhan straightened her back.

'What are you dopes doing here?' Gary asked.

'None of your business,' Siobhan said. He stepped closer, kicking the wall beside her. 'Piss off,' she added.

He didn't move, instead kicking the wall harder.

'What are those anyway?' He snatched the bunch of stickers out of Trevor's hand. Half of them fell to the pavement. Trevor began picking them up.

'Get lost,' Siobhan repeated, trying to snatch the cards back. He laughed.

'Come get them, Crangle.' Gary aimed a kick at Trevor.

'Fuck off,' Siobhan said. 'Don't, Trev.'

'Chicken.' Neil flapped his arms. He was much taller than Trevor was. She could see yellow-headed spots on his chin.

'Fine,' Trevor said. Gary stuffed the stickers in his pocket. He gestured at Trevor to attack him. Gary swung a punch at his chest, which Trevor avoided, grabbing Gary's neck, getting him in a headlock. Gary's brother moved forwards, pushing Siobhan out of the way.

'Give him a wedgie,' Gary shouted. Neil grabbed Trevor's boxers and yanked them hard. Gary scrambled to his feet. The boxers ripped and they both laughed.

Siobhan ran at Gary, punching him in the face. He staggered backwards. She kicked him hard in the balls. Twisting his arm behind, she grabbed him by the hair.

'Stay or I'll twist his arm harder.' Siobhan looked at Neil.

'It's not fair. We can't hit a girl.'

'And it's fair for two to go against one?' She twisted Gary's arm further. He roared. 'Apologize to Trevor.'

'I'm sorry, I'm sorry.'

'Give him his cards.'

'Here.' With his free arm, Gary handed the stickers back. Siobhan let him go, pushing him into his brother.

'Now fuck off,' she said.

'I guess we haven't done too bad for ourselves,' Siobhan says, smiling at the thoughts of their shared past. Trevor still looks uncomfortable. Stories of her looking out for him always make him gruff. If they're honest, not much has changed since then. It probably explains all the muscles now. Men and their egos.

'We've tucked into the bottle,' Trevor says.

'My head in the morning. Milo will be up at an ungodly hour.'

'At least you've Gete.'

'I don't know what I'd do without her. I've been trying to think of something nice to get her, a watch or bag or something that she'd have for keeps. But she'd only pawn it. They just want cash to send back home. Pity really. It's like they can't enjoy the life that's in front of them.'

'In all fairness, she's been very good.'

'Sure, look at last year, when I flew home.' Immediately, she regrets referencing the Liffey incident but it's too late. 'There's no way I could've just left the boys, with Martin away and everything. She played a blinder.'

Trevor nods. He looks down at his drink and rubs his finger around the lip of his glass. What is he thinking? She doesn't want him to feel any more guilt about what happened. Hadn't it all worked out OK in the end?

A noise from the sitting room. Siobhan glances at her phone. Shit. Gone eleven. Rocco is still not in bed. The lunatic.

'Rocco,' Siobhan calls. 'Come in here and get something to eat before sleep. Turn off that thing.'

No answer.

'Rocco. Come. *Now.*' Siobhan stands, a little unsteady as she walks to the sitting room door. 'If you don't come now, you won't be able to play tomorrow.'

She watches as Rocco saves the game and puts the remote on the couch.

'Not there. Back under the TV, mister.'

As he walks past her into the kitchen, she rubs his hair. 'Look at that tired head.' The expression on his face says he doesn't agree with her. She gets milk from the fridge.

Trevor, still at the table, has turned on the iPad and flicks through various articles.

'They've arrested a man about that girl who drowned. A Pakistani fella – a taxi driver.' The tone of his voice has returned to normal. 'The girl's name was . . . Husayin. Good-looking too.'

'Husayin.' Siobhan frowns. 'That name is familiar. I'll have to say it to Martin.' She moves over and looks at the screen. 'She must be a local. Fuck, I wouldn't want to be that man right now.'

'He might've done nothing. Innocent till proven guilty, and all that.'

Siobhan shakes her head.

'Welcome to Dubai.'

'Can I have cornflakes?' Rocco asks.

'A small bowl. But don't tell Teacher. She'll be telling off Mammy.' She lifts the big box out of the high cupboard and gets a bowl and spoon. 'Did you have fun today, pumpkin?' She rubs his hair.

Rocco nods as he pours on the milk.

'What did you think, Trev?'

'You wouldn't catch me climbing that. Not a hope.'

'It'd be great if you could get work out here,' Siobhan says again. God. She must sound desperate.

'Nana never lets me use her glasses in the cupboard,' Rocco says, looking at his cup. 'The sparkly ones.'

'That's because they were her wedding ones,' Siobhan replies. 'No one is allowed to touch the Waterford Crystal.'

'I don't like Ireland,' Rocco says.

'You didn't like visiting Nana?'

'No.'

Siobhan laughs. Trevor keeps reading.

'You hear him, Trev?' Siobhan starts looking over Trevor's shoulder at the iPad. 'What's that?'

'Video of your man today climbing up the side. Like, it's nuts.'

'Is that him? On the very top of the Burj?'

She doesn't notice as Rocco slips down from the kitchen chair, and it is some minutes before she notices the television has been turned back on.

Tahir

His left eye is sealed shut. Should he pull it open with his fingers? Something tears and a small noise escapes his throat. His hand drops. A crimson sliver of light enters the socket. The itch vanishes but now the eye burns.

How many hours? Was it days? He looks around the cell, the fluorescent light making him wince. Walls of bare block-work. A hole in the corner. No tissue or hose. The mattress he sits on is no more than an inch thick, the metal bars underneath cutting into his skull and back.

Daylight. He needs to see the horizon, to know what time it is. Days driving are agonizingly slow but here time stops altogether. Has he slept all night . . . a few hours . . . an hour?

He hears steps outside and jumps up, inching back towards the wall. Not again. He told them what he knew. He's done what they have asked. What more do they want? The footsteps stop. He waits for the key to turn in the lock. The footsteps start, growing faint again.

There are other noises at times. The shouts of prisoners. Heavy doors slamming. Footsteps through the ceiling. If only he had his phone. Where is the embassy? Has Anam got word to them? Maybe she is still waiting for him to call.

Tears fill his eyes. Dearest Anam. She tried to calm him on the phone. When was that? A day ago? Two days?

★

'All will be well, my love. I shall find the money somehow. We shall get you a flight home tomorrow or the day after.'

'I must leave now. As soon as possible. What if they come?'

'Tell them the truth. Trust Allah. You are a good man. He will take care of you.'

'You do not understand. It won't be the white man that they will want.'

The phone had cut out. He'd sat back on his bunk, unable to get comfortable. When Muhammad and the others came back to the cabin, he pretended to be asleep. He prayed. And he prayed. And he prayed. The others slipped under their blankets. Finally, the light went out.

In the bunk below, Muhammad snored. Every time he moved in his sleep, Tahir was disturbed. He watched the hours go by on his phone. One a.m. Two a.m. Three a.m. The sheets became clammy. They would come. Any minute, the doors would fling open and police would enter.

'You look ill, my friend,' Muhammad had said at breakfast the following morning. 'You must eat something. Look, you have not touched your oats. I will get you some tea. That will brighten your mind.'

But he could not eat food. Every time he brought the spoon to his mouth, his throat tightened.

'You must eat something.' Muhammad shook his head. 'Even sip your tea. It is a long hot day on the road.'

'I am sick,' Tahir replied.

Muhammad laughed.

'There's no being sick in Dubai. Pray and it will pass.'

★

If he keeps counting in this cell, then he'll know how much time has passed. Nine hundred and one, nine hundred and two . . . was it eight hundred and one? Count the blocks on the walls. Count the number of scratches on the door.

Sleep. Try to sleep. Pray. Try to sleep again. Pray again. Get up. Pace back and forth. Are there cameras in the room? Do they watch when he uses the hole? There's no hose for cleanliness. Treated like a dog. Worse than a dog.

Anam. Does she know yet? Is she worrying about the silence? Have Ibrahim or Baba gone to Foreign Affairs? If only they would let him make a call.

'You are alone.' He tries to keep these words from taking his mind hostage, but they are never far away. What if he is never freed? What if he never sees Fatima and Alayna again? Who will care for them? Ibrahim and Baba – how will they manage?

The door rattles. Tahir jumps back, crouching in the far corner. A guard steps inside, dropping a plate of food on to the floor and a plastic beaker of water. Tahir can see the baton hanging from his hip.

The door closes. It is some time before Tahir breathes normally. He looks at the food on the metal plate. Slop. Chicken, gristle, streaks of blood. The water in the glass is cloudy. He sniffs it, wondering what makes it grey. But there is no smell.

Tahir had stood in the RTA office, the first in a line of six drivers. Mr Dasti was behind the desk; he waved him forward.

'Quick, quick. Stop wasting time. You should be in your car.'

'Excuse me, sir. I must return home. My father has fallen ill and has not many days. Just a week. One week will do.'

Mr Dasti typed on his computer for a few minutes. Without looking up, he said, 'We cannot just let people come and go as they wish. If we did, there'd be no taxis. You have a contract to complete.'

'But please. This is very serious. My wife and children will be alone.'

'We all have wives and children. We must make do.'

'They will be unprotected.'

'We are all unprotected. We can only ask for Allah's mercy.'

'But—'

'You must go to your car now. There are ten men waiting to take your job in a moment. Be grateful for what you have.'

'But—'

'No more buts. Do you want this job or not? And do not appear in my office again with your shirt in such a condition. Look at the creases. Next.' Mr Dasti waved the next man forward.

Tahir turned towards the exit. He willed his legs to hold him. The doors opened and he was hit by the wall of heat. Would he be able to drive in this condition? Staring ahead, waiting, wondering.

Muhammad waved at him from five cars away and tapped his watch. Tahir gazed at his phone. Even one text from Anam would help. Something to shake the fear. Why did he ever come to this place?

He sat in his taxi, flipping down the visor and pulling out the photo of Anam, Fatima and Alayna. He tucked it into his back trouser pocket. Just in case. His phone vibrated.

Baba says we can send you some money. We pray. My love and heart. Anam.

He texted back, but the reception was poor and he wasn't sure it sent. Driving out of the parking space, he waited behind four other RTAs at the exit.

A noise began behind him. He looked over his shoulder. Mr Dasti running from the office. Was that his name being called?

'Stop that car . . . Tahir. Get out now.' The short fat man looked ridiculous, his shirt flapping. There was nowhere Tahir could drive, with cars in front and to the rear. Mr Dasti was getting closer. Tahir jumped out and ran towards the main road. All the men around began shouting.

Police sirens. Where would he go? He slipped under the barrier. The sirens grew louder. Two squad cars appeared in front. He turned back but Mr Dasti was coming with others not far behind. Running across the wet lawn, he slipped over the black sprinkler pipes and tried to climb over a wall.

Hands grabbed his feet. Something hit the back of his calves; he lost his grip and was dragged down. Something hit him a second time. Then a third.

'Tahir Nasiri, you are under arrest.'

Tahir struggled. A uniformed man punched him in the stomach. He gasped and fell to the ground. Something hit him on the back. He screamed.

'I have done nothing,' he shouted.

'Then why do you run?' Something hit him in the left eye. A baton? Warm blood flowed over his cheek. Another knock to the head. Then nothing.

★

Light. Somewhere. Overhead. He'd tried to move his hands but they were caught. What was that on his cheeks? Sticky, like fruit juice. Where was he? He tried to lift his head from his chest but was hit with a blinding pain. He . . . he was seated. He was not in bed. 'Anam,' he whispered. 'Anam.'

Water. Ice cold. Into his face. Tahir jumped; his right eye opened. His left was sealed and throbbing.

'Wake up. Enough of this.'

At the other side of the small table, a uniformed man sat with a paper file and glass of water in front. Behind, a younger officer stood, holding an empty jug, a few drips still falling from the spout on to the floor.

'You know why you are here?'

'No, sir.'

'State your name, for the record.'

'Tahir Nasiri.'

'How old are you?'

'Thirty-three.'

'And how long have you been in Dubai?'

'Almost two years, sir.'

'Tahir, if you answer our questions and do as we ask, things will go well for you,' the older officer said, taking a sip from the glass. Tahir tried to swallow but it was near impossible, as his tongue was so dry. Oh, to have one sip of water.

The young policeman leaned against the back wall, tapping his baton on his thigh. He glanced at the mirrored wall, before staring at Tahir. Tahir looked down.

'Where were you on the night of Thursday the eighteenth of November?'

'In my taxi, sir.'

'From what time?'

'Eight in the evening till eight in the morning.'

'What were you doing between the hours of twelve and one?'

'Driving my taxi.'

'Do you remember anything in particular?'

'Nothing at all. I just drive people.'

'Were you down by Dubai Marina?'

'Yes, no . . . I can't remember. I don't know.'

'You're sure?'

'Wallah. I am sure.' Tahir tried to ignore the thumps in his chest. His head began to throb.

'You are lying.'

'No . . . please, please.' The young police officer stepped forward and with one swift movement brought the baton down hard on Tahir's thighs. A gasp. His vision blurred again.

'Tell me the truth,' the older police officer said.

'I don't know.'

'We have cameras. Your car was seen close to Marina Mall just past midnight. It left twenty-five minutes later. Tell the truth.'

'Wallah, wallah . . .' he cried.

'Do you recognize this woman?'

'No . . . no, sir.'

'You lie. We have videos of her getting into your taxi.'

'She was in my taxi. But I know nothing. I did not see anything.'

'The more you lie, the more trouble you are in.'

'I, I drove a man and two ladies to the marina. That is all.'

'Now you remember. Shame on you. A liar.' The policeman

took another sip of water, moving the glass close to Tahir but not close enough. Tahir tried not to think about his thirst.

'If I could get some water,' he said. 'It would help me think clearly. I have not drunk since last night.' But was it last night? Maybe he had been unconscious more than a day. What time of the day was it? Lunchtime? Midnight? The fluorescent strip on the ceiling made it confusing.

'You can have water when you tell us the truth. Or else there'll be no water. You know what happens after two days of no water? The way your eyes and throat will feel? The way your mind will hurt?'

'Please, sir. Just a glass.'

'Answer the questions.' The policeman's calm voice grew sharp, though he stopped the younger officer just as he reached for the baton.

'I had three people in the car. A blonde woman, Russian, I think. Laila, Lamya . . . No, Lydia. And a man with a strange accent. He said he was from England. No. Not England. He said it was a very wet place. And the woman, the one from the papers.'

'And what happened?'

'They wanted to be taken to an apartment. But the woman, the woman in the papers, was not happy. She asked to get out. So, I stopped. And the man went after her. He gave me one hundred dirhams to wait, and said I will have the same again if I stay until he returned. After a little while, the other blonde lady followed them.'

'And then?'

'The blonde lady came back quickly. The man was a little longer.'

'Anything else?'

'No. That is all, sir . . . Wait, I remember one more thing as I drove off. A car. A red Maserati.' Not that it meant much. Numerous Maseratis went up and down the Jumeirah strip every Thursday night. One time, he'd even seen a monkey sitting on the bonnet of a Ferrari, its lead tied to the car mirror.

'And where did you pick them up?'

'Outside the York, sir.'

'And where did you drop them off?'

Tahir gave the address. The policeman leaned across the table and offered him a sip of water. Tahir tried to take the glass but realized again his hands were tied. The water barely wetted his lips before it was taken away. He needed more. How could he think clearly without water?

'Why did you run from the police today?'

'I was afraid.'

'Afraid of what? If you have done nothing wrong.'

'Of trouble. I want to do my work and be left alone. Where is my lawyer, sir? Am I not allowed counsel?'

'You can have a lawyer, once you tell the truth.'

'I tell the truth.'

'You are lying. We saw the messages to your wife. You were trying to flee this country, from justice. Take him back to his cell. Let him think about his lies,' the older man said, and the young officer dragged him from the room.

The cell door closed. Tahir lay on the ground, eyes closed, his head pounding. Water. He needed water. He'd drink seawater. Water from a filthy rag. Anything.

The young officer paced back and forth. Perhaps if he kept still, the officer would go away.

'Get up.'

'But.'

'I said, get up.'

The officer watched as Tahir clung to the edge of the bed, willing his legs to stop shaking as he put weight on the soles of his feet. Just before Tahir stood, the man jumped forward and slammed his knee into Tahir's chest. Tahir dropped to his knees. The pain in the crown of his head became blinding again.

'Will you tell the truth?'

'Sir, I don't know what you mean.' Tahir put his hands up and backed towards the wall. The officer grabbed Tahir's arm and twisted it high behind his back. Tahir shrieked.

'Wallah. I tell the truth.'

'See this.' The man put the photograph of Anam and the two girls an inch away from Tahir's nose. 'You want to see them again?'

'Yes, sir. Believe me. I did nothing.'

'You lie. You keep lying, to hide what you did.'

'Believe me. It's the truth. I swear on Allah. My family.'

'Your family . . .' The officer laughed. 'Your wife and girls must be careful at night. Karachi is a dangerous place.' He let go of Tahir's arm, tore up the photograph and threw the fragments on to the ground.

The stone floor was cold against Tahir's cheek. His chest shook and trembled. He watched the last of the small pieces settle across the cracked concrete.

*

No sleep. No water. He'd be dead if they didn't stop soon. He tried to sit up straight in the chair but every muscle in his body cried out in pain. The older officer sat as before across the table, the younger officer behind, the baton hitting off his thigh as he walked back and forth. Tahir could just make out the remains of dried blood on his knuckles.

'How do I know I can trust you?' the older policeman asked. 'After all the lies you have told us?'

'You can. I swear. I'll take a lie-detector test. Anything.' Tahir began to sob. The throb at the back of his eyes made it impossible to put his head straight. Squiggling multicoloured lines flashed across what remained of his vision.

'Will you sign that what you said is the truth?'

'I . . . I will. Believe me. I tell the truth.'

The older policeman opened his folder. Inside was a document. The young policeman moved forward. Tahir tensed, waiting for the blow. But none came. He heard keys. His hands were free.

'No sudden movements.' The young officer spoke for the first time. He touched the baton.

'Sign this.' The older policeman held out a pen. Tahir tried to hold it but his hand shook so hard it fell to the table. He looked at the words with his right eye but the letters were blurred by tears and mucus. He rubbed his eye with his sleeve. The language was very formal. As he tried to strain his head forward, the blinding throbs of pain became overwhelming. He was going to pass out. Breathe. Just keep breathing.

'What does it say?' he said finally.

'It confirms all that you say to us. Nothing more.'

'I cannot read clearly.' His hand, which had begun to reach for the pen, stopped.

'You want to obstruct a police investigation? You want water?'

'But—'

'No buts. You sign or you go back to your cell. Another half-day without water. You'll sign then.'

'Will I be free to go if I do?'

'There'll be no more questioning. We will be done with you.'

'I can go home?'

'You will leave the station. You can have a lawyer then too.'

Tahir lifted the pen and scribbled his name across the dotted line. His name was hardly legible. Maybe he could ring Anam. Perhaps he could get to the embassy and fly home.

The policeman directed him to sign in three more places. He nodded to the young officer.

'Stand him up.'

Tahir was dragged to his feet and the policeman spoke.

Tahir lies on the cell floor; a plate of food and cup of cloudy water lie a few feet away. The coolness of the concrete feels good on his eye. He pushes his face harder into it. He opens what he can of his right eye.

He should've known better. What is trust in this world? Surely, they have recorded his interview, his testimony? They will find out these were bad policemen. He will get a lawyer too – they can't deny him a lawyer, can they?

Tahir Nasiri. You are charged with the murder of Hiyam Husayin. The end of his freedom. He shouted, scrambled forward to get the signed papers, but it was no good. The baton came down on his legs and back. The pain and dizziness took over.

Tahir inches off the floor, moving towards the water. He sips it. It tastes of chalk. Then he gulps and gulps. The flood gets caught in his throat and he coughs some back into the glass. Falling back, he feels the water seep, as if by osmosis, through his chest and abdomen.

Gete

Thursday had seemed like a long way off. Gete spent most of the week dreaming about it. Now, until eight a.m. tomorrow morning, she is her own mistress.

She sits up and stretches. Nine a.m. The room is growing warm. Stepping into her small bathroom, she looks in the mirror, examining her skin. The air-conditioning from the main house has left it dry. She opens a large tub of shea butter – a gift from Zulfa. It had only been a few dirhams down in Karama.

Her stomach grumbles; she could get breakfast in the main kitchen, but not seeing Ma'am or any of the family in the next twenty-four hours, even for one second, is more appealing. There is an apple, some nuts and a glass of lukewarm water on the dresser. That will be enough to keep hunger at bay till after church.

After showering, she dries herself and lifts out a blouse, high-necked to preserve her modesty, and with it she wears a long navy skirt. The nylon of the blouse makes it unsuitable in the hotter months; she finds herself keeping her arms close to her sides to hide the damp patches that form. But November has brought cooler temperatures, no more than thirty degrees.

How do the men work on sites with no break from the sun? She often watches them, gazing down from the metro as she speeds past the developments. The men are crouched, fabric hanging out from under their hard hats to cover their necks, thousands of them, twisting cables, setting blocks, moving rubble, ducking around swinging cranes. Building this place out of the sand.

'We are blessed,' Zulfa said one time, as they looked around a half-open gate into a site. 'There is always someone worse off than we are. God protect them.'

Picking up her Bible, Gete examines the gold-leaf lettering on the front that is starting to fade. The congregation gave it to her when she came to her first meeting. The white lady at the entrance had been so smiley. There were women like her back in Ethiopia with expressions like they knew something secret and special, offering leaflets and magazines which asked 'Will This World Survive?' and 'Evolution – Fact or Fiction?' Most people ignored them, arms tight to their sides to prevent leaflets getting slipped into their hands. But Baba liked to debate, to see if they knew the Bible as well as he did. Occasionally he'd take a leaflet and Lemuel would read it to him later.

'Do all men get saved, if they are sincere in what they believe?' Gete once asked Baba.

'Only God can know such things. We must humbly submit to His will,' he replied.

Gete opens the Bible and turns to page 320, the page with the bookmark. Her plan to read the whole Bible while in Dubai has faltered. Though the early books were easy, she got lost in Chronicles and found herself skipping paragraphs, only to feel guilty and go back and try reading them again. She must make more effort, try harder.

'This means everlasting life, their taking in knowledge of you, the only true God, and of the one you sent forth, Jesus Christ.'

John 17:3. God forgive her.

'Gete!'

'Yes, Ma'am.' Gete tries not to get annoyed as she puts the Bible into her handbag and steps through the laundry room into the main house.

'Sorry, darling. I know it's your day off. Could you just hold Milo for one second? Rocco's going apeshit upstairs. Trevor has been winding him up.'

Siobhan hands Gete the little boy, who is pulling on a Cheestring. Gete bobs him in her arms, feeling that familiar twinge in her shoulder. There are a few shouts upstairs. Gete hears Ma'am promise chocolate. The screaming stops.

'Thanks, Gete.' Ma'am returns. 'Sorry for that. I hope you won't be late.' She takes Milo back. 'You look lovely. Is that a new skirt?'

'No, Ma'am. It was my mother's.'

'You off to mass? Sorry ... you know what I mean. Church. Your meeting.'

'Yes, Ma'am.' For a second, Gete wonders if she should invite Siobhan to come. God makes no judgements. Jesus sat with sinners. Yet, no matter how much she tries, she can't make the words come out of her mouth.

'Well, enjoy your day off,' Siobhan continues. 'Trev and I are taking the boys to Atlantis. You have your keys to get in?'

'Yes, Ma'am. Thank you.'

'If you're going to one of your friends' afterwards, you're welcome to take some of the KitKats and crisps from the kitchen. We'll never get through them. You know Trev. It's all protein shakes.'

Gete thanks her again. Siobhan vanishes into the hallway, her voice echoing up the stairs.

Gete walks to the main entrance of the housing estate, past the BMWs, Mercedes and Land Cruisers. The lawns glisten, the black irrigation pipes peeping through the grass here and there. Far off in the distance is the sound of cars, the skyline of Dubai a shimmering unpredictable line. Beyond that, patches of glimmering blue sea.

The sun warms her left cheek; she closes her eyes and turns her face towards it. Glorious. Praise God. The silence. In a house with two boys, computers and televisions always turned on, it is easy to forget how good the sound of nothing is. Not that her family back home in Ethiopia was quiet; but when she walked with Lemuel along the green hills to the south of the village, they might not talk for long stretches at a time, both absorbing the soothing silence.

In a different world, she would have liked to stay locally, with her family. The state she grew up in was one of the most beautiful places in the world, with trees and rivers and endless fields of yellow and white flowers. That was the one thing everyone who didn't know Ethiopia always got wrong. It wasn't like Dubai, all sand and no food. There was water, food, if only they had the tractors and the threshers.

She recalls one time, Baba turning up the radio, shushing them all, as the presenter bemoaned that Ethiopia could be the 'bread basket of Africa'. If only that had been possible then she might never have had to come here.

'If only' – the worst two words in the world.

In recent years there were new farms around the village, owned by foreigners from Saudi and Turkey, bought from the government, and they had brand-new tractors and irrigation systems on timers, and fields of gleaming vegetables and grains. Her family still harvested corn by hand; they watched large machinery cover whole hectares in neighbouring fields every hour.

When the machines came, Baba began to have ideas and he sat many evenings with Gete, examining the costs of a tractor, and she would work out how long it would take to repay a loan if they could increase their annual yield. He had taken these numbers to the district offices and spoken to a Mr Alebel, and came home happy. 'He took my idea. He said it was very good. He will contact us soon.'

But no news ever came, and the foreign farms around the village grew bigger with each year, and Baba shook his head and said, 'There is no future for your children here. You will need to think of something else.'

For some time after this, Gete existed in an anxious daze. She found herself placing her hands on the bark of her favourite trees or the warm backs of the cattle, wondering if she would ever touch them again. Some days, she tried to pretend Baba hadn't said those words at all. However, she wasn't a child. She was nearing twenty, a woman, and she would have to make choices for herself. This meant accepting that her future here with those she loved was no longer possible. And, as Baba said, God would not push anyone beyond what they could bear.

She spoke to Lemuel about what she might do. She could

go to Addis Ababa but what would she be there, another girl amongst thousands, who'd never gone to secondary school, looking for work in a huge city? Yes, she was good at mathematics but she didn't know enough. Her potential was worth nothing if she didn't have the certificates.

Baba had warned many times what happened to girls in cities without their families. Aunt Candace would help but she had many responsibilities of her own.

'You could become a maid? They are looking, these rich people, in many countries. You would earn lots of money,' Lemuel suggested. 'And you would live in a home with the family. They would offer you protection. Baba would not have to worry for you.'

'But I'd be so far away,' she said.

Lemuel squeezed her hand.

'You could save hard, sister. Then you might return here and get a home of your own. Think of it as an adventure.'

The motorway is far off, just a faint hum. God must exist in silence. It is in moments of quiet, like this, that Gete feels His presence most. What would it be like to be a tree, spending each day listening, no demands made beyond being present, stretching branches towards the sun?

A car drives through the main entrance of the estate. The window is down. Dance music. She opens her eyes. The spell is broken. Walking towards the gates, she sees a minibus parked to one side. She waves. Danish, from the meetings, is driving and smiles out of the window. Seated in the back are a number of faces that Gete recognizes. Zulfa opens the door.

'Come, Gete. We will be late,' she calls. Gete jumps in

beside her friend. It's a tight squeeze with all the others. But they manage. She tucks in her skirt as the door slides shut.

'You look beautiful,' Zulfa says as the bus pulls away. 'Such lovely skin, smooth and even, like dark chocolate.'

'And how has your week been, sister?' Gete asks. Zulfa looks tired, all dark around her eyes. Though Gete knows she is always glad for her day off and to be out of her uniform; Zulfa has said she feels like a nobody in it, like she doesn't exist.

'Very difficult.' Zulfa glances sideways but all the others are in conversation. 'Have you read the business about the dead lady in the marina? She was daughter of Ma'am.'

'Oh, goodness,' Gete replies. She squeezes her friend's hand but is curious to know the details. 'And how is the family?'

'Bad. Very bad. There are fights in the night. Doors slamming and shouting at me and all the maids. Master Mahmoud even hit Amalia when she spilt his coffee. She cried and cried.'

'Why are they so angry?'

'They say she brought great shame on the family.' Zulfa looks around again. She leans in close to Gete's ear. 'They say she was with a man.'

'They did not say this in the news,' Gete replies.

'Of course not. And you must not say it either. I should not tell you. We could get into very bad trouble.'

'Do they know how she died?' Gete's voice grows lower. Zulfa frowns.

'Nobody knows. A taxi man has been arrested.'

Gete shakes her head.

'Is nowhere safe? These men. If they are not God-fearing, there can be no trusting them.' She looks at Danish. He is singing to the radio while he drives. The song sounds like something from a Bollywood movie. He glances across. She looks down.

'Danish is very good, don't you think? Bringing us all to Jebel Ali?' Zulfa smiles; Gete feels her elbow nudge her side.

'He is very kind,' Gete replies. 'So tell me, sister, were there many at the funeral? Did all the family attend?'

'The youngest son returned from his studies abroad. He is very wild. He drinks a great deal and has strange tastes.'

Gete wants to ask what Zulfa means by strange tastes. Has this young man made advances on her? Some of the other maids in the congregation are not safe in their beds. Without money, there is nothing to be done but put up with it. Embassies do little to help.

Zulfa takes out lip balm, looking at herself in a small hand mirror. Light brown eyes and wonderful curves. Pale-skinned. Gete wants to ask her about her name, where 'Zulfa' has come from. It sounds exotic. Maybe back home in Indonesia, she came from a wealthy family that had fallen on hard times. Perhaps their land had been taken or their shop had closed.

'It must be a cruel thing to lose a child,' Gete says, looking out of the window. Outside, as they travel further away from Jumeirah, there is only desert and pylons. Damp is beginning under her arms. She hopes the sweet-smelling perfume she sprayed will cover any possible odour.

'Yes. Very cruel. Ma'am has barely left her room. Always crying. Always crying. Mr Sir just works and works. And the two young men, when they are home it's shouting and shouting.'

The minibus stops outside the church. Gete gets out, gives Zulfa a hand down from the seat. It's a relief to stretch her limbs and straighten her blouse. The sandstone church is simple with small round arches; the only decoration is a small cross etched on to the exterior. A couple of other people stand around outside.

'I got you here on time.' Danish stands beside her. 'Three minutes to go.'

'Thank you, brother.'

'No problem, no problem,' he laughs. He laughs so easily. Those beautiful white teeth. When was the last time she heard someone really laugh, truly, from the bottom of their belly? She wants to ask him how he can be so happy when he drives buses on the same roads all day, every day.

'Would you like me to find you two seats?' he asks.

'Thank you,' Gete replies. She and Zulfa can find seats themselves, but it is nice to be looked after by a polite man. Zulfa links her arm and they follow him up the pathway of palms; he opens the main doors and they thank him again and step inside. The air-conditioning hits the slight perspiration on Gete's brow, a wonderful feeling.

The church is half full, mostly with women from Indonesia, though there is a scattering of white people too. A simple cross by the platform is all that shows the room is not a business room but a place of worship. Nothing ornate like Dubai Mall with its fountains and sparkling lights, but Christ loved humble places and the congregation keeps it immaculate.

Sitting in the fifth row, she and Zulfa lift out their Bibles, waiting for the minister to take to the platform. She says a quick prayer, thanking God that she is placed with the Cusacks – a Christian household – not like some of the other maids, who were told they must convert by their Ma'ams. Did those other girls lie in bed at night and worry about their souls? Did they pray to God, asking Him to forgive them? God is merciful. Surely, He will forgive them. 'God is jealous too' – Baba warned her of this before her departure.

'Will you be staying long after the service?' Gete whispers to Zulfa.

'I cannot today. Ma'am told me to be back before two.'

Music starts. The congregation stands. It is one of Gete's favourite songs and Mama always said she sang it so beautifully. *'Is any among you suffering? Let him pray. Is any cheerful? Let him sing psalms.'* Some of the men sing too loud, others can't hit the right notes, but there is something joyous in the imperfection.

What a shame there are no children in the congregation. Back home, babies would cry and mothers would stand at the back, their hips bobbing little ones. Distracting, yes, but it made the service more human, more natural. Maybe one day she'll have children herself, after she's made something of her life. 'Don't have children till your husband has money. Better still, marry a rich man,' Aunt Candace had said the night before she left for Dubai. 'And make sure he does not die on you.'

She'd asked her aunt did she regret having children.

'What else was there to do?' Aunt Candace replied, distracted by those women outside the open window who were bargaining with men. 'But you sleep badly after having a child, wondering what will become of their life.'

'God's will is a mystery.'

'A mystery.' She sighed. 'Come now, the wat is burning.' Aunt Candace lifted the pot off the open flame. For some minutes neither of them spoke while she mixed the injera. It would be a feast. 'You will leave with your stomach full.'

She cannot wait to see Aunt Candace again, to taste her cooking, then travel home and hug Lemuel and them all. Yet, it is this missing her family that has given her an idea, something she might do if she can keep working and saving for just a few more years in Dubai.

She would like to have a little business, an internet café, a place for making international calls which would make a good price for people to ring their family. Goodness, there must be so many maids like her around the world who miss their families back in Ethiopia, and men too, working on the building sites and driving taxis. She could help them, and at the same time make a good life for herself.

Yes, a café that is not too expensive but enough that she could have her own money and help Baba and the family. Maybe Lemuel would come and help her. She would manage the money, as Baba said she was always better with numbers, but it would feel safer to have a man in the shop.

There have to be more options in her life than just to marry a rich man, like Aunt Candace had said. Perhaps she will be lucky; she could have her own money in time and marry a man for love instead. She keeps reminding herself, everything has its time: a beginning and an end. Patience pays. Pray to God for support.

Zulfa nudges Gete, waking her from her daydreams. The minister calls out a scripture. 2 Corinthians 5 verse 15.

'And He died for all, that those who live should no longer live for themselves, but for Him who died for them and was raised again.'

She sits with a small group and the minister at the back of the church, eating sandwiches and drinking tea from flasks. The room smells of polish. Danish is on the stage hoovering; Zulfa sprays the lower panes of glass, wiping them with a cloth. Gete rubs her palms together, dry after using the bathroom cleaner.

'Ma'am says me to clean her sister's house too.' One of the maids looks around at the others. Grey hairs spread out from her temples. 'I tell her, this is not my job. I am to clean her house but she shouts and she shouts.'

The minister shakes his head, as do the others.

'Have you spoken to your embassy?'

'We have no rights, they say. We must bear what we can. There are other maids, they say, have it very bad. Beaten by Ma'ams. Sirs abusing them, making their advances.'

'Do you have money to go home?'

'No money. I must send it home. My eldest son, he is in university there. He will become a doctor.'

'When did you last see him?'

'Three year ago now.'

Gete listens as the woman continues. She hears these stories every week. Maids forced to get up at five a.m. and not allowed to bed till midnight. The agencies, they do not care about complaints.

'When I went to the embassy,' another woman says, 'there was a very angry woman shouting. She said to the embassy lady, "She is mine. I pay her flights." As if the lady own her like a slave. But the maid would not leave the embassy. She say the husband, he rape her. She says she stay in embassy till her family can save some little money to send her home.'

'She lives at the embassy?' the minister asks, lowering his tea.

'Yes, she stay there. They feed her, but they have no money to send girls home.'

The conversation continues. Gete watches as Danish tidies the Hoover's lead and puts it into the small storeroom. She stands and excuses herself, walking towards the front door. The heat outside leaves her lightheaded. Taking a slow deep breath, she makes her way to the low wall, sitting in the shade of a palm.

The doors open behind but she doesn't look around.

'May I join you?' a voice says. She turns. It's Danish, holding a mug of tea and half a sandwich. She smiles, conscious of how small her teeth are compared to his wide smile.

'How are you?'

'I am well.' She looks at her feet.

'You are not having troubles, like the other girls?'

'No. My Ma'am is good. You are busy these days?'

'Just driving, you know!' He laughs a little. 'I go home in a month, did I tell you?' Beads of sweat are forming on his dark brow.

'For good? Are you not coming back?' Her heart beats a little faster.

'Six weeks. My mother, she is keen to see me.' He sips his hot tea. It cannot be very nice when the sun is so strong.

'And your family?'

'My family are good. My father, he says he has a girl he wants me to marry.'

'Do you know her?' Gete puts down her sandwich. Danish shakes his head. He flaps the open neck of his shirt. Gete tries to keep her heels from touching the wall; it feels like a frying pan.

'She is not from my town but it would be a good marriage, I am told.'

'Won't you have a say?'

'Yes.' He laughs again. 'I can stay here and keep driving.'

'I hope she is nice and you two are happy.'

'Nothing is certain. There may be another girl I might like.' He grins at her and she can't help but give a shy smile in return.

'You deserve a good wife.'

He doesn't reply. Her smile fades and she looks down at the ground again, wondering if he has understood her. A trickle of sweat travels from her ear down her neck. Maybe she should've stayed in the church. Outside is oppressive. Danish flaps the neck of his shirt again, trying to keep cool.

'It would be lovely to swim now, don't you think?'

Gete nods though doesn't say a word. Slipping into cool water sounds wonderful. Back home, on hot days, she swam close to her home; the boys would splash the girls and laugh as the girls told them off. The younger children would play in the shallows, picking stones.

'Maybe we should go back inside to the others,' Gete says. 'They will wonder where we have gone.'

'OK. If you think.'

She smiles and stands. As they walk towards the entrance, she is determined she won't look the other maids in the eyes, no matter what. Her eyes are stinging more than she'd like and she'd hate for anyone to notice.

Joan

The electronic doors of Cork train station open and close; orange screens glow with the times of the arriving trains; Joan glances around, looking at the compact AMT café, beside a newsagent bursting with newspapers and magazines. There's a delicious smell of coffee. People moving quickly across the highly polished floor.

No text from Stevo. He better be out of bed. A devil for keeping time, even before the drink.

'Now, you're definitely staying in tonight?' she asked the previous evening. 'I can't be dealing with you hungover.'

'What do you take me for?' he said. There was that slight slur to his words, now permanent, like he'd drunk too much alcohol over the last three decades and now he could never quite sober up.

'I'm trusting you now. You have clothes detergent in the cupboard? I've most of the rest packed.'

'Ah.'

'I'll bring some.'

'You know I'm in a new place now, Jo,' he said. 'I'm on that hill to St Luke's.'

'I haven't forgotten. I was there last time.'

'You were?'

'I was. Remember. When you had your appointment in the Victoria.'

The station doors close; the sun comes out as Joan walks towards the city centre, her small case behind her. The traffic speeds by, hatchbacks and silver saloons slipping past St Patrick's church. A purple-grey wall rises, half covered with emerald creepers and large billboards – a red-and-white Vodafone advertisement, the gold tones of a film poster, and a monochrome Guinness announcement (the lower half torn, curving like a wave). Behind, old houses retreat up the hillside, warm creams, yellows and soft pinks.

Cork is a special place. She does miss its cosiness, the way she was always near anyone if they were somewhere in the city. She stops at the top of MacCurtain Street, the facades of the buildings stitched together, various heights and colours – bright pinks, baby blues, off-whites and canary yellows. Swinging signs hang one floor up – 'Shandon Taxi Cabs', 'The Berries' and 'Coca-Cola' – while the neon lights of the Adult Store flicker on and off. She enjoys the patchwork, the noise of the beeping cars, the shopfronts; a bit rough around the edges, yes, but her native land.

She looks over at the Metropole hotel, with the yellow turret on one of its corners. Three decades earlier she stood on this very spot. In her head, the past seems sepia-coloured, but maybe her memory has been affected by photographs.

'Wouldn't you love to live in that little tower?' she'd said to Jack. They were heading towards the city centre for the St Patrick's Day Parade.

'You'd throw down your hair to me?' he'd replied.

'Not a hope.' She had tried not to smile. 'I'd take my chances with the witch.' His hand touched her backside. 'Stop that. You're desperate.' She laughed.

She didn't realize then that Jack was the sort of man who was never going to grow up: putting his finger into her nostril while she watched TV, grabbing her backside when she walked up stairs, and driving through puddles so they'd spray everywhere. 'You'll be the death of me,' she often said. Was it odd that she missed the torment?

She looks away from the Metropole and, after a few more yards, turns off MacCurtain Street and climbs the steep slope. Gorgeous Georgian houses, all the doors have stained glass above them. She passes a man in a worn leather jacket with a torn cup in front of him. A number of squashed cans are beside him, the rest scattered down the slope. He doesn't ask for change, just glances at her briefly and turns back to face the sun. She throws a few coins on to his blanket.

A beep from her phone. A message from Stevo.

I'm up. I'm up. She calls the number.

'I'm only five minutes away. Are you dressed?'

'I'll get the kettle on.'

Two side streets take her to the door of her brother's flat. Downstairs, there'd once been a restaurant, though the windows are now boarded. She looks at the green paint coming through the red at the bottom of the door. An open bottle of Corona sits by the gutter, along with a number of cigarette butts and a crisp wrapper: things to add to the 'to-do' list.

She pushes the button but no bell rings. Tapping with the rusted doorknob, she hears feet hammer down the stairs inside. The door opens and she smiles at Stevo, trying to ignore the smell of fried sausages.

'Good to see you.' He gives her a hug. 'Let me take that.' He reaches down for her case. She tries to stop him but he insists. For a moment, she has to get over the shock of seeing him. It's a fright every time, her little brother, an old wreck of a man, thin as a pole, teeth the colour of nicotine, lines on his face like the bark of a tree. That awful denim jacket which has seen better days.

He talks but her mind drifts. He can't have many years left. Nothing left of the boy she knew. She tries not to dwell on the ever-growing realization that she will be 'that old woman', the last of her generation, popping to the corner shop alone, back hunched from the arthritis. Yes, it's horrible to die, but surely it's worse to be the last one left behind?

What if Siobhan and the boys never come back, and possibly Trevor too? She'd asked Siobhan what would they do next, and Siobhan had broken her heart when she said, 'Martin said there's great jobs in Singapore but he'd love New York really.'

'What about Dublin when things pick up? It'll be grand in a few years.'

'Not a hope, I'd say. Martin has no interest any more. Sure, we'll be back anyway every year for holidays, and you'll come out to us.'

'Oh.'

'Mam . . . you there?' Siobhan had asked.

'Yes, love.' Joan finally caught her breath but she still felt like she'd just taken a punch.

'Great. I thought the reception had gone.' Siobhan began chattering on about something else.

'Come on upstairs, get in out of the cold,' Stevo says. She steps inside and he closes the door.

A wheelie bin is under the stairs and there's a sweet smell, like when cider gets spilt and isn't cleaned properly. The grey carpet has traces of white paint all over it. Wouldn't you put down an old sheet and save the floor?

Joan grips the rail as she climbs the stairs. The whole house slopes towards the river. Where to start with this place? Better to flatten it.

'You wouldn't want to be drunk going up these steps,' she jokes.

'The place has character, Jo. Who'd want to be livin in a perfect world?'

She watches each step, holding the balustrade tightly. The dust is an inch thick between the rails. That can't be good for his lungs, not that it'd make much difference with the forty Bensons he smokes each day.

'Won't you have a cup of tea, Jo?' Stevo asks. 'You'll break your back like that.'

Joan stops wiping the inside of the shower doors, rubbing away a few strands of wet hair with the back of her hand.

'Ten minutes,' she says. 'I've the toilet and floor to go, then it's done in here.'

'I don't know why you bother when it only gets dirty again. I've the kettle on.'

'Has the machine finished?' she asks. 'I'll need to get the bedding on the radiators.'

'Yes . . . no. The door isn't opening on it.'

Joan squirts more Cif on to her cloth and works it around the small grooves in the shower floor. Curly hairs are in the plug, the grout a dark brown. She would say something but what's the point. She keeps rubbing, her wrist starting to ache. It'll never really be clean. Bodge job of a bathroom. Half the paint is falling off the ceiling from the damp.

'I've the tea made,' Stevo shouts. 'It'll only be going cold.'

After a minute the bathroom door opens.

'Come on now, Joan,' he says. 'You and the cleaning. You're nearly as bad as Mammy . . .'

Joan smiles but doesn't reply, her arms still vigorously moving.

'. . . you remember when Mammy used to get the library books, Jo, and she'd be crossing out all the swear words in them? I was tellin the boys about that. They were crackin up.'

Joan laughs. Stevo keeps talking nonsense, without any intention of helping her. Finally, after a rinse, the shower sparkles. She's a miracle worker.

'You're done now?' he asks.

'Nearly.' Standing, she squirts a large quantity of bleach into the toilet bowl. 'You men are an awful breed. I'll have to come back to this, once the Domestos has had time to kick in.'

*

'The tea has gone cold,' Stevo says, as she sits down in the living room. He lights a cigarette. She'd love to scold him, but it is his place after all. He still has one of those TVs with fake wooden sides. Across the dining table is 'stuff'. It can only be described as stuff, as it appears to be everything from old ESB bills to rusty bolts to old cigarette packets.

'Would you ever let me get a skip bag?' she says. 'We could clean the place out?'

'Relax there. I barely see ya and you'd rather have your head in the toilet bowl.'

She laughs, but is unhappy she does. It feels like collusion.

'How's Trevor?'

'Great. He's having a ball with Siobhan in Dubai. Though he's burnt the face off himself. I keep telling him to put on sunscreen.'

'Siobhan and the two boys? Make sure to send them my regards.'

'No fear of her. Though Martin is never about. He's always working but she's well able to spend his money, so maybe they are a good match after all.' Joan laughs again. There's no point in telling Stevo her concerns about how isolated poor Siobhan is. God knows what Martin's up to away travelling. Of course, there are great bursts of excitement down the phone when an event is coming up, Siobhan describing the dress she bought or where she got her hair done, but in between are great spaces where Martin is away, Rocco is off at school, and poor Siobhan is at a loose end.

Of course, there was the incident with the messages on Martin's phone. Siobhan had rung her one evening while she was watching the news. It must've been one a.m.

Dubai time, and Siobhan was on her mobile, not Skype. She asked a string of questions which could've been done at a reasonable hour and not at a rate of three euros a minute.

'How are you, Mam? How is Maggs? The hospital?'

Of course, Siobhan hadn't been raised in a ditch; she always asked how things were in Ireland before going on about herself. There was a long pause. Knowing an avalanche of information would follow, Joan asked, 'How are you, love?'

'Good. The boys are grand. You know . . .' Another pause.

'Is Martin OK?' They'd be talking all night at this rate. Siobhan could fly home for the money she was racking up on her phone bill.

'He's . . . Now, I don't want you saying, "I told you so." Honestly, I feel sick.'

'What happened?'

'Martin has been messaging a woman.'

'Oh.' Twenty questions had jumped into Joan's mind. But all she could think of was Martin's old bedroom at Richard and Shirley's. All those naked women, tits out and fingers God knows where. *I knew it.* She hated that those words came immediately into her head.

'What did they say?'

'Saying how good-looking she was, great legs and jokes about her rear.'

'Was there lots of messages?'

'Five. But I dunno. He must've deleted the ones that came before.'

Sonofabitch. Joan's nostrils flared. Thank God Siobhan wasn't there to see the colour of her face. She took a deep breath, knowing from experience that getting knee-deep in other people's relationships never ended well.

'What do you think you'll do?'

'I dunno, Mam. He says it was all innocent, just buttering up a girl who works for a company that he's trying to get a contract with, and they just got a bit flirty at a party. But like . . .'

'Don't be apologizing to me. You've every right to be upset.'

'What do you think I should do?'

Dangerous territory. Joan hadn't wanted to say what her gut was telling her, that the texts were probably the tip of the iceberg. There'd only be one loser if she said what she thought and it wouldn't be Martin. Anyway, Siobhan always did what she liked. Even Jack couldn't talk her round to things. 'You have to do what's right for you and the boys,' she'd said, finally.

'Yeah. The boys.' Siobhan was silent for a number of minutes. Joan felt terrible, but the idea of Siobhan and the two boys flying home and them all cooped up in her house, Rocco's video games so loud the windows rattled, filled her with dread. She knew what would be the outcome. Fifteen years later, they'd all still be there, the wallpaper hanging off the walls. Course, she'd do it if she had to, but that didn't make the prospect pleasant.

'Look, sleep on it and talk to me in the morning,' Joan had said finally. 'I'll always be here for you, love. No matter what.'

'Thanks, Mam.' A sigh down the phone. 'Christ, my head is splitting.'

'Cup of Barry's.'

Siobhan laughed. A blow of the nose. It wasn't till then that Joan realized Siobhan must've been crying. They chatted for a few minutes longer, until Siobhan said she'd better go before she'd need a loan to pay off the phone bill. They hadn't talked about it since. Siobhan never brought it up, and Joan knew from experience that if Siobhan felt she was interfering without being asked, she'd get her head bitten off.

The news was still on mute; a plane had vanished off the coast of Brazil. What would Jack say about it all? Truth was, she knew what he'd say. 'She's made her bed, now she must lie in it.' Maybe he was right. Last thing she wanted was for the two boys to have no daddy around. He might be a waste of space, but at the end of the day he could provide for them in a way none of the rest of them could.

'You didn't hear? She's due her first,' Stevo exclaims. Thank God. The chats are beginning to flow. The silence was starting to get awkward. Joan would like to ask him about his life, but every time she goes to say something she realizes the answer will include a reference to alcohol.

'She isn't? That didn't take her long. What age is she anyway?'

'Eighteen. It doesn't take long at that age if you are looking for it.'

'True. The father?'

'God knows.'

Another silence.

'Any man on the scene?' Stevo asks.

'Of course not. The cheek,' she laughs.

'As long as you're happy. It's been long enough.'

She takes a sip from the Man United cup. It's definitely one of the mugs she washed earlier.

'Do you want a sandwich, Joanie? I'm famished,' Stevo says.

'Will we go out for a bite?' Joan had seen a packet of ham in the fridge was already open and didn't trust it. 'Lunch in Luigi's? My treat.'

Thankfully there is nobody in Luigi Malones that she knows; the lunch crowd have already gone back to their offices. Stevo still has on that old raggedy denim jacket. The notches on his belt don't go small enough, so he's stuck a few more holes in it with a knife. It's like she's sitting across from a tinker. Same time, she's happy that he'll have a good feed.

The waiter comes, and she orders a bottle of water for the table and a carbonara. Stevo orders bacon. He looks around at the surroundings like he's a sailor lost in a foreign land. He scratches his ear. She tries to ignore the bits of dry skin that are flaking off on to his jacket. She hates herself. It's awful to be embarrassed by her own family.

'Are you still going to the group each week?'

He nods.

'Dry shites, but I go all right.'

'Have you had any . . .' She's not sure how to finish the sentence. Benders? Falling off the wagon? Lapses? His drinking came in bouts. Sober for a month or more, then vanishing for a week. He'd show up when the money ran out, smelling of sweat and stale beer.

'I'm doing OK,' he replies. A politician's answer if ever she heard one.

The food arrives. The pasta is divine. She'd murder a glass of Pinot Grigio. Stevo cuts into the pork. She tries not to look as he licks his knife, resisting the urge to slap his hand down.

Where had it gone wrong? Mammy and Daddy had reared them right. She'd always studied hard, avoided drinking more than a glass or two, and had never been arrested. It was like some switch had flipped in Stevo's head somewhere in his teens and things began going wrong. Chasing Blossy from number twenty-nine, and she a married woman. Picking fights, Daddy collecting him from the station. Motorbikes. Smoking God knows what.

If he'd just gone to England and got a job on one of the sites, he might've worked up the ladder, got a trade, made something of himself instead of hanging around Cork. 'Signing on, pouring back the pints and hunting for the female flavour of the month is not a profession,' she once told him. He told her to 'fuck off and stop being so nosy', that it was his life to live how he wanted.

Thirty years ago. *Thirty years.* Where did the time go? A slow change from telling him to cop on to doing her best to keep the train from going completely off the track. He'd been no use when Mammy got sick, or Daddy. A drunken wreck at both funerals. Though maybe it was all destined to be. The doctors called the drinking a disease these days – maybe it was all in Stevo's genes.

The night after Daddy's funeral, she took Stevo home in a taxi. Jack offered to help but she wouldn't hear of it. This was her blood, not his responsibility. Wasn't she a nurse? Heaving Stevo out of the cab, his eyes floating in different directions, he laughed as a middle-aged man passed them.

'Look at that fella, the fat fella with the big arse on him, ah he's not the worst, I don't judge anybody. I know the Bible. Put the eye of a camel through a needle.'

She helped him on to the bed upstairs. He grumbled and shoved a bit but then he began to settle. Pulling the duvet out from underneath him, she yanked off his shoes and helped him out of his jumper. It was half soaked with lager, as were his pants. As she helped him slip his trousers off, his boxers accidentally came with them. And she saw it. She saw her brother's penis.

Now, as she sits across from Stevo in Luigi Malones, she tries not to think about that image. But it feels burned into her brain. Of course, barely a day goes by in the hospital when she doesn't see one or two of them, but her brother's? She hates him for having that memory.

Stevo puts down his fork. 'That was, what does young Trev say? Savage. That was savage, Jo.' The meat and potatoes are gone. The broccoli sits on the edge of the plate.

'My pleasure.' She gives him a smile, trying not to look at those washed-out, crinkled eyes.

God forgive her for lying. She told Stevo her train home was an hour earlier than what it actually is. A day in that house is enough to make anyone turn to drink. At least she can head back to Dublin safe in the knowledge he's clean sheets, the bathroom and kitchen are in order, and he won't burn down the flat with cigarettes falling out of ashtrays. There is no point in worrying beyond that. Crisis management is the best that can be hoped for.

Rather than heading straight to the train station, she goes towards the Opera House. It's getting dark. The early winter evenings. People pass as she pauses at the Bank of Ireland ATM by Paul Street, some with Tesco shopping bags, some on their way home from work.

Across the walkway, box hedges frame a blue statue of the Virgin Mary outside Saints Peter and Paul's, her head tilted, arms outstretched. The gates to the church are open. An old woman stands with her hands out. Joan gives her a coin, glancing at the woman's flowing amber skirt.

Standing at the last pew, she gazes at the objects crammed together like an overfull attic, despite the size of the church. She walks to the bronze altar table at the far side. There is a scattering of candles on the rack. Slipping a two-euro coin into the slot, the noise echoing around the church, she lifts out a tealight and straightens its wick. It flickers as she lights it off one of the other candles. She gazes at the flame.

Even though she's lived in Dublin decades, this has always been her favourite church. She made sure both Trevor and Siobhan were christened here, despite the hassle it caused for everyone. Mammy loved coming here whenever they were in the city. She always went to the same little rack of tealights.

Someone coughs. It echoes. An old woman stands at the other side of the church by a rack of proper candles rather than simple tealights. In the past, Joan was tempted to go to the grander altar but she never did, wanting to keep the ritual her mother began. She glances at her tealight one last time before she turns to leave. Her attention is caught by a picture of the Virgin Mary in the altar beside her. Mary is surrounded by gold, greenish-coloured. Poor Baby Jesus is not so much a sickly-looking child but a strange small man.

God, mind poor Stevo. And please look out for Trevor, she thinks, though she wonders if there is any point in praying for Stevo. It feels like his chances are over. His mind will never go back to the way it was when they were young and he'd all the guff and gab of a cocky young lad.

But Trevor. Goodness. He better not go the same way. It'd break her heart to see him at fifty, she an old woman in her eighties and he still floating along, nothing done with his life – no family, no proper job, no home of his own. Whatever about his gruffness, he's a sensitive soul and this world is not made for sensitive sorts, no matter how big their muscles grow.

Last year, when he'd come home from the hospital, he was a ghost for a number of months. It was like he wasn't there. No smart answers back. No telling her to get out of his face. A nod of the head, as if agreeing with her words that he'd be the death of her. 'You're putting nails in my coffin.' Her favourite phrase got an airing.

This defeatist attitude was the worst of all. Part of her had wanted to shout, 'Yeah, life is difficult. Don't you think I miss your father all the time? But you keep going. That's what you do. You're alive. You thank God you're alive. You look out for each other and you make the most of it.' But another part of her felt shaky at the thought of the Liffey. Had the emergency services not fished him out, Trevor would now be buried alongside Jack. All she wanted to do was keep him close. She whispered to herself, 'You better not die before me, Trev. I've had my fill of deaths this life-time. My turn next.'

Eventually she did ask him the question that she'd hoped to avoid asking. They'd had another fight, her doing her best to get him off the couch so he'd make his shift at work, his red face like he'd had when he was eleven. She might as well have been kicking a puppy.

'Trev. Please. What's wrong with you?'

Trevor's eyes were glassy but he said nothing.

'I don't know what to say, my love. You're so young.'

Still no response from him. Yet, the pain was written across his face.

'Just try, Trev. Honestly, don't you think the day your father died I wanted to hop into that bed and not get out? But you know what? I thought about you two and little Rocco, made an effort and good things followed. Get out there. Do something. Otherwise, what's the point?'

He stared into space. Were the words going in at all? After a moment, he sat up, leaned across and hugged her. No tears. But the hug was tight. Funny thing was, she started crying. He remained still and steady as a rock and it was in this solidity that she realized something of Jack was still alive.

'I love you, Mam.'

'I love you too.'

The train is quiet. Joan is happy. She has four seats and a table to herself. Outside the windows, it's dark. She feels like she is on a plane, cocooned in artificial light. Lifting her phone out of her handbag, she sees a number of messages. The first is a picture of a grey floaty top from Siobhan.

Mam. Will I buy one for you? One left in your size and half price? Siobhan is a good girl really. Generous to a fault.

Joan glances out as the last of the lights of Blackpool Shopping Centre vanish from view. The city is very small. There's something claustrophobic about it – well, maybe not so much the place but rather being around Stevo. She can't relax in his company.

Her phone rings.

'Hi, Mam.'

'Hi, Trev. Is all OK?'

'Grand. Just checking in.'

'This'll be costing you a fortune.'

'I'll be in bed before you get home on Skype.'

'Did you have a lovely day?'

'Great. Siobhan has everything organized. We're heading out for brunch tomorrow. Bit of a piss-up, like.'

'I was down with Stevo today.'

'How is he?' Trevor's voice grows hard.

'No different. I helped him with a few house bits. The usual.'

'Fair enough.'

'The halfway mark for you in Dubai. You missing your mammy?'

'Ah, would you stop.' Trevor laughs. There is a pause.

'Mam,' he says. Another pause. 'I . . . I was chatting to the lads in Siobhan's gym. They were saying they might need another guy to help with the personal training.'

'Oh.'

'They were saying they could get me out here for a while. We'll have to see how it pans out, but, I dunno. What do you think?' He continues talking but Joan is distracted by her thoughts. Trevor gone. The idea of it makes her feel sick. That clean house all to herself in Dublin. She wants to tell him that he has a home, a job and a warm meal each day in Dublin.

'Trev, I think that's a great idea,' she says.

'Are you sure? I'd be worried about leaving you, Mam.'

'Don't be silly. What do you take me for?'

The conversation continues for a short while longer. Now that he has told her his news, his voice relaxes and they chat about the usual silly things. She replies, doing her best to sound normal, but she is thankful when he says goodbye and hangs up. Warm tears flow down her cheeks. She knows she's done the right thing but Christ, it hurts.

Lydia

Those stupid girls keep laughing, all crowded on to one bunk. How can they be joking in such a place? They are silly, silly creatures. No wonder they get caught by the police. Nylon skirts. Denim jackets. Sparkly earrings and necklaces from a cheap accessories store.

One of the girls burps. A man's noise, deep and low. Disgusting. The rest of the group are giggling like children again. There is a smell of body odour as another lifts her arms. How long can they keep her here? Will she end up like those women, stupid and dirty, making the most of it?

Lydia puts her cardigan over her legs, leaning against the exposed-block wall. The mattress does little to cushion the metal frame underneath it. Is there no air-conditioning? She glances at the bunk above her. A woman snores. Some hair falls over the side of the bed. Lydia wonders what would happen if she yanked it. Because right now she'd love to fight. She'd love to hit something – someone – hard. Every time she tries to get her life on track, something always goes wrong.

It had started well, the weekend approaching and James, a regular, in the mood to celebrate a business account he had won. James: good-looking, small dick, but impressive technique. Moaned a lot when she sucked his cock.

Afterwards, he wrapped the used condom in a piece of

tissue and put it in his pocket – some men do that, worried a girl might use the sperm. Lydia sat on the bed, wondering if he would want to chat or if he would leave straight away.

'You are busy with work?' she asked.

'It's stressful,' James replied, looking for a sock. 'Though I'm feeling less so now.'

'I hope you . . .' Lydia stopped. There was a hammering on the apartment door. 'Bianca. The door,' she called. No answer.

The hammering again. James looked at her.

'You know who that is?'

Lydia shook her head. She hoped it wasn't an old client returning. Sometimes they rang her or showed up drunk, saying they didn't have the money this week, but they'd definitely have it next time. Or worse, those men who thought they were in love with her because the sex had been so good.

Lydia slid off the bed, putting back on her clothes. She looked in the mirror, stroking her fingers through her hair. James closed the final buttons on his shirt.

'All right. All right. I'm coming,' Lydia called. She reached the door and glanced through the peephole. Men in green-and-red suits.

'Open up!' one shouted.

'Fuck.' She glanced at James.

'What?'

'Flush the condom,' she said. 'Do it.'

The hammering continued. The door was rattling hard. Not much more and it'd be taken off the hinges. She heard the toilet then turned the lock. Five officers stormed into the room. She staggered backwards, knocking a lamp on to the tiles.

'What took so long?' one of the men asked.

'I was looking for my top.'

'Who is this man?' The policeman looked at James, who reappeared from the bedroom.

'A friend.'

'Your name?'

'John Matthews.'

John. Of course. Like all the others.

'Are you married?'

A pause.

'I am.'

'Well, Mr John, you must leave. Or should we call your wife?'

'No, no.' John grabbed his coat and, without looking up, walked straight towards the door. Coward. No interest in what happened to her. To think about the number of times they'd fucked, how he'd told her she was the most beautiful woman he'd ever seen, how he hated his wife and wished he could leave her.

'You are Lydia Sushkova?'

'I am.'

'Miss Sushkova, I am under orders to bring you to the station for questioning in relation to the death of Hiyam Husayin.'

'Who?'

'You'll come with me.' He held her arm, the grip tightening, pinching the flesh.

'I need my jacket. You're hurting.'

'Get her coat.'

'What are you doing? These are my things.' Lydia turned

around, watching as police officers searched the apartment. 'What are you looking for?'

'You must come with me now.'

He handcuffed her and pushed her towards the elevator. Mrs Sarkis from number sixty-seven, with the hips of a hippopotamus, stood at her front door and shook her head. 'Your poor mother,' she said. 'The shame you bring to your family.'

'Your poor waist,' Lydia shouted back. The officer shoved her into the lift.

What would Igor say about her now, trapped in a Dubai cell with a bunch of giggling hookers? He has a temper. When he was eight, she'd pretended to squash a fly with a piece of tissue. She squeezed it down hard on the windowsill – 'Didn't you hear it crunch?' As he watched, she ate the dead fly. Of course, the fly had only ever been a raisin that she'd planted before. He began crying. Eventually, she told him it was a joke and he'd punched her hard. Her shoulder was blue-black for a week.

His temper. His sister, 'the whore'. And Mama. 'My daughter a harlot. Oh God, what have I done to deserve this torment?' Then endless lines from the Bible quoted:

'Just as Sodom and Gomorrah and the surrounding cities, which likewise indulged in sexual immorality and pursued unnatural desire, serve as an example by undergoing a punishment of eternal fire.'

Mama loves the scriptures where people are damned, burning in hell forever. God does not forgive; nor will she. Not that it matters. Even if Mama did want to help her, it would be of no benefit. She has no money.

But Igor. He would get over his temper in time. The humiliation would pass. Feelings like his are too strong to last. Lydia sighs. She is not alone in the world. She closes her eyes, feeling a warm trickle of sweat travel down to her jaw. The women on the other bunks continue to laugh like schoolgirls.

Veronika's witchy pointed face. Lydia opens her eyes. Veronika would slip ideas into Igor's head. 'What about our baby, Igor? Can we really have him knowing an aunt who is one of those sorts of women?' And Igor frowning, the idea sinking further till eventually he would shrug and say, 'Lydia has made her own bed, now she must lie in it.'

What can they charge her with, truly? She knows nothing of this girl. They could've gained nothing from her questioning. How many hours had she been kept in that chair? It felt like forever, the wooden seat digging into her flesh.

'What is your full name?'

'Lydia Sushkova.'

'No middle name?'

'I was christened Maria but that is not official.'

'How long have you been in Dubai?'

'Three, no, four years now.'

'And what do you do for money?'

Lydia was silent.

'I repeat, what is your occupation?'

'I model. I have money too, from my savings and family.' A smile on the older man's face. He looked at his hands. His cuticles were splitting.

'And what sort of modelling is that?'

'I do it back in Russia,' she lied. 'For magazines. Does that surprise you?' She smiled, wondering if her looks might appeal to him.

'We ask the questions,' said the younger officer, who stood by the door. He was handsome, in a tired sort of way. What were his hands like? Stocky fingers. Cock. Seventeen, eighteen centimetres? These Arab cocks could be thick too.

'Could you clarify your work?'

'I thought I was here to talk about a girl who has died.'

'You are.'

'I do not know her.'

'You met her. We have footage of you getting into a taxi with her on the day she died.'

'I would like a lawyer before I answer more questions.'

The officer laughed.

'You are not on a *CSI* show, Miss Sushkova. This is Dubai.'

'I do not know this woman. I do not lie when I say this.'

The officer opened the file of papers. He slid a photograph across the table. There was a picture of an Arab girl. Those eyes. Lydia tried to ignore the sudden feeling of light-headedness.

'You know her?'

'This is the woman you are looking for?' Lydia asks. 'This is Hiyam?'

'Have you not been reading the papers, Miss Sushkova?'

'I have no interest in the news. But I have seen this woman before. She did not call herself by that name. It was something else. Hiba. Something like that. She said she was from Turkey and we shared an RTA. But that was it. She left the taxi early and I travelled onward.'

'Slow down, Miss Sushkova. Much slower. Where did you meet this woman?'

'Outside the York.'

'And what were you doing in the York?'

'Dancing.'

'Alone?'

'My friends were there. We were having fun.'

'Drinking?'

'No.'

'And then what happened?'

'I was to meet a friend at the front of the York.'

'A girl.'

'No. A man.'

'A boyfriend.'

'A friend.'

'You know him well?'

'I know him over a year. He was outside with the Turkish girl. He asked if she could come along to my house for a drink.'

'A drink.'

'It'd been a long night.'

'And you said yes? Were you not concerned about bringing a strange man to your apartment?'

Lydia smiled. So, this was the game they were playing. They would not catch her out. She was no fool.

'As I said, he was a friend.'

'Tell me more about him. Your "friend" that you have known for a year.'

'He . . .' Lydia paused. What did she know? 'He is Irish. He is a businessman.' She tried to remember what business he was in. He talked for a while after the fourth time they'd had sex. Nearly all of them did eventually. 'He works for a marketing company. They market real estate. He said he was going to Egypt and we met to celebrate a new account.'

'What is his name?'

Lydia was silent.

'You do not know his name? This "friend" of yours? Can you tell me a bit more about the nature of your "friendship"?'

'He was called . . .' He'd never given her his real name, but Lydia had seen a memo in his briefcase while he was in the shower. 'Martin. His name is Martin. I do not know his second name. I have his number. You can ask him questions.' It felt wrong to give his name but she would not get in trouble for this woman's death. How stupid could this man have been, to have got involved with a local girl?

'That will be very helpful,' the officer said. For a second, she thought she saw a faint smile. 'Remember, your cooperation will help your defence, should you need one.'

'What else do you want from me?'

'Your phone. Of course, we can unlock it in time, but things will go easier for you, if you give us the pin.'

'But?'

'Miss Sushkova. We know what you are. We have all the evidence we need, with or without your phone. However, with your help on this, I will make sure you are well treated.'

Lydia looked at the table. Cheap wooden ply. Black metal legs. She could be in a classroom in school. What could she do? Bianca had once said, 'Get to an airport if things go wrong. If they want to get you, they will, one way or another.' It was too late now. All she could do was cooperate and hope.

'You can have my phone details, but you must let me talk with my embassy,' she said. 'This woman who died, she was not Turkish?'

'No. She was Emirate.'

Chto za khuynya. Martin, you stupid, stupid man.

'Am I entitled to a break?' Lydia asked. 'I need water.'

The policeman laughed.

'You can have water after you've answered our questions.'

'Tell me again, what happened when you got into the RTA outside the York?' the policeman asked. Lydia swallowed. The lack of daylight was disconcerting. How long had she been sitting there? Was it morning yet?

'I have answered your questions already. We three sat in the back of the car. The driver was to go to my apartment.' Lydia tried not to think about her thirst, which was beginning to grow maddening. Her tongue felt large in her mouth and it was getting harder to swallow.

'And how was Miss Husayin?'

'She would not look at me. She would only talk to him.'

'Why was that?'

'Jealousy. Women are always jealous.'

The investigator smiled. The younger officer, who had been pacing back and forth behind him, stopped as she said this before continuing to walk. There was no smile on his face. What a boring man he must be. What a friendless life he must live.

'And how was the mood in the car? Happy? Angry?'

'I do not know. She was very quiet. He was trying to make her laugh but his jokes were stupid.'

207

'And you.'

'I do what I do. Nothing more. It does not matter if I am happy or sad.' The officer kept writing in his notepad. She strained forward but all the words were in Arabic.

'The driver. What did he do?'

'Nothing. He drove. Martin told him to turn up the radio – a song he liked was playing – but that was it.'

'And then what?' More notes. Papers neatened and turned over.

'When we got to the marina, the girl, the Emirate girl, said she didn't want to come with us. Martin tried to calm her, but she said no and told the driver very strongly to stop the car.'

'And?'

'She jumped out. Martin told the driver to stay and gave him money. Then he ran after her.'

'What did you do?'

'I stayed in the car for a number of minutes. The meter kept rising. Till I said to the driver, "I will be back," and I got out and went down to the marina to see where they had gone.'

'And then?'

Lydia frowned. How many times could he ask that same stupid question? How many times could she say the same thing over and over again?

'They did not see me. I stood back, behind the barrier. There was building construction and sand was going into my shoes. The girl was shouting a lot and the man said things to calm her down, his hands like this.' Lydia held her palms up.

'Did you hear any words?'

'Just him saying "only one drink". This fight was not my business, so I slipped away and went back to the RTA. Martin, he returned about five minutes after and said the girl was going home, and for the taxi man to drive.'

'And?'

'That was it. The taxi man dropped us home.'

'What happened there? Was the man behaving differently than usual?'

Lydia smiled.

'Different. What way you mean, different?'

'Was he happy? Angry?'

'He seemed agitated but he calmed down after a drink.'

'And then what?'

Hours. Hours and hours and hours. How long would they have her sitting here? Was she allowed to go to the bathroom?

'How can we trust what you have said to us?'

'The taxi driver will confirm my story. I was not outside the RTA for more than five minutes.'

'A lot can happen in five minutes, Miss Sushkova.'

Why did he keep saying her name like that? The formality was unpleasant. A pause for what felt like half an hour, though it might've only been a few minutes.

'I need water,' Lydia said again. The light gave her a blinding headache.

'In time. After the questions.'

'Which way did the driver go after he left you and the man at your apartment?' the younger officer asked.

'I don't know.'

'Did he turn around? Go back towards the marina?'
'I could not say. I did not look.'

'We are almost done, Miss Sushkova.' The older officer looked tired. The young policeman, after leaning against the back wall with one leg, then the other, then both, finally took a seat beside his partner. Lydia squeezed her bum cheeks, trying to get the circulation working again. She could feel pins and needles in her calves and feet.

The older policeman lifted a series of stapled pages out of his folder and slid them towards her, placing a pen on top.

'What is this?'
'A statement confirming what you said today is true.'
'It is in Arabic.'
'I can explain it to you.'
'I will not, *will not*, sign anything I cannot read.'
'Miss Sushkova, you do not understand. We make the demands here.' His voice was quieter, more forceful, but she was unmoved.

'I will not sign.'
'Do you want to leave this room and get water?'
'I will die in this chair before I sign that. I want to speak to my embassy.'

'Miss Sushkova, I thought we agreed to cooperation.'
'Am I under arrest?'
No answer.
'Am I under arrest?' she shouted.
The police officer frowned.

'Not for now. You will be held for further questioning.'

'I shall say no more till I have spoken to the embassy.'

Lydia touches her cheek to the exposed-block wall, enjoying the coolness of the stone. An Emirate girl, of all things. Even if Martin hadn't been involved in her death, he was ruined. Everyone knows the rule, surely, that above all else, you do not upset the locals.

Who is the girl's father? He must be a man of some wealth, going on the bag she was carrying that night: Louis Vuitton, Autumn 2010 collection.

'Hello.' A head appears from the top bunk. Lydia smiles but doesn't reply. 'You in trouble?'

'Some,' Lydia replies. What a stupid question.

The woman climbs down, sitting on the edge of Lydia's bed. She is wearing a baggy T-shirt. Probably Indonesian or Filipino. Her nails are black with dirt and her eyes don't line up quite right.

'I am Sarah,' she says. 'My Ma'am said I robbed her jewellery. I didn't but nobody believe me.'

'I'm being questioned about a girl who died.'

'They don't believe you?'

'Do they believe anyone?'

'You sleep a long time,' the girl says. 'They be questioning you?'

'Yes.'

'They question me again and again. I do not know what more I can say.'

'How long have you been in here?'

'Months and months, I think.'

'Months. Are you not arrested?'

'I don't know. But we never get out of here.'

Lydia looks over at the group of young women on the far bunk. They still giggle. One plaits another girl's hair. Another laughs, hitting her friend with a pillow.

Glancing down, Lydia touches her calf. Still smooth. Yet, they won't be like that in a month's time. Her nails – the Chanel Graphite polish will all be chipped in a day or two. Already, her hair feels greasy. She touches its limp tendrils – thank goodness there is no mirror.

'I can plait your hair, if you like,' Sarah offers.

'Maybe in a little while. Thanks.'

The young woman smiles, picking her nails and lifting out some of the dirt.

Trevor

'Did you talk to Mam?' Siobhan asks, smearing her lips with gloss, glancing in the car mirror. She's wearing a green strappy dress like she's ready for a night on the batter. Her hair is all blow-dried like she's a film star. 'You boys got your seatbelts on?' she calls into the back.

'Yes, they have, Ma'am,' Gete says, who sits between the two boys' seats. Poor Gete. After her day off, she's back dressed like she found the clothes in a skip.

'I spoke to Mam last night,' Trevor says. 'She didn't sound herself but she was on the train.' He hopes it wasn't what he said to her, but then, how could it not be?

'Don't worry about her. She's always odd after a Cork trip.' Siobhan fixes her sunglasses.

Trevor glances at his watch. The bloody traffic jams are driving him bonkers. The sun is making his arm sizzle through the window. It's been nearly twenty minutes and they've barely gone five blocks. Worse than Terenure, and that's saying something.

Siobhan's phone beeps, her bag at Trevor's feet on the passenger side.

'Will you check that?' she asks. 'It could be Martin.'

Trevor glances at the screen, smiles and reads the message out.

'how are U love? Chattin to Trev last nite. Heard his news. On Skype this evening? Kiases xx.'

'Tolstoy,' he says with a laugh.

'I'll call her later.' Siobhan inches forward. 'If I get back now, I'll be stuck messaging half the day.'

Finally, they clear the last set of JBR roadworks and make their way down Al Sufouh Road. The sparkling sea looks glorious. The humidity is lower than the day before. Cranes and unfinished apartment blocks rise up to the right.

'Are we nearly there, Mam?' Rocco asks.

'Not far now. You OK, Milo?' But Milo has already gone to sleep.

'Nice shirt. Where'd you get it?' Siobhan glances at Trevor's top.

'Hilfiger.' He flips down the visor and looks in the small mirror. Wraparounds like James Bond. Blue striped shirt, short-sleeved with the guns out. Nice pair of Diesel jeans, though already his balls are sticking to his thigh.

Could he live here? Really? There's something about the place that drives him kinda mad. A feeling of being trapped which comes, not on the first day, or the second, or the third. Just a gradual sensation that creeps in. A feeling like he wants to do something illegal, just for the heck of it.

Fuck. His shoulders tense. He *has* done something illegal. The Russian in the bar. He'd crossed a line he never thought he would, not even in strip clubs on stag nights.

What would Mam or Siobhan think of him if they knew? It's one thing for them to roll their eyes at him being a bit of a lad. But this? When he closes his eyes and the images of his time with Anna return, he doesn't get a flush of arousal, thinking how hot she was. Instead, he gets that horrible wincing feeling, the kind of feeling he gets when he thinks back to that night he ended up in the Liffey. He can just imagine Siobhan's face. Mam wouldn't believe it of him.

He needs to put this image aside, think rationally, and make a list of the pros and cons of Dubai. Great job, flash car, great apartment. He'd be a few thousand miles away from Lucy Quirke. Yes, it might all be a bit hollow, but if he saved enough he could start his own gym back in Dublin in four or five years. Like, it isn't exactly the place for him – in fact, he isn't sure he likes it at all – but it could be the stepping stone to getting his life together.

He glances down and touches the new 'Rolex', thinking that could be the real thing if he wanted. He'd be a pearl diver, taking the plunge. Fuck it. Maybe he should move. A 'fresh start', like Mam said.

Siobhan drives through the entrance and Trevor looks at the golden horse statues 'playing' on a lawn. Passing fountains and landscaped gardens of evergreens and palms, they stop outside the ornate hotel entrance. There are seven or eight uniformed doormen in the portico.

Trevor and Siobhan get out and one of the men takes the keys from her. A Bentley pulls up to the hotel entrance beside the Jeep.

'Doesn't matter how much you have,' she says with a smile. 'There's always someone richer.'

Trevor gently lifts Milo out of the back seat. The little boy rests on his shoulder, his drool wetting the Hilfiger shirt.

Gete takes Rocco's hand while Siobhan picks up her Birkin bag and holds Trevor's free elbow.

'Isn't it great Gete is here? I'd murder a mojito.'

'What about the car?' Trevor asks.

'We'll collect it tomorrow.'

They walk through the lobby and Trevor gazes at the Venetian crystal chandeliers that hang from five storeys above, the gold mouldings, the marble tiles in every colour making swirling Arabic patterns on the floor. Receptionists, bell boys, maids and waiters bustle around. A huge fish tank is the central feature, beyond which are the hotel gardens.

A waiter takes Siobhan's name and checks his list.

'This way, Mrs Cusack.'

They are led through a series of rooms, filled with marble columns and gold-leaf finishes, low couches and tables like something from a French chateau. Caucasians and Arabs drink tea and place orders. Asian waitresses and waiters disappear in and out of swinging doors.

Finally, French doors lead on to the terrace, where tables are scattered between palms and umbrellas. At the corner of each table, bottles of champagne sit in buckets. The tinkling of cutlery and crystal, conversation and laughter, travels over the gentle breeze and blends with the soft sound of outdoor air-conditioning.

'Siobhan,' a voice calls. Rebecca waves. She's wearing designer shades and looks as rich and thin as a footballer's wife. Beside her is a balding man.

'Sorry we're late.' Siobhan kisses Rebecca's cheek.

'Trevor, this is my husband, Mike.'

'How you doing, mate?' He has an accent like an English

soccer fan. In front of him is a plate of oysters, caviar on crackers and lobster claws. Trevor leans over and shakes his fat hand.

'Marta has taken George to the play area,' Rebecca says. 'He can't sit still.'

'Rocco, you want to go with Gete and find George and Marta?' Siobhan asks. He nods. Gete takes Milo from Trevor and walks in the direction of a small bouncy castle.

'Gete won't be eating?' Trevor asks.

'She will in a bit,' Siobhan replies.

As they sit down, a waiter appears, takes the champagne off the ice and pours them a glass. Taking a sip, Siobhan sighs.

'Heaven.'

'This is your first time out here?' Mike asks Trevor.

'I was here shortly after Siobhan and Martin came out, but I haven't been out much since.'

'It's some place. What do you do?'

'I'm a personal trainer.' Trevor takes another large mouthful of champagne. The first thing he's asked by everyone here is, 'What do you do?' when most likely they would rather ask, 'How much do you earn?'

'There's good money to be made out here, plenty of bored housewives. All the men get fat, busy making money, while the wives spend their days in the gym.' Mike laughs, patting his round stomach.

'He's thinking about making the move,' Siobhan says.

'You'll never regret it, mate. The money.' Mike leans in. 'The women. You'll never go home.' His cheeks are already flushed. Trevor wonders what ladies he means when he says 'the women'. Does Mike go to bars alone? The memory of Anna flickers through Trevor's mind and he flinches, as if he's touched an electric fence.

Siobhan flags a waiter.

'Will you bring a jug of mojito for the table and one of those watermelon vodka things, yeah, the scooped-out ones. Great. Thanks.' The Indian waiter nods and vanishes. 'Isn't this the life?' She swallows the last of her champagne. As soon as the glass has touched the table another waiter appears and fills it, topping up the other three also.

'You want to go inside and get food?' Siobhan asks him. Turning back to Rebecca, 'I can always tell when Trevor is getting hungry. He gets a right scowl on his face.'

Trevor walks through the French doors, under a large archway and into the first kitchen. Lining the walls are hundreds of types of baguettes, bagels, loaves, pitas, tortillas and pastries – white, seeded, wholegrain. It smells unreal, like a bakery in Paris.

'Stay away from the bread. Wait for this,' Siobhan says, leading him to the far end of the room. Mountains of ice are keeping oysters, lobsters, prawns and shellfish cool. A side of cooked salmon is on a bed of leaves and lemon slices, while beyond it are rows of oatcakes and brown bread smeared in cream cheese, caviar in large platters, and smoked fish arranged on staggered silver plates.

'You must try one oyster, at least one,' Siobhan says. Trevor grimaces, though he takes a number of lobster claws.

'After another drink or two. A bit more Dutch courage.' Already he can feel his body warming from the alcohol.

They continue through another arch to tables laden with cheeses: Doolin, Carrowholly, Gleann Gabhra, Kerry Blue, Gubbeen, Port Salut, Le Coutances, Saint-André, Raclette, Saint-Nectaire, Kirkham's Lancashire, Yorkshire Wensley-dale, Stilton and Somerset Camembert.

'How the hell do you eat all this?' Trevor asks.

'We're here all day. There's loads of time to try everything.'

Next is the English roast dinner kitchen; trays of roasted onion, parsnips and sweet potato, glazed carrots, boiled sprouts and red cabbage, fluffy Yorkshire puddings, and gravy brown and smooth. Chefs carve chicken, beef and lamb.

Queues form at the kitchen beyond where a chef flips stir-fry in a pan. Green, yellow and red curry. Korma. Dopiaza. Madras. Vindaloo. Boiled rice. Fried rice. Noodles. Prawn crackers. Sauces. Dips. Sweet chilli. Soy sauce.

'There's more?' He turns to his sister.

'We're only halfway through the kitchens,' she says. 'Wait till you see the dessert room.'

'We finished that quickly,' Siobhan laughs. The mojito jug is empty; a bed of mint leaves remains at the bottom. She has a glazed look.

'We're worse than the Romans,' Mike replies.

Trevor looks down at his fifth helping of food, the remains of a Mexican fajita and tortilla crisps.

'I'd get fat if I lived here,' he says.

'The Dubai stone. It's legendary,' Rebecca replies.

'There's not a pick on you,' Siobhan says, glancing at Rebecca's waist. 'What I'd do to get rid of this.' She pokes at her belly. Mike lifts out a pipe from his pocket and a little box.

'What is that? Weed?' Trevor asks, leaning in, looking around, glancing at the green clippings in the box.

'No. I've not a death wish! Only tobacco. Strong stuff though.'

'Would you get a bang off that?'

'A bit of a kick. Want to try?'

Trevor nods.

Jesus. That stuff nearly blew the head off him. Trevor sits back into his seat, gazing out at the landscaped garden that leads down to the beach beyond. Rebecca and Siobhan giggle to each other, both sipping from the vodka watermelon.

A band plays the kind of songs you'd get at a fancy wedding. Trevor watches a few pissed middle-aged women dance, big rosy cheeks on them. A few of the little kids join in. Maybe he should ask Rebecca if she wants to throw some shapes.

Siobhan's bag vibrates. She puts down the watermelon and picks out her phone. 'Martin,' she mouths, putting the phone up to her ear, her finger in the other.

'What . . . yeah . . . I'm at brunch with Trevor and the boys . . . Course, I'll send you a picture . . . Rebecca and Mike. You're what? What's up? When are you getting back? Text me . . . text me. I can't hear a . . .' She puts the phone down. 'He's gone.'

Christ, she must be pissed. She'd never let Martin off the phone so easy if she was sober.

'Martin is well?' Rebecca asks.

'Great. Working like a mad thing. To be honest, I'm raging with him. He promised this week to be around with Trev here, but something came up.' Siobhan sighs. 'Still, you've got to admit, he's quite a specimen.' She shows Rebecca a picture on her phone. Trevor looks sideways. It's of Martin on the beach, with a tanned lean torso.

'See that, Mike?' Rebecca points. 'Martin hasn't any extra weight and he works as hard as you do.'

'Nobody works as hard as me,' Mike laughs. He wiggles his stomach. 'More of me to luuurve.' Rebecca shakes her head at the others. Then her eyebrows rise, as if remembering something.

'Did you hear about that girl who died in the marina?' she asks.

Siobhan nods.

'Nuts, isn't it?'

'I was talking to Sandra, you know, Sandra from—' Siobhan is cut off by Rocco, who has run back from the bouncy castle.

'Mammy, can I get ice cream?'

'What's that on your face? Are you Spider-Man?' Rebecca asks.

Rocco touches his cheek, as if remembering the face paint.

'Of course you can have ice cream. Does Gete have Milo?'

Rocco nods.

'Trev, will you bring Rocco in for ice cream?'

Trevor stands. That's what happens when Siobhan pays for things for him, like a seven-hundred-dirham ticket for brunch. It makes it hard to say no – even when he isn't sure his legs will hold him. That's something to add to the list of pros to living here. He could pay his own way.

'So, Sandra was saying to me that she'd heard . . .' Siobhan's voice fades as Trevor makes his way back through the crowded tables.

Three fountains: dark, milk and white chocolate. Marshmallows, cut strawberries with blueberries and pineapple, biscuits and mini muffins all ready to be dipped. Trevor lifts Rocco as he inches marshmallows under the flowing chocolate, his hands and mouth covered in the brown sauce.

Behind the fountains, Trevor gazes at the rows of mini cakes, ten, twenty, thirty . . . easily fifty varieties. Half these names he couldn't even pronounce. Morsels of flaked chocolate; glazed summer fruits; lemon, strawberry and chocolate mousses; blackberry tartlets with vanilla-flavoured mascarpone cream; flaky and shortbread pastries; fruit tarts; salted caramel croquembouche; fresh fruit flutes; éclairs; perfectly round macaroons in a rainbow of colours; gold-leaf chocolate cakes; gianduia-filled profiteroles with double chocolate sauce and toasted hazelnuts.

A crêpe stand; chocolate syrup, banana, nuts, sprinkles, marshmallows, honey, summer fruit. Beside it, an ice cream stand: mint, mocha, praline, divine vanilla, choco-orange, pistachio, rum and raisin. Trevor's plate remains empty as he looks, unable to move. Where to start? Other diners seem to be having the same trouble: 'What will I choose, darling?'; 'That looks delicious!'; 'I'm such a pig.'

Rocco has no problem picking ice cream flavours and crêpe toppings. Maybe that's the secret: to be comfortable in

Dubai, you have to be born here. How would he, as a six-year-old, have reacted to so much dessert? There was that time he was left groaning on the carpet after he'd eaten too much birthday cake at Eoin's party.

Trevor smiles. In the end, he takes a cake with gold leaf on top to see what it's like. He holds the mound of food that Rocco has picked, the sticks with marshmallow and chocolate sauce, the chocolate chip ice cream, and the crêpe oozing toffee and syrup.

'Mam will never let you eat all that,' he says. He realizes how fuzzy his vision is.

'She's had lots of mogiteos,' Rocco says.

Trevor straightens up, but by the time he's ready to say something the young boy has run off.

'The RTA is outside, come on now.' Trevor tries to lure Siobhan away from the harp in the main foyer of the hotel. Siobhan has full-on drunkface – eyes drifting, half-pursed lips, chin vanishing into neck – and pays him no attention. Gete rocks Milo in her arms next to the doormen. Rocco plays on his game console, George looking over his shoulder.

'Molly, my Irish Molly, my sweet and much-loved dear . . .'

Trevor and Mike direct Siobhan away from the instrument, trying to be as inconspicuous as possible. They get a few glances from other guests but the staff ignore them.

Gete, Siobhan and the two boys pile into the back of the RTA, Milo on Gete's lap. Siobhan mumbles about feeling sick but then is quiet. Trevor closes the front passenger door and gives the address. Rebecca, slightly unsteady, leans in the window and gives Milo a kiss. Trevor can smell her perfume.

'Wonderful to see you, guys. Are you here much longer, Trevor? We'll have to do it again soon. Get back for the holidays. They pull out all the stops for Christmas brunch. It makes today look like nothing.'

'Good to meet you.' Mike gives Trevor's hand a shake through the window. 'I hope the job works out – I'll sign up for some sessions.'

'I shouldn't have had that piña colada,' Siobhan says. Trevor looks in the mirror. Her eyes open briefly and she yawns. They've turned off Al Sufouh Road and appear to be heading inland. For all Trevor knows, the taxi driver could be doing a loop of the city. Siobhan is always warning him to keep an eye on them. He glances back at Gete, whose gaze remains fixed on the horizon. Milo snores lightly.

There's something in Gete's eyes. What does she make of all the Westerners, pissed as fuck? Do the lads back in Ethiopia get drunk on the weekend? The maids deserve a bloody medal for the shite they put up with.

Imagine if he ever had to confess to her all of the things he's done in his life? Tell her about the women he's fucked, including Anna. The times he's got drunk and picked fights with fools outside bars. The amount he's wanked to porn online, every type imaginable: threesomes, girl-on-girl action, guys fucking girls in the ass, skipping all the intros to get to the bit where the girl got fucked senseless and moaned like a bitch. This is the state of his mind.

What does Gete even think of him and his accident last

224

year? What does she know about the Liffey? When Siobhan had been rushing around, throwing clothes in her case to fly home, had she told her anything? Does Gete know that he'd been sculling pints all that night and bemoaning Lucy Quirke? Probably not. She'd got on with it and cared for the boys while Siobhan came home to sort out the mess he'd caused.

Lucy-fucking-Quirke. He is destined for a life with a Lucy-fucking-Quirke. The couple of nice women he'd tried to date never worked out. He told the boys he'd cheated on Beata when he hadn't. Somehow, it seemed less shameful than saying he was impossible to date. 'Why do you not talk to me?' she asked. 'You do not let me in.' But how can he let someone in? Lucy has given his heart enough of a battering for one life.

He looks out of the window, gazing in between the break in the skyscrapers. Far inland, beyond huge pylons, he can make out the first hints of unfinished housing estates. Villas with no electricity or water. Thousands of properties abandoned – the part of Dubai kept hidden from view. Siobhan has mentioned the property crash once or twice, but 'at least Martin still has his job'.

Could he live here? Maybe it's just the Catholic guilt that means he finds it hard to enjoy living it up, spending money, having one-night stands, and not giving a damn about how messed up the place is. Whatever happens, he is never paying for a woman again. But can he trust this to be true? How many times has he said he'd never do something again and then gone and done it? These mistakes hurt just as much the second time, and the third, and the fourth.

Dubai. Dubai. Dubai. There is no place like it.

Siobhan yawns again. Trevor turns his head and smiles.

'Good day, eh?' she says. She seems brighter. The alcohol is wearing off.

'Really good. Thanks a million.'

'If they make the offer, you have to take it,' Siobhan says. 'We could do brunches every week.'

It's nearly dark by the time the RTA pulls into the housing estate. His head is starting to pound. He'd give his right arm for a pint of water. The fucking traffic in this city.

Siobhan, somewhat sobered up, directs the driver through the series of small roundabouts and junctions to the house, passing by the gleaming 4x4s, palm trees and sleepy villas. As they turn on to their road, there appears to be a commotion. Crowds are standing on the kerbs. Blue-and-red lights from three police cars.

'What's going on?' Trevor asks. The taxi driver comes to a halt. Siobhan hands him a note.

'Probably a domestic.'

They get out. Trevor lifts Rocco into his arms. Gete keeps hold of Milo. Walking down the street, something becomes clear.

'Oh my God, that's our place.' Siobhan looks at him, her face turning white. She instinctively reaches for his forearm.

'It's probably a mistake. Don't panic yet.' Though Trevor can already feel his own pulse increase.

'Gete, will you stay here with the kids?' Siobhan asks. Gete nods. 'Trev, give her Rocco. We'll sort this.'

★

Gete sits with the two boys on a neighbour's wall. Siobhan's nails are digging into Trevor's bicep but he doesn't say a word. Men in green-and-red uniforms are walking in and out of the front door of the house.

Siobhan lets go of his arm and runs forward.

'What are you doing?' she calls out to the closest policeman.

'Are you the occupier of this home?'

'Yes. I'm Siobhan Cusack.'

'And who are you?' The man looks at Trevor.

'My brother. He is here on holiday. What is going on?'

'We are looking for Martin Cusack. He is your husband?'

'Yes. What's this all about?'

'You come with me, madam, to speak to the Superintendent. You stay here, sir.'

'But—'

'Trev, do what he says.' Siobhan puts her hand against his chest. Her demeanour has transformed. It's like she's never had a drink.

Trevor watches Siobhan being escorted across the front garden towards an older-looking officer. Siobhan's dress – could it be any shorter? And her upper arms are exposed. He can see her getting animated but the words aren't audible. He looks around. People are staring, though none have taken out their phones. What the fuck is going on?

Trevor glances at his watch. It's been fifteen minutes. He looks over his shoulder. Gete and the boys are still sitting on the wall. Gete seems to be staring at nothing. Rocco is fixed watching the flashing lights of the cars.

'Can I get a coat and flat shoes at least?' Siobhan's voice

echoes over. Trevor turns back. She and the officer are moving towards him. 'You're not arresting me, are you?'

'This is only for questioning, Ma'am.'

'What's going on?' Trevor asks.

'It's Martin, that's what,' Siobhan replies. Her cheeks are flushed. 'You know that girl on the radio. The one who drowned.'

'What's that got to do with—'

'Come, Ma'am, we must go now.'

'I'll come with you,' Trevor says. 'What station are they taking you to?'

'No. Stay with the boys,' she replies. 'This won't take long. I'm sure this won't take long.' All he can see in her face is fear.

Aasim

Aasim glances up and down the hallway. Baba and Mahmoud will be at the office for many hours to come; he stayed in his room till he heard the comforting sound of their cars slipping out of the driveway.

Stuck to Hiyam's bedroom door is a ceramic nameplate, a series of swirls and roses surround 'Hiyam', which is written in gold. Mama had bought it at a fair in London and Hiyam stuck it to her door, apparently delighted, but later, as she and Aasim sat on her bed, she shook her head and said, 'Mama thinks I am still a child.'

'Be thankful for it,' he'd replied. 'You can get away with so much.' Hiyam smiled, continuing to paint her toenails French grey, the shade Aasim had seen models wear on the Chanel runway.

Mama has been in her room all afternoon; Aasim glances over at her bedroom door. Was she sleeping all this time? Or is she lying on her bed, thinking about Baba's words at lunch, or worse still, imagining the future – all the days that now lie before her which Hiyam will not be part of?

The police haven't searched Hiyam's room; Baba's doing, no doubt. His influence is beyond what Aasim had imagined. They'd come to the house mid-morning and Aasim thought they might want to question him, but they hadn't.

After they left, the family had been summoned to Baba's office. Mama, Mahmoud and he fell silent as Baba raised his hand.

'I want no questions,' Baba had said. 'You all listen and do as I tell you. I have had a long conversation with the police. I don't know what you've all heard but the truth is this: Hiyam was coming home from a friend's house when the taxi driver attacked her and left her for dead in the marina . . .' Aasim was about to speak, the various rumours coming to mind, but Baba put his hand up again. 'Let me repeat myself: if anyone asks you, Hiyam was coming home from a friend's house when the taxi driver attacked her and left her for dead in the marina. She was alone. She was not at the York. We have a confession from the driver. That is all.'

'But, what about—'

'But nothing.'

They all turned to leave. Baba called after them.

'If I hear that any of you says anything other than this to anyone, you won't want to know the consequences.' His tone was chilling in its calmness. 'For now, say nothing, and you two must stay at home.' He pointed at Mama and Aasim.

Aasim inches down the gold handle of Hiyam's bedroom door. There is an ever-so-slight creak, as the springs inside the mechanism contract. Even this small noise echoes. The house is like a mausoleum.

How long can this continue, locked down at home with no one to talk to? He's tried to call David, but David is in Lahinch. Though, of course, what could David say from thousands of miles away that would be of any help? *Love you, snugglelord. Can't wait to see you, Prince Charming. Think your Aasimazing xx* Typical David-y messages.

The bedroom door slips inwards. Plush purple curtains are pulled back on golden hooks, the inner blind pulled down. Soft light travels across the sheepskin rug to the voile that hangs from the corners of the bed. 'Princess Hiyam' is carved into the painted headboard. Purple satin sheets are perfectly tucked in; the cushions on top – sequinned, heart-shaped, one reading 'Love' – sit three deep.

An Apple computer sits directly across from the door. Nana had never approved of it. 'Shameful. Like a window into her room.' Hiyam rolled her eyes but did not react.

Aasim inches the door closed. The comforting click. He glances at the white towelling robes that hang on the door's reverse. The smell is sugary, like one of Britney Spears's perfumes. Typical Hiyam. His eyes water. The feelings that arise startle him. For some unaccountable reason, for the first millisecond after he inhales that fragrance, the memory of her is so strong it's like she isn't dead.

Enough. It is pointless being sentimental. He lets go of the sleeve and walks to the dressing table. A pink GHD lies beside an open make-up bag. Lightening cream, tweezers and eyeliner slip out.

'You look stupid, like you've just been punched,' he'd said to her the first time he'd seen her apply make-up.

'This is Dior,' she replied. 'Kim Kardashian uses it.'

'Does Mama know you have it?'

'She gave it to me.' Hiyam smiled, vindicated. Those Cleopatra eyes, lit by film-star bulbs that surrounded the dressing-table mirror, glistened like sapphires. Her phone vibrated. She glanced at the message, replied, but didn't say a word as to who it was.

Baba always complained about her phone. 'You pay me no attention,' he said. 'You show no respect when I'm talking.' But even at that moment she didn't seem to be listening, glancing at the television over his shoulder, her phone resting on her lap, where she waited for it to vibrate.

'Aasim.' He jumps, puts the picture of Hiyam and Fadiyah back on the dresser, and turns around. Mama. She's almost unrecognizable. Without the charcoal lining her eyes, they've become dots; her hair, normally blow-dried and full of shine, is tied back in a simple ponytail. 'A woman's hair is her glory,' Nana often said, 'that is why it is not for all men to see.' Hiyam gave her usual groan and mouthed, 'Because I'm worth it.' Nana shook her head and muttered something about young people.

'To think. Just a week,' Mama says. 'You and I were having lunch in London.' She looks at the floor, lost in her own thoughts. 'Life . . .'

'I hate it.'

Mama walks to the corner of the bed and touches the voile, running her fingers down the seam.

'We promised her this bed, do you remember, when we moved to this new home.'

'She always wanted to be a princess.' Aasim picks up another photograph: Hiyam with three girls from her school. Each flashes their handbag: Fendi, Prada, Gucci.

'So beautiful,' Mama says. 'Too, too beautiful.'

'Do you ever miss our old house?'

'Yes . . . No. I never liked the dust. But things were simpler. You children were small.'

'Hiyam was never simple.'

'Like her great-aunt who married the Christian.'

'She died too.'

'She did. And young.'

They stand, staring at the bedroom space. Aasim touches her bedside table, half expecting to feel dust.

'It's strange being in here,' he says. 'What are you going to do with everything?'

'I don't know.' Her lip trembles.

'You think you want to stay in this house?'

She shrugs.

Mama opens the door to Hiyam's walk-in wardrobe. Aasim lifts *Marie Claire* from the pile of magazines that sits on the dressing table. Victoria Beckham in a shoulder-padded swimsuit. He's reminded of their family holiday in Qatar the previous spring. Baba had won a large contract to build a new hotel in Doha, Aasim was on mid-term, and they'd all been flown there on a private jet.

Shortly after they arrived, Hiyam was banished to her suite. She refused to take off her Agent Provocateur black-and-white one-piece with cut-out sides. Truth was, she looked incredible – she could've been in *Marie Claire* herself and ultimately that was the problem.

'I won't wear it,' she cried, glancing at the burkini that lay on the bed beside her.

'Baba insists.'

'We're in the hotel. Why not?'

233

'Because he says so. He's your father,' Mama said.

'Won't you talk to him? Please.'

Mama smiled kindly but didn't say a word. Her own bur-kini peeked out from underneath the bathroom robe. Hiyam, in a fit of temper, pushed the pile of clothes off the bed.

'I'll look like a fool. All the other girls are wearing normal swimsuits.'

'They are foreign girls. They don't know better,' Mama replied. 'You must respect your father's wishes.'

'What harm does it do? Fadiyah's parents—'

'There are men at the pool.'

'Fine. I won't go. I won't swim.'

For the rest of the holiday, Hiyam sat in the nearby terrace, watching the others while they swam and splashed about in the water. She sipped on iced tea, flicked through magazines, her phone resting on her lap, unmoved by Aasim's begging that she join them.

Towards the end of the trip, after the others had gone to bed and she and Aasim watched *Glee* on his laptop, she had said, 'We're in prison. What's the point in having all this money if we can't do what we like?'

'What will we do with all this?' Mama reappears from the closet. She is holding a pair of black Manolo Blahnik heels. 'Some of her friends might like a few things? Fadiyah perhaps?'

He walks over and takes the shoes from his mother, glancing at the soles.

'These haven't been worn.'

'She was saving them for a special occasion. But now . . .'

Mama's nostrils flare and her eyes become wet again. He touches her shoulder and she regains her composure. 'You remember her buying them?'

'Yes.'

'She never told you who the man was in London last June?'

He shakes his head. It'd been unlucky, Baba answering the hotel phone, instead of her. Hiyam had been in her bathroom fixing her make-up, and Mama was tying the laces on her shoes. Prayers at the mosque would start in half an hour.

'Who is this? What do you want with my daughter?' Baba had said. Aasim and Mama looked up. Baba gazed at the phone, which had gone dead, before putting it down. 'Hiyam!'

'Yes.' Hiyam appeared from the bathroom, holding her GHD.

'A man called for you. From reception. Who was he?'

Hiyam had protested her innocence. Baba didn't believe her. Instead of letting her stay with Mama, he insisted she return to Dubai with him when he left the following day. When Aasim asked her about it later, she shook her head and said it was none of his business. 'One day, I'll be gone from this family,' she said. 'No one will tell me what to do.'

Aasim's phone vibrates. He hands back the shoes to Mama and lifts it out of his pocket.

'David?' she asks. He won't look up, but he can feel his cheeks and ears grow warm.

'It's Khaled.'

'Are you meeting him again?'

'Later.'

Mama doesn't reply. Aasim senses something in the silence.

'Is that not OK?'

'Your father does not think Khaled good company. He wonders about the places you go.'

'He wonders.' Aasim exhales. He thinks about the strain between Baba and Mama since Monday's row. Did they pretend he hadn't called Baba a hypocrite?

'You are his son. It is his business.'

'He can't stop me.'

'There is much he can do – your cards, your phone – and he will. Mahmoud is determined.'

There is something in Mama's tone. Aasim straightens up.

'He has spoken of it to you?'

'Yes.'

'But my cards . . .'

'I know.'

'What do you think I should do?' Aasim's heart thuds. He feels hot.

'I cannot tell you.'

'You think I should go?'

'Don't say. I don't want to lie if they ask me.'

Aasim shakes his head slightly.

'This is bull—'

'Please . . .' He isn't sure if her pleading is about his language or if she's hoping he won't make a scene.

'Did he say when?'

'Any time. Maybe even today.'

'Fuck . . .' Aasim glances at the door, but before he moves he sees his mother's face. 'Sorry, Mama. Sorry.' He steps over and kisses her cheek, hugging her. 'I love you, Mama. I know you may not think it . . .'

'I love you,' she replies, tears beginning to flow down her cheeks on to his shoulder.

Then, after a moment, he pulls away and walks towards the hallway, giving one last look over his shoulder. Mama: a slim ghost in a dim room. Little more than a tomb, not unlike the whole house. Whatever life there had been before, whatever family had existed, was now over.

His cards don't work. His cards don't fucking work. He tried to buy that new album on iTunes and it was declined. Then the T-shirt on the Armani site. Same again. Aasim dials David's number. No answer. Dials again. No answer. Come on. Come on. Where the fuck is David?

He rings Khaled. After a call that lasts twenty minutes, Aasim pulls his suitcase from the end of his bed, dragging it towards the walk-in wardrobe. What should he bring? He could ask Zulfa to help him pack, but what if she tells Baba about his plans?

It doesn't seem possible that life could get any worse. His emotions all jumbled, there aren't even tears, just red-hot cheeks and frowns and nostril flares as thoughts rush through his head. How will he get all his clothes into a 23kg case? How will he survive when he gets back to Dublin with only two thousand euros in his Irish bank account? Will he have to work? How will he manage to study if he does?

Vicky. JodieB. Will they even give a shit about him if he has no money? Being rich is his thing. He brings the champagne and coke. David likes that he can splash out for dinner in Chapter One or Guilbaud's, or flash his card in Brown Thomas and say, 'Happy birthday,' even when it isn't David's birthday for months.

Khaled – at least there is one person to be thankful for. How will he pay him back? He was so kind on the phone: 'Don't worry about it, man. You can hit me back when things work out.' Yet, with so little in his account, there is no way he can repay the flight any time soon.

Why can't he stop his hands shaking? He needs to pack. He needs to get the fuck out of here before something else goes wrong. No. What he fucking needs is a drink. Anything. Right now he'd drink the alcohol out of Hiyam's nail varnish remover. Anything to stop the trembling.

He stops. Damn these stupid tears. Hold it together. Only another day. Get back to Dublin. Why isn't David fucking answering his phone? Answer, goddammit. Answer.

Deep breaths. Don't give in. Don't give in. Hold your shit together.

Flared nostrils. More tears.

He is going mad. He is actually going mad.

'Where the fuck have you been?'

'What?' David sounds startled. 'I'm just out of the shower. I'm sopping wet.'

'I've been calling for hours. Why haven't you answered?' There is a slight echo as his voice bounces off the tiles in the ensuite. The bathroom door is closed; Baba and Mahmoud returned home an hour ago.

'I'm in Lahinch. You know I'm away with the gang. What's wrong?'

'Fucking everything. That's what's wrong.'

'Hiyam?'

'No. Me. Things are seriously fucked up.'

'What happened?'

Aasim doesn't answer. He pulls a tissue from the box by the sink, wiping his nose. Finally, he continues, 'Everything's a mess. I have to get back to Dublin. Mahmoud. Baba. They're acting crazy. They've stopped my cards.'

'You've only been a few days at home.'

'I can't stay here. I can't. And Mama, she can't help. They've stopped my cards. Can you believe it?'

'What are you going to live on?'

'I don't know. My scholarship.'

'But your apartment.' David's tone surprises him. There's a pause. 'Sorry, that's not helping.'

'Who gives a shit about the apartment? They're asking questions. They're trying to take my phone too.'

'But . . .' David tries to interrupt Aasim's flow but to no avail.

'They know about Hiyam. They know she wasn't alone. If word got out . . .' Aasim trails off for a second. 'You know who my father is? You know what this could do to the business?' Aasim's voice grows louder again.

'But who was Hiyam with? Don't they want to know?'

'Some white g—' Aasim remembers his father's warning from earlier. 'This guy works for a company that was contracted by Baba. Knowing her, she probably stalked him online. That's Hiyam for you.'

Another pause.

'Aasim. She's dead,' David says. Aasim doesn't reply. He

sobs. 'Aasim . . .' David sighs. 'Look, get back to Dublin. We can talk properly here.'

Aasim hears the sound of a car beeping.

'Who's that?'

'Eva. We're just getting ready to head back to Dublin. It looks like it could snow.'

'Snow . . . but my flight . . .'

'You're coming back?'

'Haven't you been listening to me at all? Wake up, David. I don't even know if I can get out of this house. Bloody Khaled had to book a ticket.'

'What ticket?'

'The flight. Wake up. I'm flying back today.'

'You're what?'

'I have to get out. What if they take my passport?'

'They can't do that.' The line goes dead momentarily. 'Aasim. Are you there?' David's voice sounds panicked.

'Yes. The reception in the bathroom . . .' Aasim sniffs, taking a deep breath, comforted by this spontaneous concern.

'What time is your flight?'

'I'll be in Ireland tomorrow lunchtime. I'm flying KLM. In actual economy.'

'Oh.'

'What will I do?' A deep sigh. Aasim shifts on the edge of the bath, his legs going dead.

'Just get back. It'll all work out OK.'

'You won't . . .' Aasim's voice trails off.

'I won't?'

'You won't . . . nothing. It doesn't matter.'

'No, tell me.' David waits. No reply.

'Do you know what's really weird?' Aasim says finally. 'I keep looking at her profile online. It's crazy it's still there.' He pauses. Is someone knocking on his bedroom door? 'I've got to go,' he whispers. 'Love—'

But the call has ended. Aasim glances at the phone. Did the signal fail? Fuck. Fuck. Fuck. A fear grows within him, unsure about what future he has in Ireland or anywhere. David is only human and maybe Eva has been right all along – there is no middle ground between his world and theirs.

Alone. He is utterly alone. The feeling leaves his knees weak and he slides down from the bath to the floor. He can hear the sounds of knocks growing louder, but he doesn't respond, looking at the phone, hoping that it will ring and it will be David.

The minutes pass. There's no call back. The urge within him to dial is overwhelming but he can't bring himself to do it, waiting for it to ring. It was unfair to test David in such a way, but there is no other way to be sure that David wants to help.

Tahir

Four beds. Nine men. Tahir sits in the far corner, half hidden by a bunk. What time of day is it? Has an hour or five hours passed? How long will this continue? The fluorescent light flickers; he knows its cycle as if it were Morse code. Perhaps if he counts the number of cycles, he'll know what hour it is.

Others lie on the floor of the cell; they fight over who will get the beds. Manish, who is propped on the concrete wall beside him, has a black eye. The skin on his knuckles is torn.

'Don't let blood get on you,' he'd said when Tahir first arrived. 'There is AIDS in these places. They try to infect you, to punish you.'

Tahir nodded. Surely it was just a rumour.

Manish snores, just like Muhammad did in the old dorm room. Tahir closes his eyes but the snores seem to grow louder. Allah, it appears, has cursed him to a life of interrupted sleep.

At least he is no longer isolated. This cell is more unpredictable – he is never sure when violence might erupt – but being with other men has made the madness of being alone retreat.

Of course, the fear hasn't vanished. His eye, still sore, now opens a little, though part of his vision is pinkish.

'You must have done something very bad,' Manish had

said when the policeman shoved him into the cell with the others. A couple of the prisoners had looked up, but most turned over and went back to sleep. He'd slipped between the bodies, glad there was no mirror to see what had been done to his face.

'Caught selling drugs?' Manish had the look of a sand cat, grey but quick-witted.

'No.'

'Stealing?'

'No.'

'Sex . . . rape?' Manish raised his eyebrows.

'No.'

'No problem. You do not want to talk. You will be here for some time, see. I am here three months now. We all talk sooner or later.'

Tahir was silent, looking through the bars of the cell. In the corridor outside, more men slept. How many had he counted? Fifty? One hundred? And beds only for a handful.

'Why are you here?' Tahir had asked.

'They say I steal.'

'Do you?'

Manish smiled.

'You are from Pakistan too?'

'Lahore.'

'You have family?'

'No family.'

'Then why are you in Dubai?'

'I take a chance and say "who knows". A roll of the dice, my friend.'

★

243

Tahir drags his index nail under the others, lifting out the dirt and flicking it on to the floor. Manish's snores stop. After a few moments, his eyes open. He stretches and yawns.

'Another day in paradise, eh?' Somehow Manish seems content.

Tahir smiles briefly. His back aches from lying against the concrete; his uniform is blackened with dirt. He tries to ignore the smell as he lifts his arms; perhaps, if he is here long enough, the damp smell from the showers and the odour from the men will appear to vanish.

Outside the metal bars, voices become raised. A prisoner accuses another of taking his book. Punches are thrown. The men in the cells move close to the bars, hammering them with their shoes, goading them on.

Tahir stays back with Manish. The noise grows louder. He waits for officers to appear. Someone will get a beating. What if he never escapes this cursed place? What if Anam, or any of the family, believes he is guilty of the crime? He sits up, finding it hard to breathe. Manish grabs his arm.

'Stay still. You don't want the officers to notice you.'

'But—'

'But nothing. Do not draw attention to yourself.'

'But when do I see a lawyer?'

Manish laughs.

'You have money for this lawyer?'

'I am innocent. I did nothing.'

'We are all innocent men in here.'

'But I am.'

Manish continues to laugh. Tahir would love to hit him.

'Did you sign anything?' Manish asks.

Tahir nods.

'That is very bad . . . then again, does it really matter? Pakistani, Indian, Indonesian. We are always guilty. Accept your fate, my friend.'

Somebody is whimpering somewhere. It sounds like a boy. The police have taken away the two men who were fighting and the cell block is full of low whispers.

'What is that noise?' Tahir asks Manish.

'That is Shao. From China, I think.'

'Why is he crying?'

'He was . . .' Manish gives Tahir a look.

'What?'

'Some of the men, they attacked him in the showers. You know what I mean. Be careful. Don't go in there alone.'

The cell door opens. A white man with yellow hair is pushed inside. The men playing cards on the floor become quiet. He looks confused, as the floor space is all gone and the bunks are full. He staggers through the group, who swear as he knocks into the pile of cards. He slumps against the wall next to Tahir.

A smell of alcohol and perfume. The man bends his knees, pushing himself up. Before long he is asleep.

'They put white men in this place?' Tahir glances at Manish.

'Everyone goes in here. Doesn't matter who you are. We stay away from the white men. They have their lawyers. They get out.'

'When do I speak to the embassy?'

'Our embassy is useless. Not if you sign what they want you to sign. Make peace with yourself. This is your home for now and for the future.'

'But my wife. My girls,' Tahir replies. How will they all survive without his wage each month? Baba is too old for labour. Ibrahim is too fragile for responsibility.

'Pray to Allah.'

'Allah.' Tahir doesn't trust himself to reply. There are enough sins in the world without him adding another. Who would associate with the daughters of a convict? What shame this will bring on them all. They will be outcasts.

Fatima – how will she fund her studies? How will she become like Najma Hanif? She could never run for parliament with a father in jail.

'Try not to worry about tomorrow's troubles,' Manish continues. 'It can be hard, very hard, but we survive with the help of God.'

'There is no God in this place,' Tahir replies, looking out at the men squashed together, gambling, swearing, talking about drugs.

'God is everywhere. You just have to look hard.'

Tahir is silent. He resists the part of him that wants to blaspheme. The side of himself that would like to ask, 'What God? The one who lets a man be raped in the night? Who does nothing when innocent men go to jail, leaving their wives and children to starve.'

Life makes no sense. The harder he works to improve his family's lot, the more it pushes against him, as if it wants him to fail.

'How do you do it?' Tahir finally asks. 'How do you manage to smile in all this?'

'We must be bigger than the problems we fight.'

One of the card players is taken away with a broken nose. He
is unable to pay his debt. Tahir queues for the canteen. Bare
block walls. Metal tables screwed down. Fluorescent lights.
He picks at the food that's stuck in the grooves of the metal
tray he's been given. He can guess what dinner he will get.
Lunch: rice, some sort of meat, maybe a piece of fruit. He
swaps his weight from one leg to the other, still in the queue
after forty-five minutes.

Five hundred mouths. Forty tables. The men shove
against each other when the police aren't looking. Moving
towards the kitchen window, his name is taken. The police
do a count three times a day, though he cannot imagine how
anyone could escape.

'Pavan, my friend,' Manish says to the man who serves
them. He's a prisoner too; the canteen staff are all convicts.
'Make sure to be nice to them,' Manish told Tahir. 'They'll
keep you the nicer pieces of meat, give you more rice.'

Tahir smiles but it appears all the men in the queue
have the same idea, trying to chat to the men serving. No
response. Rice, meat, sauce. 'Next.' He walks down the aisle,
looking for a place to sit. The men grab at their food, a bit of
bread to mop up the liquid, and sip water in plastic cups.
There's a low murmur of voices.

'Hurry,' a prison guard shouts. Tahir looks around. More
men wait their turn to be seated. His forehead is wet from
the heat of all the bodies. What if there is a fire?

The only space is at a table close to the officers. The white man sits there, alone, strange and exposed. That morning, when washing his clothes in the large sinks with the others, he'd seemed helpless, dipping his shirt in and out as if it would get clean from simply getting wet. One of the other prisoners shouted 'Khaneeth' and the others laughed.

As Tahir goes to sit down at the table, Manish shakes his head, urging him to sit elsewhere, but Tahir ignores him. He gives the white man a nod.

'You have just arrived here?' he asks.

The white man stops eating. He is childlike with his hands, pushing the food into his mouth.

'This week.'

'Me too. Why are you here?'

'A stupid reason.'

'Oh.'

'Did they beat you?' Tahir glances up at the guard. But the officer is paying no attention.

'Yes.'

'And you have a lawyer.'

'The embassy.'

'Ah, you are lucky. I have no lawyer. Where are you from?'

'Germany.'

Tahir opens his mouth to speak. However, the only thing he knows about Germany is World War II. Hardly a thing the white man will want to talk about.

'You live here?' he finally asks.

'No. On holiday.'

'And you are in jail. You have no luck, my friend.'

The white man looks down, trying to scoop up his food. Clumsy fingers.

'Is it drugs why you are here?'

'A woman.'

'Ah.' Tahir smiles. Some things are the same everywhere. 'A beautiful woman?'

'My fiancée.'

'And where is she?'

'In a different jail.'

'Oh.' Tahir blushes. He takes a mouthful of meat. It is chicken. Maybe turkey, as it is very dry. He dips it into the spicy sauce.

'I am married too. A beautiful woman. Her name is Anam . . .' Tahir's voice trails off when he sees the white man's expression. A very arrogant look – that line in between his brows. Tahir sighs. Even now, when they are both prisoners, the white man thinks he is better than him.

'Tahir Nasiri?' A prison guard walks down the corridor, shouting his name. His baton rattles along the metal bars. The men in the cell move backwards. Tahir tries to think about what he might've done to get noticed. The cell door opens.

'Yes . . . yes, sir.'

'Come with me.'

A murmur goes through the cell and up the corridor.

'Trouble. Trouble,' someone shouts.

'One black eye to match the other.'

A couple of the men laugh. The policeman turns around, baton raised, his eyebrows high. Silence.

'You have a phone call,' he says to Tahir. 'Come. Enough of this time wasting. It is a call from Pakistan.'

The men part as the officer walks along the corridor. He taps on the large metal door at the end. A looking hole slides across, then the door clicks and swings open. Three corridors on, Tahir is led into a small room. A series of telephone booths are on the walls. Two other men are talking quietly.

'Number three.' The guard points to a booth. 'You have ten minutes.'

Tahir lifts the phone.

'Hello?' he says. 'Who is this?'

'Tahir, is that you?' Anam's voice is sweet like honey.

'It is me. It is me.' Tahir tries not to shout with joy.

'My love,' Anam says. He cannot form sentences for some time. He can't stop the hot tears streaming down his cheeks and neck. 'What is happening? They say you have been arrested, that you killed a woman.' She switches to speaking Punjabi.

'I didn't kill anyone.'

'But . . .'

'You believe me . . . you do believe me?' He tries to stop the sobs, but his voice keeps coming out in all different volumes.

'Of course. You don't even need to ask that. We don't have very long. I haven't many rupees and there's much to talk about.' Her voice, though kind, grows firm.

He sniffs, wiping his nose on his sleeve, as there is nothing else to hand.

'Tell me, how are the girls?'

'They know nothing,' Anam says. 'It's best not to tell

them. When they ask why you have not rung, I tell them it is because you are very busy and that you will write. You will write to them?'

'Of course, of course . . . and they are still studying hard?'

'Of course.'

'But how will you survive? I cannot send you money.'

'We'll manage. We will, don't worry. Ibrahim is doing what he can. Baba is not very strong but he has helped a lot. He goes to the Foreign Affairs offices every day, waiting from morning till night to speak to an official. They tell him they are very busy but he does not care. He sits and says he will sit till someone listens.'

His tears return. He tries not to let the shudders in his chest take over. God bless Baba. How can he ever repay him?

Anam continues, 'Baba tells you to be strong and to remember the blood in your veins. We have survived worse. You will overcome this.'

Tahir scrunches his eyes tight, pushing his knuckles hard into them, willing himself not to cry out. What has become of his life? Why did he come to this godforsaken place?

'Do not worry for us,' Anam says. 'Even if I must get a job and Ibrahim too. We are your family. I am your wife. You must keep yourself safe and strong. Allah will protect you. You will get justice.'

'But . . .' Tahir stops himself. He cannot tell her his fears, that there is no justice to be had, that it's likely he'll spend many years in prison. Or even death by firing squad; it hasn't happened many times, but there have been cases.

He must put this thought out of his head. It doesn't bear thinking about.

'We will get you home, my love,' Anam says again.

'But—'

'No buts.' There is strength in the way she speaks, something Tahir has not heard before. 'Do not worry for us. Keep yourself safe till we find a way out.'

'I love you,' he says, a half-whimper.

'I love you too. Nothing will change that.'

'Will you say to the girls—' But the phone has gone dead. He shouts down the receiver. But Anam is gone. He turns to the officer. 'She . . . the phone. It's dead.'

'Your time is up.'

'But—'

'But nothing. You come now.'

The cell closes. He slips back through the men on the floor. A couple are sleeping, top to tail, on both bunks. The usual group crouch around in a circle, a couple of coins and a few piles of cards between them.

Tahir sits next to Manish.

'You look better. You are standing straight. Your colour has returned.'

'It was my wife. She called from Karachi.'

'And is she well? Your daughters?'

'They are managing. My wife. She is a great woman.'

'You are a lucky man. I have no wife nor have I ever.'

'Did not your parents arrange it for you?'

'It was not meant to be. And now, with my situation, the will of Allah has been proven wise.'

'My father, he is working for my freedom.'

'That is good.' Manish smiles but his eyebrows rise. Tahir

senses how hollow the last sentence sounds. He clears his throat.

'Have some water. Here.' Tahir takes a sip from Manish's bottle. He feels the cool liquid spread out from his chest. Manish hands him a rag. 'Dry your eyes. Don't let the others see you weak.'

Tahir pats them dry. He can smell the sweat on the cloth but it doesn't matter. To hear Anam's voice, her sweet voice, like an angel. It stays in his head. It will comfort him for many days.

How much does such a call cost? What food could have been bought with such money? She must not call often. Especially now they have so little. Fatima and Alayna must not want for anything because of phone calls. He will tell her next time to write, to spare every rupee she can. He will not have their lives ruined. They must have everything they dream of, good educations and happy lives. Whatever way they can manage it.

He inhales, wishing to help them. What can he do while at the mercy of others? He can neither help his girls nor protect them. Who thinks about how the families of prisoners survive – their wives and children? If only he could send his prison meals home to them.

He leans forward, closing his eyes, tucking his legs underneath him. He tries to be inconspicuous as he starts to recite prayers. He repeats the verses, finding comfort in the assurance of their rhythms. In these recitations is his personal prayer:

'Lord God, care for Anam, Fatima and Alayna. Look after Baba and Mama. Keep Ibrahim strong so that he might provide for them all. Please, may justice prevail. May the truth win out. Though, if this be God's will, I will submit to it and ask only for the strength to endure.'

Maybe all will be well. He might even escape, cut the metal bars with a nail file and dig through the sand, then find a boat to freedom.

Freedom: standing on the roof of his building in Karachi, feeling the light breeze on his face, the noise of the traffic below grown faint. Anam comes up behind him, touching his side and slipping her head in under his shoulder.

'Only a few minutes to sunset,' she says.

'Where are the girls?' he asks.

'Mama is reading to them.'

Tahir leans his head sideways, kissing her hairline, his mouth touching the silk. She smells of almonds; he inhales deeply, the perfume travelling far into his lungs.

He opens his eyes. The bars. The fluorescent light flickers. The men play cards or half sleep. Somewhere, in the corridor, are the echoes of a fight. If only he could keep his eyes closed forever.

He sits up. The image of Anam and the girls grows stronger in his mind, not them as they were, but as they will be when he one day returns to them. Anam might be grey by then. Maybe the two girls will be women with children of their own. But this is something to live for.

Trevor

White noise: the fridge purrs soft like a tractor; the television's hum is so high-pitched it's almost silent; and the fan in the laptop occasionally sparks to life. Rocco sleeps, tucked into Trevor's arm. One of Milo's baby blankets is over his legs. Trevor taps the keys quietly, trying not to move his elbows. The laptop is hot on his knees.

No word from the police station. They are as bad as the muppets back home. 'She will be released when we are finished.' A nice way of saying fuck off. Course, he could ring Mam but he doesn't want her to worry when she couldn't do anything anyway. He'll hang off till he hears something.

Refresh. Nothing new. If only his friends would post something. What time is it back home? Three a.m.-ish. The lads will still be in Coppers. Or maybe they've gone to the Wright Venue and are now hunting for cabs somewhere up the north side.

Lucy Quirke's page. The make-up is laid on thick. He often told her she looked better off without it. 'Tan makes me look thin,' she'd said, pouting away in the mirror. Women. Hard work. He opens another picture. What's this? By the Luas stop on Harcourt Street with a few of her girlfriends, with a dazed look on her puss. Underneath, one of the girls has written #drunkface.

Could he really have spent over a decade pining after this woman? There never was such a creature. He has to get free of her. Things have to change. Reaching for the tab, he clicks 'unfriend'. *Are you sure you wish to unfriend Lucy Quirke?* He pauses, his finger hovering above the pad. For a moment, he wonders if his arm will tense and refuse to do it. Then he clicks 'yes'.

Relief. Trevor glances away from the screen over at the other couch. Gete sleeps, head to one side. Milo is curled into her lap but there's no snoring. He must be sleeping light tonight. Trevor looks back at the computer, closing down his profile. He prays his new resolution will last, though it's hard to know when he's failed so many times before.

The queasy feeling returns. Trevor glances at his phone on the armrest. Nothing happening. No luck with Martin's number, no response after all the missed calls. He's probably in bed. Or up to fuck knows what else. Daddy had been right; he'd got the sum of him the first time they'd all met. Pinstripe suits.

Trevor opens the news page. He presses 'refresh', as he's done every five minutes for the last nine hours, but it's the same few articles. 'Girl Found Dead in JBR Marina.' 'Taxi Driver Arrested in Connection With Marina Drowning.' Trevor frowns. Some Pakistani fella looking to get his hole and not prepared to ask for it. That's what happens when these religious nuts make a big deal about sex. It all goes arse-ways.

How on earth is Martin stuck in the middle of it? Does he know that girl? What the hell does he have to do with that taxi driver? That knob-end has no interest in people making less money than him.

Siobhan. Come on. Come on. Come on. What's keeping the police? Surely, it's obvious she doesn't have a clue what's going on. God knows what they're doing to her. He'd be straight over to the station but . . . Trevor glances at Milo. Gete's hand is around his waist.

Gete's head dips to one side. She looks more like a statue sleeping than a human. No noise, no dribble. Lids shut lightly, as if she's having a long blink. Maybe that's the way they sleep in Ethiopia, with one eye open, ready for anything.

She'd tried to tidy all the things that the police had pulled out of the presses. 'Leave it. I'll help you in the morning,' he'd said as she continued picking up the overturned boxes. 'We'll worry about the boys for now.' However, maybe Gete wanted to tidy up, to keep busy rather than be left with her own thoughts.

Trevor sighs. He'd love to move right now and stretch out his joints. His arm has gone dead from Rocco but he'd hate to wake him. Poor Rocco at the top of the stairs a few hours earlier, hovering, uncertain. No computer games. No smart-mouth. No 'I want'. Rocco, a young boy whose eyes were wide, worrying about his mother.

'You OK?' Trevor had asked.

Rocco's lips twisted a little.

'Come down here. You don't have to stay up there by yourself.'

★

The sun is beginning to rise. Has he slept? His eyes feel dry. He glances at his watch. Does it look cheap? Siobhan had said a gold one would start looking chipped and fake soon enough. This one should last a bit, she said, as long as the studs didn't fall out. 'Who'd believe it's a Rolex, on me?' he'd said to Siobhan. 'Just tell them I bought it for you,' she replied.

The sun is warm on his left cheek. He blinks, trying to get moisture into his eyes. His laptop is dead on the arm-rest. Why the hell are they keeping her so long? Milo will be awake any moment. He's beginning to fidget. Gete strokes his arm with the tips of her fingers. Is she awake? Or is that unconscious, a mother's instinct while she sleeps?

The front door clicks. A key turns in the lock. Trevor jumps forward, before rubbing Rocco's head where he knocked it. Gete opens her eyes, slightly dazed. Milo frowns, his lids opening a fraction. The front door swings open.

Lifting Rocco to one side, Trevor clambers up. The alcohol from the brunch hits and a pain pulses through the crown of his head. He does his best to ignore it and in three large steps he's in the hall.

Siobhan stands in the doorway. Her hair is tangled behind her. The dress from the night before is marked and creased. Black eye make-up has run down her cheeks. Her nose flares. She begins to cry.

He hugs her. Her torso shakes. It's some time before sound comes out. He thinks about saying something but decides against it.

'Mammy?' Rocco stands in the sitting room doorway, uncertain, picking at the Transformers print on his T-shirt. She pulls away from Trevor and bends down, opening her arms.

'Baby,' she says, hugging him. She glances up at Milo.

'He's just woken, Ma'am. He slept right through.'

'Good . . . good. I wouldn't want . . .' She squeezes Rocco tight and holds his hand as she stands and kisses Milo on the head.

'What happened?' Trevor asks.

Siobhan glances down at Rocco.

'Would you help Gete make a cup of tea for me?'

He nods his head.

'You're a good boy.' She leans down and kisses his cheek. Trevor takes Milo from Gete, following Siobhan upstairs to the master bedroom.

Siobhan closes the bedroom door, making doubly sure it clicks shut. She sits on the edge of the bed, tossing aside a few of the pink silk cushions. Her GHD is still on the tiles beside the bed from getting ready for brunch. Trevor sits on the dressing table chair and reaches out his hand to hers. Milo picks at the gold-plated swirls on the seat.

'Fuck. Things are not good.'

'But—'

'Martin . . .' His name bring tears to her eyes. 'Martin has been . . . you know that girl. The dead one. He's been, you know.'

'What? But what about the taxi driver?'

'I don't know, Trev. Something fucked up is going on. The police are gunning for Martin.'

Trevor's not sure what else he can say. He glances down at Milo. Normally, Siobhan would tell him off for that sort of language in front of the kids. He strokes Milo's soft curls.

Milo puts his arms out for Siobhan and she hugs him in close, putting her palm over his exposed ear.

'Martin must've been seeing this girl for a while,' she whispers. She wipes her nose with the back of her hand. 'They were chatting online . . . Like, a local girl, of all people.' The words come out in bursts.

'What were they asking about?'

'They were trying to say I knew more than I did. Hours they had me in a room, hours. Asking the same questions over and over. At least I was here with Gete that night. They couldn't deny that.'

'He's hardly the first man to mess around and his wife none the wiser.' Trevor frowns. He could've phrased that better. What bothers him most is, though the news is a shock, some part of him is saying, 'I knew it.'

'And they think it was Martin who killed her?' Trevor asks. He doesn't like Martin but he doesn't seem like an actual murderer.

'They wouldn't tell me hardly anything. It was like they didn't know themselves. Apparently, her family are big shots. Who knows what's the truth.'

'What about the taxi driver?' Trevor asks again.

'Trev, I said I don't know.' Siobhan sounds exasperated. 'All I know is they'll lynch him, even if he hasn't done anything. Messing around with an Emirate . . .'

'He'll—'

'Trevor. Seriously. You've no idea. These guys mean business. You should see the inside of that police station.'

'You'll manage.'

'Doing what? Don't you get it, Trev?'

'Get what?'

'If Martin loses his job, we can't pay the bills. There's no bankruptcy in Dubai. Martin will go to jail and I could too. Then what'll happen to the boys?' Siobhan kisses the top of Milo's head, squeezing her eyes shut.

'Are you sure about this?' Trevor says. It must be about the tenth time he's asked her.

'I've been going over it and over it. There's nothing else to do.'

'This is your life.'

'Don't you think I know that? But what other option is there?' Siobhan's lips keep trembling. 'Fuck. I can't believe it.'

'There must be some other way.'

Siobhan sits up.

'Don't you think I'd take it, if there was? Trev, this is it. We cut our losses.'

'But your life here?'

'With the boys at risk? If we have to leave on camels, we're going.'

Trevor can't help but laugh, and Siobhan does too before her face turns serious again.

'I'm not joking, Trev. You saw those parked cars covered in sand.'

'Whatever you think.' He squeezes her hand. Siobhan's forehead wrinkles and there are more tears. It is some minutes before she can talk again.

'How could he do this?' She holds Milo tighter than ever. Trevor picks a packet of Kleenex off the dresser, handing her a few sheets. They are the soft ones. He can smell the aloe. Eventually she is able to blow her nose.

'Ma'am, your tea.' Gete taps on the door.

'One second,' Siobhan calls. She blinks a couple of times. Dabs her eyes. Another kiss on Milo's head.

'How soon do you want to go?' Trevor asks.

'Today.'

Siobhan showers in the next room. Trevor sits on the bed with Siobhan's laptop, Rocco beside him. Siobhan has given him his console but he is more interested in what Trevor is doing. Milo is at their feet, drawing with crayons. Trevor can hear kitchen cupboards open and close downstairs.

The VPN on the laptop is switched on. Trevor checks KLM and then British Airways for the cheapest flights. Emirates is out of the question. Too expensive. A national airline too – who knows what information they're passing on.

'You don't mind booking them?' Siobhan had asked. 'They'll check my cards.'

Trevor nodded and said it was fine. Would the bank ever allow that amount to go through? If he switched over his savings then maybe his Visa debit would take it. There'll be smoke coming off it. Still, if it has to be done, as Daddy would say.

Siobhan kissed his cheek.

'I'll pay you back, honestly, as soon as I can.'

'Don't be silly. Anything for you and the boys.'

'Could you book us to London, or even Amsterdam for now,' Siobhan said. 'Can you stretch to return tickets? One way is a red flag.'

Trevor inhaled. But family was family.

'What about Gete?' he asked.

Siobhan picked a pair of jeans from the wardrobe.

'What can we do?' she replied. 'She has no visa.'

'The flights are booked. We all leave at midnight,' Trevor says as Siobhan leaves the ensuite. Her wet hair is tied back in a ponytail. Her face looks shiny, like she's applied a thick layer of cream.

Trevor watches as she puts her handful of toiletries back on the dressing table.

'Any luck with Mam?' she asks.

'No. I didn't say anything in the messages, just for her to give me a ring. You know her. She'll freak.'

'She's going to get some shock tomorrow.'

'How's the head now?'

'The shower helped.' She reaches for the open bottle of Evian on the bedside locker. Her eyes look like they've been stung by bees.

'What are you going to take?'

'I don't know. How much space do we have?'

'Twenty-three kilos each. Same for the boys.'

'One hundred kilos . . .' Siobhan glances around.

'It's only stuff.'

'I know . . . but . . .' For a moment, as she glances around, Trevor realizes that for the first time in her life Siobhan is without words, her mouth ajar.

'You can always get more stuff.'

'I suppose.' She turns back to him and squeezes his hand. A faint smile, glancing at her sons. The sight of them brings colour back to her cheeks.

'You boys mind going home to see Nana for a while?' she asks, her voice returning to normal. Rocco nods. Milo pays no attention.

'It just fucking happened?' Siobhan shouts. Trevor glances out through the sliding door to where she stands by the pool. If she held the phone much tighter, she'd crush it.

'Rocco, will you take your games up to Gete,' Trevor says, handing him a bag of leads and CD cases. 'Go on. She's upstairs in Mammy's room.'

'I don't give a shit . . . You've ruined everything . . .'

He stays kneeling at the press, fingering through a drawer of papers, mostly old bills and a couple of *Now* magazines. Nothing necessary. There's a set of crockery in the cupboard below. Trevor recognizes it – a Christmas present from Mam. A fine pink ribbon travels around the rim of the mugs; the dust on the saucers is clearly visible.

He should leave the sitting room. Mam would clatter him for eavesdropping. But he stays put, pretending to look for items worth packing.

'. . . go fuck yourself, that's what you can do. Did you even think about me? About the boys? What about their friends? Rocco's school. No, you didn't think, did you? You're a selfish prick. I should've listened to Daddy and Mam. They knew what you really are, you son of a bitch . . .'

Siobhan walks away towards the far wall. Her voice grows faint. She turns, pacing back again.

'. . . you knew, didn't you? Your fucking BS story about getting delayed with work. You were too chicken-shit to fly back here. You knew they'd lynch you . . . am I right?

Am I . . . answer me . . . am I right? Huh. Well, that says it all.'

Siobhan's voice grows louder. Trevor can feel her eyes on him. He pretends to look busy, lifting out the plastic parts of a toy.

'Don't worry about that, Trev. That's rubbish,' she shouts in the door. 'Yes. That's Trevor. He's still here. Thank fuck he is. Could you imagine if he wasn't?'

Her voice becomes muffled. Trevor resists turning around.

'. . . oh, you didn't do it, didn't you? It just happened. Oh, well that's better now, isn't it? Then what about the prostitute?'

Trevor leans forward into the press. His heart pounds.

'. . . I don't know what they meant. They were being weird and asking . . . Yeah. As if I could believe you. Are you a fucking toolbag or what? What the hell were you thinking? A local girl. Your client's daughter. What kind of a gobshite are you? Some young wan bats her eyelids and gives you a bit of attention and you've her flat on her back. No . . . led by your fucking cock . . .

'No, I don't want to see you again. I'll hang you out to dry. Every penny I'll take. Go fuck yourself, Martin. Go fuck yourself.'

Trevor walks upstairs. Siobhan is still tearing chunks out of Martin on the patio. He pauses on the landing, gazing into the master bedroom. The wardrobe doors are open. On the bed are three large suitcases. Gete folds a T-shirt. Milo runs over to her, holding a colouring book.

'Very good,' she says, rubbing his back.

265

'Can I bring this?' Rocco walks out of the bathroom, holding a toy Transformer.

'If you have space. Put it in your case.'

Trevor clears his throat and walks into the room.

'How are you getting on, Gete?'

'Good, sir.'

'Do you need a hand with anything?'

'No, thank you.' She smiles briefly, before glancing back at the pile of clothes.

'When the cases need to be moved, I'll get them. You don't go near them. They're too heavy.'

'Thank you, sir.'

'So . . . you'll be OK while we're gone?' Trevor asks.

'Of course, sir.'

'I'll give you my number. If there is any trouble at all, you call me. We wouldn't want to see you in difficulty, would we, Milo?' The little boy shakes his head.

'Gete is the best,' Rocco says. Trevor is unsure of what to say next.

'I better pack my own stuff,' he says.

As he leaves the room, he hears Rocco ask Gete if she'll come to Ireland, that 'Mammy could get some flights,' and Milo says, 'Please, please, please.' It isn't right, leaving her. What would Daddy say? 'It's a bad business.'

He lifts his suitcase off the floor. Most of his things are still packed. There are a few bits still in bags from shopping: some cushion covers for Mam, Turkish delight for the gang in the gym, the box for the knock-off watch, and the pair of Vans from Dubai Mall that Siobhan bought him on the sly.

*

A knock. Siobhan is in the doorway.

'Speak to Martin?'

'That's one word for it.'

'What's he gonna do?'

'He won't be coming back here.' She isn't far off crying again.

'Just as well,' he says.

'You think?'

'The boys need a father, even if he is a prick.'

Siobhan doesn't reply. She strokes her eyebrows.

'Fuck, I'm wrecked. How the hell is this actually happening?'

'One step at a time.'

'How did this happen? I keep trying to think about what I've done. What did I do to deserve this?'

'Nothing at all. This is not your fault.'

'Didn't our vows mean anything?'

Trevor's not sure what to say. He can't bring himself to ask about the prostitute. Is there an answer to Martin's sort? Probably not. Some men are like that; there's no reining them in. He just hopes he isn't one of them.

Sad thing is, he probably could've told Siobhan the truth about Martin on day one when he came over to the house with those shite lilies for Mam.

'Why didn't I say no?' Siobhan says, thoughtful.

'What do you mean?'

'Oh, nothing. You know, he asked me out loads in Tunisia before I got with him. I only gave him a score because he'd bought me and the girls a load of fish bowls one night.'

'You have Rocco and Milo now. It's not all bad.'

Siobhan smiles. This seems to satisfy her.

'Any word from Mam?'

Trevor shakes his head. He opens his mouth to say something, then frowns. Gete's voice echoes in from somewhere in the house.

'What?' Siobhan asks.

'I dunno . . .' He decides to say nothing.

Lydia

She'd be better off dead. If there was a painless way to do it that would leave her body unmarked, she might've tried something long ago. Yet she's watched crime shows, all blood and bullet holes, and swollen bodies floating in water. There's no way to be dead and keep your looks.

A policeman hands her a large plastic box. Inside are her jacket, phone and bag. She'd forgotten about her Dior. There are fingerprints all over the sleeves and she thinks about filthy hands on her things.

She slips on the jacket. It is beautiful, the way it slips perfectly over her shoulders, the fabric smooth as silk, snug at the joints. How could she live without beautiful things?

Her hands are a mess. She'd love to pick at her cuticles, pull at the dry splitting flesh. *Dermatitis artefacta*: 'picking at skin as a cry for attention'. Her doctor at the time had suggested antidepressants. Mama said it was idleness and told her to study harder.

She puts her hands down, thinking about the sting, the drop of blood that pulling her skin would release. The policeman in the cloakroom continues gazing at her and she pulls up the collar of her jacket, turning sideways towards the metal door. 'Five minutes, then they will come get you,' he says. There is a look in his eye she doesn't like, like he has a right to stare. In a bar, she might've told him to 'pay or look away'.

She pulls at the bottom of her dress. As she lifts her arms, there is a faint smell of sweat. The first prickles of hair are showing on her legs. Soon she will be home, feeling the heavy jets of water descend from the wide showerhead. But what if she's convicted and is sent to prison for a year? Two years, even? She'd regress to a cavewoman.

'We have arranged bail, pending your trial,' the man from the Russian embassy said. He looked like a used-car salesman. Shiny suit. Cheap. An ugly paisley tie.

'Are you the ambassador?' Lydia asked.

He smiled. He had small teeth that were yellowed from nicotine. 'No, but I work for the consulate.'

'Oh.' Lydia inhaled. She'd been fobbed off with an office clerk. The fate of a prostitute wasn't high on their agenda.

'Are you sure you do not want us to contact your family?'

Lydia shook her head.

'I did nothing in all this. I know nothing of this girl who died.'

'I know. We have negotiated with them. But they are charging you with sex outside of marriage.'

'But . . .'

'Be thankful they are not charging you with more.'

'They tried to get me to sign a document. I refused, even when they said they would not give me water. Surely, this is torture. They cannot proceed.'

The representative smiled.

'Have you ever tried to breathe while someone stuffs sand in your mouth?'

'Of course not.'

'Be grateful. It could be much worse.'

Lydia leaned back in her chair. Behind the diplomat was a mirrored wall.

'We are alone here?' she asked. 'Surely, there is discretion when talking to the embassy?'

'Yes,' he said, glancing over his shoulder. His voice did not sound convincing. 'There is good news,' he added. 'They will give you bail. But you must surrender your passport till after the trial.'

'What other choice do I have?'

'To stay here.'

'Then I must agree. Anything else?'

'That is all. They will release you tomorrow.' He stood. She followed his lead.

'You have many more cases?'

'There are always cases.'

'Thank you for your efforts.' She put out her hand. He smiled but didn't take it.

'You are welcome, Ms Sushkova. Try not to worry. Even after a conviction, quite often women are pardoned, with enough pressure from our government. Are you quite sure you don't want to contact your family?'

'Absolutely not.'

Why didn't he shake her hand? Did he not want to sully himself, touching the flesh of a prostitute? Why? Was she unclean? Because she fucked for money or because she was caught fucking for money?

The metal door opens and Lydia walks into the main lobby of the police station. The noise startles her. Free people. How easy it is to take freedom for granted, until it's taken away.

The sunlight. The feel of it on her skin makes her shoulders relax. The fresh air. The sense of space. The bustle of life, being part of it again. Relief. Joy. She can never go back to those cells. Nothing is worth it. She'll escape somehow – hijack a boat – whatever it takes. Without freedom, life is nothing.

She puts out her hand. A taxi stops, a Pakistani man doing the same thing he does every day. How do they do it? Is driving in the same metal box for twelve hours a day, seven days a week, any better than being in a cell? Her hands rest on her legs as she sits back in the car. She is acutely aware of where her palms and fingers touch her knees. Since the swab, she hasn't wanted to think about anything touching her inner thighs or her private area.

'Lift your skirt,' the masked lady had said. At least she was a woman. Two police officers were stationed outside the door.

'You are a doctor?' Lydia asked.

The woman nodded. Lydia glanced at her hijab.

'Nurse, get me a swab.'

'I do not want to do this.' Lydia's voice grew louder.

'You must. It is an order.' The doctor had a tone of impatience.

'I do not want it.'

'We must get swabs in all sex-related cases.'

There was nothing else to do. Lydia held her top lip between her teeth. She closed her eyes and lifted her skirt, pulling down her purple thong. The doctor put on gloves.

What did she think of her hair-free vagina? Did she go home to her husband and talk about what whores white women were? Did she speak to her daughters, telling them to stay away from degenerate fair-skinned races?

Lydia opened her legs.

'Wider.'

Lydia held her breath while hands examined her area. Then she felt something dry. Like a cotton bud.

'Now, turn over, please,' the doctor said.

'What?'

'We need to swab your rectum too, Ms Sushkova.'

'But no one . . .' Words failed her. She turned around on the bed; the doctor pulled her hips back. Anal bleaching. What would she think of that? Something fine and dry was inserted and her muscles clenched at the discomfort.

'You may turn around.' As Lydia sat back, she saw the cotton swab being placed into a glass tube.

'That is all. You may put on your . . . underwear.' The doctor did not look up. She got a pen and began writing. Lydia glanced at the words but it was all in Arabic.

'Lastly, I need a swab from your mouth.'

'Won't all these tests be inaccurate?' Lydia asked. 'Much time has passed since I was arrested.'

The doctor didn't look up but continued sticking labels on the samples.

'Ms Sushkova, please open your mouth.'

A swab was dragged across her throat. The dry feeling on her tonsils made her want to cough. It was over quickly.

'When are the results?'

'In due course. Pull down your skirt, Ms Sushkova. I will call in the officers.'

★

The taxi is almost at her apartment. She glances at the road-side posters advertising Danone Activia, a new Mercedes and Pantene shampoo. A celebrity with a mane of glossy brown hair says her locks have never felt thicker. Though the posters are within arm's reach, there is no graffiti. Back in Russia, cocks would've been drawn on the celebrity's lips, with filthy slogans. *Hooyesos. Suka.*

She'd like to draw a dick on the girl's mouth and watch people's faces as they drove past. Her insides feel tight and tense. She hates this place, all veneer, all bullshit.

She crosses her legs, trying again not to think about the doctor's hands touching her private area, the feeling of swabs pushing into her, dry and dragging across skin. It is stupid. How can this bother her so much? She lets men fuck her for money.

'How long have you been in Dubai, boss?' she asks the driver. Anything to distract her.

'Two months now.'

'You like?'

'It's OK. Very long days. Very long.'

'And where are you from?'

'India, Ma'am.'

'You think you'll stay here long?'

'Four years, Ma'am. Maybe more.'

'You have a family?'

'Yes, three boys.'

'You miss them.'

'Very much.' He pulls a picture out of his visor and she looks at the three children: sun-faded clothes, overlong hair, bright eyes, like a clichéd picture from a charity poster. She smiles.

'Handsome boys,' she says. She glances out of the window. Her building is only a few hundred feet away. 'Next on the left, boss.'

She pays him forty dirhams, though the price is only thirty. She steps out. He is about to pull off but she puts her head back inside the RTA.

'Don't stay too long,' she says. 'Don't miss your boys growing up.'

The cupboards in her room are all wide open. Her duvet is pulled back. Did they take samples from this? She always uses condoms, so there is little chance they will find DNA on her swabs. But her bed? Did they look for stray hairs? Take samples of curious stains?

A glass lies smashed on the floor. There's been no attempt to tidy it. These policemen are thugs, worse than the criminals. Where was their warrant? She picks up the shards, trying not to cut her fingers. At least her laptop had been in Bianca's room. They hadn't taken that.

The others are not at home. She couldn't bear their questions. Putting the broken pieces of glass into the bin, she steps into the bathroom and turns on the tap. Hot water flows. *Hvala bogu.* She can shower.

Tigi shampoo. Two rinses. A deep-conditioning hot oil treatment. Yves Saint Laurent Natural Action Exfoliator for face and neck. Jo Malone body wash applied with Dermasuri Deep Exfoliating Mitt. Rinse. Allow the shower jets to pummel her shoulders. Skin cleansed and soft. Step out of shower.

Pat skin dry with large soft towel. Tie hair back. Clarins eye serum. Elizabeth Arden Eight Hour Cream. Kiehl's Crème de Corps. L'Occitane hand cream. Brush teeth. Floss. Listerine mouthwash (mild). Check eyebrows for new stray hairs. Pluck. Cotton-bud eyes. Remove remains of nail polish. Book a leg waxing. Towel-dry hair. Add TRESemmé mousse. Blow-dry. Smooth with John Frieda serum. Spray of Elnett. Put on loose grey Juicy Couture tracksuit pants and hoodie.

Ritual complete. She feels human once more.

The sound of the washing machine echoes from the kitchen. The cushions on the couch are overfull and her neck feels sore from being at such an angle. She takes a blueberry from the plastic. It's warm. She puts the packet back on the coffee table.

How long has she slept? An hour? No, two at least. She glances at the television. The muted presenters are all glossy hair and smiles. Wouldn't it be lovely to throw something at them?

What will she tell Bianca and the others? Maybe they haven't noticed the police were at the apartment. She could say she stayed with a client for a number of days. It is better for them not to know. How would they react if they discovered the truth?

The washing machine cycle starts a vigorous spin. Maybe it would've been better to throw those clothes away. Now they'll hold the memories of the jail, the smell of sweat and the steam of burnt curry. Her bed sheets too. Maybe she should've thrown them in the garbage chute. To think of those unwashed policemen's hands touching the satin, hands that picked noses, scratched testicles and wiped behinds.

She turns up the volume of the television as loud as she can bear it. It is over. She is home. Who can say what will happen next? Maybe the embassy will get her a pardon and she'll never have to go to jail. 'There's no point in worrying about the future,' Bianca said to her once. 'Anything can happen before it.'

Maybe Bianca was right. A sense of hope rises in Lydia's chest before vanishing almost immediately. Yes. Anything can happen, but when does 'anything' really happen? When does the most likely thing not happen?

Keys in the front lock. Lydia puts down the packet of blue-berries and fiddles with the television remote. The door swings open. It is Bianca. She jumps at the sight of Lydia.

'You are back?' Bianca puts down the Carrefour bag on the tiles. There is lipstick on her teeth. The yellow string vest she is wearing does not support her breasts correctly.

'Yes. I'm back. You know that guy, Stefan, he—'

'What happened? The police . . .' Bianca's voice becomes quiet, waiting for the front door to click shut.

'You saw?'

'They said they arrested you. They search everywhere. They have released you?'

'I am back now.'

'Are you well?'

'Yes.' Lydia finds it hard to remain composed.

'Why were they here?'

'Nothing. Just some trouble with a client.'

'Mrs Sarkis talk to me. She say they here about the death of that girl.'

'Sarkis is a gossip and a liar.' Lydia finds herself getting angry. 'I am free now. All will be fine.'

'Do they have your passport?'

'Yes, but . . .'

Bianca shakes her head. 'This is very bad.' She leans against the back of the sofa, then straightens herself up.

'It will be fine. They have not charged me. The embassy have sorted everything.'

Bianca doesn't seem to listen. She folds her arms, her head still slightly shaking. She looks at the wall, gazing at the Japanese print.

'I don't think you can live here any more,' she says. 'It's too dangerous with police coming to the house. That is bad. So bad. They might do anything.'

'You can't—'

'I am sorry, very sorry, but you must go.'

'The other girls?'

'They are the same.'

'You've talked to them?'

Bianca looks uncomfortable. She nods her head.

'I'm not going to get you into any trouble.'

'But what if they come back?'

'They won't. They have my passport.'

'No . . . no . . . I am very sorry.'

'But where will I go?'

'You can find somewhere new.'

278

'With what money?' Lydia's last word ends with a dry croak. Bianca shrugs.

'You have no savings?'

'A little.'

'Well . . .'

Lydia shakes her head and swallows hard. 'I cannot believe you. You said you were my friend. You are all bitches.'

Bianca folds her arms.

'Fine. I will go.' Lydia walks towards her bedroom. At the last moment, she turns. 'Fuck you, Bianca, fuck you.' She slams the door and sits on her bed. The pillows feel dry without their covers. She opens her laptop. It flickers to life. Where will she go? How will she find two more girls to live with? Has word got out about her? Is she now marked?

Too many questions. She opens her inbox. Thirty new messages. The phone company has sent her a statement. A client asks when she is next free. She scrolls down, stopping when she sees an email from Igor.

Lydia,

How are you? I hope you are happy in Dubai. Veronika and I have been worried about you. We called many times but no answer. We've left voicemails – what is wrong? Why don't you call us back?

Things are not good here. Mama has been ill for some time now. She did not want us to talk to you but you need to come home. She has not long, the doctor says to us. She has a growth in her lung and it has spread to the liver. They think they can

279

*slow down its progress with treatment. But it is not good. She
will not live more than some months, they say.*

*Mama does not know this. Veronika thinks it best not to tell
her. Please call us when you get this.*

Your brother,
Igor

Lydia inhales. No 'Love, Igor'? Veronika probably wrote this.

Mama has cancer. For a moment, Lydia feels a strange
relief. Mama might never have to know about this mess in
Dubai, though why does Mama's opinion concern her when
they have not spoken in months and she is thousands of miles
away?

Lydia frowns. Mama is dying and all she can think about
is herself. She is horrible. No wonder everything has gone
wrong. She doesn't deserve to have good people in her life
when she cares nothing for anyone else.

She picks up her phone, scrolling down to Igor's number,
but as she looks at the +7 digits she feels hesitant. What can
she say? If they ask her to come home, she cannot go. They'll
think she's doing it to be cruel, and there'll be nothing she
can say to change their minds. She puts down the phone.
Mama, forgive me, she thinks. She wouldn't be as cold-
hearted as this if she had a choice.

The past was the past. Had Mama truly been so awful?
She'd scolded her and Igor, yes, warning them about the mis-
eries of life, but she'd always made sure they had a meal to
eat. They'd never been without a bed. What had Mama said
about the world which hadn't been proved right?

'Forgive me, Mama,' she says, powering off her laptop. She slips sideways on to the unmade bed and closes her eyes.

Her phone beeps. Lydia's eyes open. Ten p.m. Her head hurts as she sits up, groggy from oversleeping. She cocks her ear. The house sounds silent. The others must have gone out looking for clients.

You free this evening Anna? the message reads. Eric – 'Mr Cocky'.

The memory of her life one week ago makes her want to cry again. *No,* she types back immediately. But something holds her back from pressing send. How will she live in Dubai if she has no visa to work and she cannot fly home? She will have to eat some way.

Delete. Delete. Blank message. She begins to type again: *Hello Mr Cocky ;) I am free later but my apartment is busy. We can go to your place?*

Wiping moisture from her eyes, she presses send.

Siobhan

The bags are piled in the hallway: Trevor's Dunnes Stores suitcase, and her and the boys' Samsonites. Siobhan puts her Louis Vuitton over her shoulder, trying to focus on the tasks at hand. Now is not the time for falling apart.

'Hopefully we won't be away too long, Gete. Family emergency.' She refuses to look at Trevor, his face like a dog after being told off.

'Yes, Ma'am. I will wait for you to call.'

'I'll be in touch.' Siobhan gives her a hug. 'You are the best, you know that?'

Christ, now she's crying. What is she like? If only she could do more to help. How can she with the boys? Sometimes you have to put those closest first. Gete is a grown woman, not a child that needs mammying. Doesn't she have her own family back home? She must have plenty money saved at this point. She's no expenses. Back in Ethiopia, she'd be minted.

'Look, take this,' Siobhan says. She hands Gete an envelope with dirhams inside. She shouldn't be giving away her money – who knows when the next pay-cheque will be coming? But fuck it. Gete is Gete.

'You come back soon, Ma'am?'

'Of course, of course. If anyone asks, you tell them that.' Siobhan wipes her eyes with the back of her sleeve. 'Come on, boys, say goodbye to Aunty Gete.'

Rocco's usual shyness vanishes as he hugs Gete's waist. For a second, Siobhan worries she might have to peel him off her. The last thing they need is a scene on top of everything else.

Gete takes Milo in her arms. Milo cuddles in, as if ready for sleep. She smiles, looking at Siobhan. 'It's past his bedtime.'

Lights come through the windows. A car engine.

'Our lift,' Trevor says. He reaches for the front door.

'Oh, Gete.' Siobhan squeezes her arm again, rubbing Milo's back. 'Come now, young man, we have to get a taxi.' He's too sleepy to react.

Siobhan turns, Milo warm against her chest. She looks into the sitting room at the books scattered across the couch, the plastic toys and the DVDs in piles in front of the television. All to be left behind.

'One last quick runaround,' she says. Trevor takes Milo from her. She climbs the stairs, glancing down at the bikes lined up against the wall. Fuck. Her home. What will happen to all these things? She glances in Rocco's room. Gete has taken off the Spider-Man bedding. The wardrobe doors are open, as are the drawers, as if thieves have been searching for something valuable.

Her bedroom. The expensive linen. Madonna's lyrics about satin sheets come to mind. What a silly song to come into her head at such a moment. Martin. Martin. Martin. How could you? All his protesting on the phone.

'You know I love you. I love you, Siobhan. Listen to me. Please. It was a mistake. It was just sex. It just happened.' How could he say he loved her? Half of her wants to hit him hard, again and again, see him cry out in pain. The other half . . . what does the other half want? The last time she felt like this was at Daddy's funeral, the horrible knowledge that something was gone which could not be brought back.

Daddy had been right. The signs were there: the WhatsApp messages, the loving a bit of attention. She can see it now. Him flirting, testing the waters, then a bit more, till he'd gone too far and the only option was to save face and see the thing through. And the excuses to himself afterwards to overcome the guilt: 'You only live once . . . Isn't life for living?'

This Emirate girl was hardly the first, no matter what he said. These things happen gradually, not overnight. A few messages. Pictures going back and forth. A series of compliments. Chats about how unhappy he was with his wife, while the girl talked about how she loved European men and that she wanted to live, to experience everything. Flirting, describing what they would do in bed together, then finally a secret meeting and all was lost.

Oh, Daddy, why aren't you here? For in a better reality – in a TV show – she'd call him now, confess that he knew better, and his coldness would vanish in an instant. Daddy could never resist an apology. She'd be his girl again, he'd figure out what should be done next, and everything would come good in the end.

She stands for some time at the end of the king-size bed, looking at the covers, thinking about Milo sleeping between herself and Martin. Sometimes, on a Saturday morning, Rocco would hop in too and she'd tell him stories about growing up in Ireland and what Nana and Granddad's house was like in Cork. Martin, panned out from the week's work, would pretend to be a grizzly bear if Rocco jumped on him or shook his shoulders, trying to wake him up.

Good times. Gone times. Were they even real times? Siobhan turns away. She has to stop torturing herself. The RTA is waiting. Downstairs, Trevor is talking.

'Now if you need anything, you have my number. Siobhan has a lot on but I'll do what I can. All this carry-on . . .'

'Thank you, sir.'

'Please, Gete. It's Trevor.'

Siobhan smiles. She said the same thing to Gete on her first day, not to call her 'Ma'am', but Gete looked terrified and said she couldn't – 'What would the other maids think if I did?'

God. All her gorgeous clothes thrown into landfill. Designer jeans. Silk tops. Flowing dresses. Though Gete might be able to flog some of it. Plenty of maids would give their right arm for one of those ball gowns. What does it matter about a few dresses? She's worn most of them anyway.

'That's the last of them,' Trevor says, lifting the smallest case into the boot. The taxi driver keeps trying to help him with the luggage, though with Trev's muscles, he could probably strap the luggage to his back and walk to Ireland with it.

Siobhan sits into the back seat, Milo on her lap. She hands Rocco his computer console. He doesn't seem that interested, dragging his fingernail along the bottom of the car window.

'It's a beautiful evening,' she says, looking at the villa. The red sky rises up behind it, slowly turning deep navy. At what point does it become actually dark? There's no line, it's all so gradual, and yet somehow it does.

'It is very nice, Ma'am. Is that all?'

'Yes. We're ready, boss.' Trevor sits into the front passenger seat.

'You have your safety belt on?'

Rocco nods, the strap cutting under his neck. Siobhan clings to Milo.

The car slips backwards. She looks at her 4x4. It was a dose collecting it from the hotel, but it would've been a red flag to leave it there. How long will it be before sand lies a few millimetres thick on the bonnet? When will the lease payments bounce or the police come back looking for her?

Number fifty-six's gorgeous Mercedes is outside. The kids from fifty-one are playing on the lawn; the young girl is trying to make her hula hoop spin. They'll get soaked by the sprinklers before long. Siobhan can almost hear the young girl's surprised screams when it happens, like the kid's slow-mo laughter at the start of *Terminator 2*.

She wants to shout for the taxi to stop. She wants to stamp her feet and say, 'No, you will not take my life.' Yet what can she do? They have to move on. Soon the gap between her life and this world will be thousands of miles. Still, it's better that than being trapped behind iron bars.

Neither she nor Trevor speak as they pass by Jumeirah Beach Residence. The traffic is heavy. Saturday night. Horns blare if cars delay more than a second when a red light turns green. Ferraris and Jaguars overtake them. Siobhan takes out her phone, locking and unlocking it. Anything to avoid being totally still.

Trevor turns around, phone in hand.

'Still no word from Mam. I texted her again.'

'You think she's OK?'

'I'm sure she's fine.' There is a tone to his voice and she wonders if he is tired of her. 'Creating drama where there is none' – that's what he'd probably say if he was looking for a fight. What is it with Irish men, always pretending situations are smaller than they actually are, saying something is nothing when actually it's a big deal?

'She was meeting Pat, you said?'

'They were heading out for the day. Pat wanted to see a ruin or a graveyard or something.'

'Wild date.'

Trevor smiles.

'Having the ride.'

'Ah, stop.' Siobhan glances at Rocco. He's staring out of the window in a strange daze. What is he thinking about? Is he aware that in a day he'll likely be wearing a thick coat, looking out at a grey estate and bare trees? Will he fit in? Has he been 'Dubaied' – too accustomed to chewing gum-free pavements, no homeless, no waiting lists, no drugs, no bullying in schools? Where everything, as long as it works, is essentially perfect?

The red in the sky is retreating. The sun sets quickly, close to the equator. A half-hour and the only light will be the blue-green haze of the glowing skyscrapers, the flash of headlights, maybe the occasional couple of fireworks from a hotel.

Fuck. It's likely the last time she'll ever see this place. She isn't ready to leave. What will she do when she gets back?

She'll be one of those awful pram-pushers that she always joked about in her teens. A drain on the world.

A text comes through. It's Rebecca.

I'm in an appalling state from the brunch! You still on for tonight? The girlies are coming at ten. Msged on FB. No reply. All OK hun? x

'What a difference a day makes.' Another stupid lyric. Then again, there is truth in every cliché. This time yesterday, they were pulling up outside the house. All night in that chair, question after question. What could she tell them that she hadn't told them within ten minutes?

'Are you going to charge me with something?' she'd kept asking. 'You can't keep holding me here if you aren't going to charge me.'

'You Westerners always say the same,' the seated policeman had replied.

'What's your name?' she'd asked.

'It's irrelevant.'

'I'll report you.'

Both officers laughed.

'Now, tell me again about what happened on the night in question.'

'But I've told you a hundred times. What more do you want?'

'Mrs Cusack, a woman has died. We will ask questions until we are satisfied.'

'You can ask me questions till you're blue in the face, but I can't tell you things I don't know.'

*

Siobhan's phone vibrates.

We need to talk. Please pick up. xx

Why is he doing this? He needs to stop. And the kisses at the end. Is he trying to drive her mad? She puts the phone down, turning the front over on her lap. Trevor swings around.

'Who was it?'

'Guess who?'

'What the fuck does he want?'

'Pretending he gives a damn.' Siobhan glances at the taxi driver. No point in swearing.

'He's got some fucking neck.'

'I suppose I'll have to talk to him eventually.'

Trevor faces back to the road.

'Yeah, but he can sweat it out for a while.'

Trevor hasn't said a word to her since Media City. He gazes at the Burj Khalifa, which rises up on his right. His brows keep moving like he's having a conversation with himself. He spins his phone between his fingertips.

The driver stares straight ahead at the horizon of sky-scrapers. He must be bored as fuck. The poor guy. Is it the start of his shift or the end?

Trevor swings his head but then he half turns back again.

'What's up?'

'You think Gete will be all right?'

Siobhan tries to ignore her annoyance. She rubs Milo's back.

'She'll be fine, Trev. I paid her enough. She still has the laptop and everything.'

'You know they have her passport? The agency.'

'All she has to do is ring them and they'll give it back to her. They'll line her up a new job straight away.'

'But with who?'

'Honestly, Trev, I've done what I could. She's a grown woman. She's well able.' Siobhan's stomach grows tighter with each sentence, her eyes dry like she could sleep for a decade. She glances at Rocco. He's asleep.

'I don't like leaving her like that.'

'Trev. Please don't put this on me right now. I did what I could. I've two boys to consider. I can't be worrying about every maid in the Middle East.'

The RTA stops outside the terminal. Siobhan hands the driver one hundred dirhams. He nods slightly and thanks her, helping Trevor with the bags. Siobhan holds Milo. He stirs a little though doesn't wake. Rocco leans into her leg. She can feel the warmth of his cheek on her side.

The breeze is cool. You'd know it was November, the weather finally becoming bearable. She looks at the cylindrical terminal, watching families walk in and out through the entrance, those exiting pale and excited, those entering tanned and relaxed.

She goes to take her first step but pauses. Airports are horrible places. 'Places between places', that's what Martin calls them. She could be standing outside any terminal in the world right now, the same glass fronts, curved roofs and blinding lights. If she could just be home in an instant and have a hug from Mam.

'Come on, Sio.' Trevor is standing at the far side of the pedestrian crossing. She begins to walk, holding Rocco's hand.

'You OK, my best boy?' she says.

'But what about Milo? Isn't he your best boy?'

'Don't be silly. You both are.'

They walk through the main entrance; her gaze lands on a group of four security men chatting beside the escalator. Trevor leans in.

'You sure you won't have trouble getting through?'

'Fingers crossed. You go through first on your own. Just in case.'

'Me first?'

'Best thing, no?' Surely he isn't changing the plan now. If they go through together and get stopped, who will be able to go and get help?

'I was thinking it'd be better for me to go second. I won't be able to help if I've gone through security.'

The girl at check-in smiles, takes the tickets and puts stickers on their bags. Siobhan feels like she's going to throw up. She wonders if the girl has noticed her cheeks glowing red or the droplets forming on her forehead.

'How old are you?' the girl says, smiling at Rocco, but Rocco is shy.

'He's tired. Long day,' Siobhan replies, trying to seem natural but not sure quite how to do it. The more she tries, the more her voice sounds strange to her.

'Here are your tickets. Watch the screens to find your boarding gate.'

Siobhan thanks her, glancing over her shoulder as she walks away. She turns a corner and walks through the crowds of people, gripping Rocco's hand firmly. Milo is already making her shoulder ache but she has to 'suck it up' – that's what Mam would no doubt say.

The security barriers are next. Fifteen queues in a row, ten people deep. She gazes at the men behind the passport counters in their white robes and red keffiyehs. She finds the youngest-looking and joins in behind an Asian family. Five rows over is the counter for business class passengers. No queue. A pang. The aisle she knows best, simply cruising through, not stuck with the masses in economy.

What if they catch her? Could they arrest her? She wasn't told she couldn't leave. Then again, Dubai laws have nothing to do with common sense. What about the boys if they did arrest her?

Damn. How much worse her life will be (and it already feels bad enough) if this passport guy, ten people away, frowns when he sees her name, types something into his computer, and calls his supervisor over. Please, God. She doesn't ask for much. She isn't even asking for herself. But for her boys, let this go OK.

The queue inches forward. People in front whispering like they're on death row. Come on. Come on. Get it over with. Her legs feel like jelly. She kisses Milo's head. Rocco holds her jeans pocket, looking around at people taller than him.

'Hail Mary, full of grace. The Lord is with thee. Blessed art thou amongst women, and blessed is the fruit of thy womb, Jesus. Holy Mary, Mother of God, pray for us sinners, now and at the hour of our death, Amen.

'Hail Mary, full of grace . . .'

What is the rest of the prayer? She can't keep repeating the same four lines. Fuck. Is she actually saying the rosary? Oh, God, if you're there, please, keep the boys safe.

Five people in front. Two people. One person. Her heart feels like it's going to jump out of her chest. If she could only take a deep breath to steady herself, but how suspicious will she look if she's heaving away like an asthmatic.

'Next.' The young passport man has a blank expression. She steps forward and hands him the documents for herself and the two boys.

'Going to?'

'London.'

'Going home?'

'No. A holiday. I live here.'

He looks at her passport. She can't quite see what he's doing. Hail Mary. Hail Mary. Hail Mary. Jesus Christ and all the saints. Let it be OK. Her foot is tapping. Stop fucking tapping. She clings to the collar of Rocco's T-shirt. Why the hell is it taking so long to scan the passport?

She looks at the young Arab's face. Not a muscle changing. Fuck. If he knows something, will he ever just get on with it? What will she do? Run? Run where? Come on, say something or give her the passports.

'Here,' he says, handing back the documents. She smiles for a second, hurrying on.

She's through. She's through! It should be clear sailing now. She smiles, giving Milo a squeeze as she takes off her shoes for the security scan of her hand luggage.

'Rocco, you've no coins in your pockets?' she asks, as he goes to walk through the X-ray machine. He shakes his head.

'Good boy.' Her voice is croaky. She'll get some tea at the gate.

She walks through the machine. Milo is not happy to be woken, but other than that, it's only a couple of minutes before she's in the main duty-free hall. Sitting on a bench, she takes her phone out of her Louis Vuitton. A message from Trevor: *Are you through OK? x*

Siobhan smiles. He never 'x's his messages. She dials his number and the phone rings a few times. No answer. She calls again. Still nothing. She sighs. Short of credit, as always.

Yes. Through security. No problems. Ireland here we come! She frowns. It reads like she's going on holiday, but the relief that she is free makes everything seem wonderful. The chatter of people buying alcohol and perfume is joyous to her.

Her phone vibrates. It's Trevor.

Phew. Relief. You sure ur through all right? She hits reply.

Everything is fine. All sorted. On way to gate.

She calls Rocco back from touching the stand of toys. Milo plays with the pattern on her top. 'I've stickers in my bag when we get on the plane,' she says. 'Bob the Builder. You like some Bob the Builder stickers?' He nods.

If Trevor gets here soon, she can go to the bathroom and give her face a rinse. Her eyelids feel like there's glue underneath them.

Her phone vibrates.

Glad you are OK. Will see you back in Ireland. Don't mind me. All good. Get home safe xx

Siobhan dials his number. Rings out. Tries again. This time the phone has been switched off. Voicemail.

'Trevor. What the hell? Where are you? Answer your

goddamn phone . . .' She keeps shouting until the voicemail runs out. A beep. The phone hangs up on her. A few passengers nearby are staring. Milo looks like he's about to cry. She starts texting.

WTF???? What are you doin? Srsly, get through security.

No reply. What is going on? Can she go back through? But what about the boys? Panic threatens to overtake her but there's nothing to be done.

She inhales, trying to calm herself. Anger creeps in and it helps to banish the fear. Typical. Trevor is off doing whatever Trevor wants to do. The chips will fall where they may. Either way, she and the boys must get on the plane.

Joan

Joan checks the front pocket. She searches the main part of her bag again.

'Christ, I've forgotten it,' she says. They're well on their way to Blessington.

'Didn't we survive before without them?' Pat replies, giving her a grin. She does her best to look around the broken tooth. He's cleaned up well: a nice blue-and-white check shirt, a bit of pomade in the hair, polished brown boots and belt, and freshly washed Levi's.

'But if Trevor calls.'

'He's well able to look after himself.' Pat indicates off the main road. Lord knows what he has in mind.

'It's getting late,' she says. The clouds are low. Not a single star.

'You'll love this, Joan. It's only on once a year.'

'You won't tell me?'

'Don't you trust me at all?'

Joan gives him a sly look and they both laugh. She feels silly in her cocktail dress and Pat driving her out into the sticks. It'd been so long she could barely open the bottle of nail polish, twisting the top with her teeth.

'You better not have me walking through fields or puddles in these heels,' she warns him. Brown Thomas. Siobhan had talked her into buying them. They came in a beautiful silver box and the red Prada letters were gorgeous. Every now and again, she takes the shoes out of the tissue paper and walks around the house in them.

Taking a right, Pat directs the car through the tunnel of trees towards Blessington town, the road nearly black. A few shadows flutter down in front of the beams. Snow? No. Just dry leaves.

'A heavy night on the way,' Pat says.

'We won't be outside?'

'Not at all.'

'Should we be heading out so far? I'd say there'll be snow.'

'Trust me now, Joan. Look, only one more mile to the town. We're only going a bit beyond it.'

As they drive through the town, Joan admires the Christmas decorations filling the shop windows. People run back and forth across the main street, wrapped in coats and thick scarves. The scene reminds Joan of the advert that's always playing at Christmas. *Holidays are coming, Holidays are coming . . . always Coca-Cola.*

'Would your family be from this neck of the woods?' Joan fixes her rings. Hopefully Pat isn't an anorak. She's met the local history types before, the kind who hammer on about scattered rocks in a field.

'My family are from Straffan. We go back a good few generations.'

'I'm the first of my family in Dublin.'

'You were down to your brother?'

'In Cork, yes.' Joan hopes he won't ask more questions.

'How is he?'

'Grand. You've no siblings?'

'Just myself. It would've been nice to have a brother, a partner in crime growing up.'

'True,' Joan replies. She doesn't want to burst his bubble.

'Have you heard much from your gang in Dubai. Trevor is enjoying himself?'

'He is. A bit too much, no doubt. You know young lads these days, breaking their mothers' hearts.' She laughs. 'He might have landed a job out there, would you believe.'

'Oh.' Pat keeps his eyes on the road, the last of the town lights ending, and they drive back into dark countryside.

'It's the best thing really. They have great opportunities out there.' Joan pauses. Her voice sounds strained.

'Still, it can be hard, family away. Since Mammy died, the house is very quiet.'

'I've people at me all day in A&E. I'm glad for a bit of peace when I get home.' She tries to laugh again. She glances sideways at the shelf in the door. A few books squashed in. She picks out a red one. *The Golden Book of Ireland.*

'You travel much?'

'I'd like to do more,' he says. 'But I don't fancy heading off by myself.'

'You're a great man for reading.' Joan picks out the other books: *Wicklow Uncovered*, James Joyce's *Dubliners*, and *The Pocket Book of Irish Writers.*

'Probably too much. Mammy always said I should spend more time in this reality.'

The road continues to meander, weaving through trees. Where on earth is he taking her? She probably should've told

Maggs she was heading out. There are enough stories about women being dragged into the woods.

'Nearly there,' he says. 'You've no idea?' She shakes her head. The tunnel of branches seems never-ending. She puts her wrist to her nose, smelling her perfume.

Then, as if out of nowhere, the road opens out. A wide entrance of three Greek archways appears on the right.

'You know where we are now?'

She shakes her head.

'Russborough House . . . where the robbery was in the eighties.'

'Oh, yes.' She nods, though she hasn't a clue.

'They open the place once a year and put on a dinner.' The car slips beneath the main archway; gravel crunches underneath the tyres. Glittering light from the Palladian mansion travels across the large parkland. Joan inhales.

'Well, Pat, you're a man of many surprises.'

The house is something else. Chippendale this, Louis the Fourteenth that. No wonder the IRA were mad to get their hands on some of the loot. Joan keeps her elbows in tight as they walk from room to room. Imagine folks living like this. Gold on everything, and the hardwood floors are to die for.

Down in the basement, a girl takes their coats and serves them a glass of mulled wine.

'Thank you . . . Jesus, not too much, I'll be on my ear,' Joan says, though she doesn't move her hand as the girl continues to pour. 'Isn't this wonderfully Christmassy. You're very good, Pat.'

He grins. His cheeks are pink from coming in out of the cold. His ears the same.

'I thought you might like to try something new. There's not a speck of dust in this place, Joan.'

'I know. Nearly as good as my home.'

'Nearly?'

'Not quite,' she jokes.

A woman plays on one of the Steinway pianos in the drawing room. Sitting beside Pat, Joan closes her eyes and listens. She has no idea who it is. Mozart, Beethoven or somebody. She can't ask Pat. He might think her stupid.

His leg touches hers. She can feel the heat of his thigh and she's surprised that she doesn't mind it. It doesn't feel pushy or like he's trying something funny. In fact, it is almost comforting.

Jack wouldn't have been seen dead in a place like this. A holiday in Spain once a year was about as much as they did together; she'd drag him through the souvenir shops of Benidorm.

She opens her eyes, gazing at a portrait of a red-haired boy above the fireplace. He's the head of Trevor – not the Trevor of now but the Trevor pre-Lucy Quirke. It was only a few weeks after that yolk stayed over for the disco that he came home from school and started hammering on about joining a gym.

'You're too young for all that,' she'd replied.

'Ah, leave him be, Joan,' Jack had said.

'Mr Muscles, eh?' Siobhan had laughed. 'Trying to impress the ladies?'

★

What would Trevor think of Pat's efforts this evening? She feels guilty – 'Pat and his broken tooth' – as if that's all he is. She can be awful when she wants to be. It's too easy to be cynical.

She glances at Pat. What had he been doing all those years, caring for his mother? Heading into the library each week to get her Mills & Boon, picking up a few biographies and history books for himself? Staying up and reading a few pages after she'd fallen asleep and stopped pestering him?

She feels a strange glow of pride on his arm, going from room to room. The tour guides are wonderful. They answer all the questions he asks about the paintings and bits of furniture. She doesn't understand half of what they're saying, Lord this and King that, but it's nice to listen to someone who does.

The restaurant is lit with candles. There is a soft murmur of voices from the tables around them. Joan is delighted to see her name written on a card at her place setting.

'White or red?' Pat asks her, opening the menu. 'I'm driving but you tip away.'

'Goodness, no. Three glasses and I'm in bits. Trevor calls me a lightweight.'

'Have one more glass. That'll only be two.'

She smiles.

'Why not?' There are butterflies in her stomach. What is she like? You'd think she was sixteen again. Jack was never one for going to fancy restaurants. They'd sometimes go for a bite to eat in Coman's or Howards Way (getting the two-course fifty-euro special with a bottle of wine) on a Thursday evening. In all fairness, Jack was right; it was good food without costing an arm and a leg.

Vegetable soup was the starter, with melt-in-your-mouth soda bread and room-temperature salted butter.

'Would you not try the goat's cheese?' Pat asks her, scooping up the crumbling white stuff on his fork with a bit of rocket and pastry.

'It's a bit heavy for me,' she says, taking a large mouthful of wine. Is she actually nervous? She can't even remember the last time she was.

'You've been a good bit to Dubai?'

'I have,' Joan replies, appreciating the effort Pat is making with the conversation. She keeps on trying to think of things to ask him, but somehow or another his mother always seems to be at the centre of them. 'Some people love it. I'm not sure I could stick it for long.'

'It wouldn't be the place for me,' Pat says. 'I've a fondness for trees.'

'It's not perfect, but then, where is?' Joan takes another sip of her wine, flagging the waitress and getting another glass.

The couple at the table on the far wall laugh loudly. Next to them, a white wine bottle is upside down in a silver bucket. Joan gazes at the tealight in the frosted glass. Her cheeks have that pleasant warmth.

'This is wonderful, Pat. I know I've said it already. I can't even recall the last time I dressed up for an evening.'

Glowing. The only way to describe Pat's face.

'Hopefully, we'll do it again,' he says.

'Yes. As long as I've *Corrie* on record.' When was the last time she laughed this much? Probably some story from Trevor about a young one he was seeing. She'd be slapping his arm and calling him a gurrier.

'Any more wine?' The waitress has a lovely smile, the freckled face of a teenager.

'No, just a coffee after dessert,' Joan says. 'No, Pat, I couldn't have a drop more.' Normally, a man cajoling her to drink would be very off-putting. But there is an innocence about Pat, like he's working on the logic that giving her more of everything will make her happier, which is oddly endearing.

Crème brûlée – she'll be as fat as a house. On with the trainers in the morning. Maybe Maggs will walk as far as the canal with her.

'It's a beautiful spread they have on.'

'Top notch,' Pat says.

'It must've cost you.'

'Don't worry about that.'

'I couldn't leave you with the expense of it.'

'Don't be silly. No . . . no. I won't hear another word.'

'You're a terrible man,' she scolds him. He smiles and she thinks, for a second, she sees a hint of the young man underneath the lines. Something in his eyes perhaps.

'That was a wonderful evening,' she says as she gets out of the car, wrapping her coat tight. How many times has she said 'wonderful' tonight?

'My pleasure, Joan.' Pat gets out of the car. She protests.

'It's bitter. Keep yourself warm. Can you believe it actually snowed?'

'I'll see you to the door.'

'Honestly, I'm OK.' However, as she speaks, she slips a little on the beginnings of ice.

'Here.' He comes around the car and gives her his arm. Opening the gate, they walk up the path.

'My peonies will be ruined,' she sighs, looking at the flowerpots. 'They should've been stored a month ago.'

'I'll give you a hand with them one day, if you like.'

'You're very good.'

The doorstep. She fumbles for her keys. Is that her breath fogging? She can't feel her feet but maybe that's the wine.

'My fingers are numb,' she says, trying to get the key in the lock. He laughs, as if a bit nervous. He rubs his hands together.

The key slides in. She glances at him hovering. He isn't thinking about coming in, is he? Well, there'll be none of that.

The car engine is still running. No, he isn't presumptuous. The front door clicks open and she's about to step inside but turns back towards him. He remains uncertain, like a boy in those teen movies when she was growing up. She leans in a little. No harm with a bit of encouragement.

Trevor had mocked her, wondering if her lip would be cut by the chip in Pat's tooth. No, though he is nervous, a bit shaky with his lips and hands, it's a kiss that wouldn't shame any self-respecting man.

It's a brief kiss. His hands stay on her shoulders and arms. He steps back, embarrassed.

'I'll say goodnight to you, Joan.'

'Night, Pat. And thanks again.' Joan glances across the fence. All the lights are off next door. The net curtains are still. She feels fuzzy.

'I'll text you in the morning.'

The gate creaks as it opens. Some oil is needed. Pat salutes as he sits into the car and she waves back.

Joan closes the door. Beams of light, as the car turns, travel across the hallway ceiling. She smiles, flicking the switch. She'll bring a glass of water to bed and hopefully she'll be OK for the morning. Really, she's worse than a schoolgirl. She shakes her head, putting her coat on to the hook. Taking off her shoes and catching them in her right hand, she stops in front of the hallway mirror.

A middle-aged woman. Auburn hair. Good cleavage. A bit of a belly – the ten pounds she's always trying to lose. Good skin, well, a few wrinkles but she still has a bit of a glow in her cheeks.

Funny how she can look like this and feel like she did back in the eighties. Time is a funny thing.

The tragedy of old age is not that one is old, but that one is young.

Siobhan had given her tickets to that Oscar Wilde play one Christmas. She enjoyed it overall but that one line stayed with her, the horrible shock that it was.

Pat's kiss. When was the last time she'd been kissed like that? A real romantic, film-type of kiss? Jack gave her kisses when he came in from work and they did do the deed here and there. But romance – that'd been a while.

She smiles again. She can't help herself grinning. To have a man chasing her, giving her attention. Ask her only half a day ago, and she'd have said she wanted nothing to do with romance. However, now her lot are all grown up, why not? She's only herself to please. It is no one else's business. The tooth could be fixed easy enough.

Her phone. It must be in her bedroom where she took the bits out of her handbag and put them into her clutch. Stopping on the stairs, she straightens a print of Fota House. Are there fingerprints on the glass? Somewhere in the back of her mind, she can hear Trevor's boots clattering as he rushes down, him touching off the picture, then the front door slamming. The print is faded now – not surprising as it had hung in Daddy's house for decades. Nothing like the gold-leaf frames in Russborough.

What a house. Joan is slow climbing each step. The money those type of people have is scandalous. All the people the family knew: Churchill, film stars and aristocrats. It's like the same few people have always ruled the world, living outside recessions and God knows what else, while everyone else goes along with the status quo.

Her phone is plugged in on the bedside locker. And there she was, always scolding Trevor for leaving his iPhone charger in the socket, saying he'd burn the house down. She opens the wardrobe and puts her shoes neatly back in the box, placing the tissue paper carefully around them.

She pauses as a thought crosses her mind. Pat. He can't still be a virgin, can he? She swallows. For a moment, she's not quite sure how she feels about this. If they were ever to,

306

you know, would she have to guide him? Would it be the sort of disappointing encounter that she and Jack had that first time?

No. It doesn't matter if Pat is or not. What he doesn't know, he'll learn. And, as she recalls how she looked in the hallway mirror, she's glad it's unlikely there is a string of women to be compared against.

Sitting on the bed, she lifts her phone and unplugs the lead. She turns on the bedside lamp, puts on her glasses and unlocks the screen.

Seven missed calls from Siobhan, five from Trevor, and a rake of texts.

Siobhan doesn't answer. The phone isn't even ringing. No luck with Trevor's phone either. What the hell is going on? Joan reads the messages again.

Hi Mam, call me when you get this. Urgent. Trev.
Mam, ring me. Sio xx
Where are you? REALLY need you to call.

Why don't they say what's wrong? That's Trevor, no doubt, not wanting to worry her. What could've happened? Not a crash. Those eighteen lanes of traffic. Please don't let Rocco or Milo have run out on to a road.

She tries Siobhan's phone again. Nothing. Trevor's. Zilch. There's no other option but to ring Martin, a prospect she doesn't fancy. She can't remember the last time she rang him specifically, probably the hour after Milo was born. Does she even have his correct number?

Scrolling down her contacts. *Martin – Siobhan.* It rings though. She sighs with relief. Thank God someone has their phone on and can tell her what the hell is going on.

'Hi, this is Martin Cusack's phone. I can't take your call right now, but if you leave your number . . .' All hint of the Cavan accent is eradicated from his voice. Joan hangs up and dials again, only to ring out to voicemail a second time. She rings a third, then a fourth time.

Finally, on the fifth attempt, the phone is answered.

'Hi, Joan.' She can hear noise in the background. Where is he? In a bar?

'Hi, Martin. I've missed calls from Siobhan and Trev but I'm having no luck getting through. Have you heard anything?'

'Joan—' Martin breaks off. What's that song going on behind him? Westlife or something. His silence begins to frighten her.

'Talk to me. What's happened? Not the boys?' Her voice grows progressively higher.

'No. They're not hurt.'

'So, you've heard?'

Silence. More Westlife.

'Yes. They are not answering because they're on a plane.'

'A plane? Where?' Her head is foggy, her eyes dry. Why did she have that extra glass of wine?

'Back to Ireland.'

'What's happened? There's not been an accident?' She knows she's asked already but Martin's voice is so odd.

'There's nothing wrong with the boys, or Siobhan, or Trevor.'

'What is it then?' Joan frowns. 'Are you out? Have you

been drinking? Martin ... Martin ... what's wrong? Tell me.'

Silence. Will he ever start talking? Is that the clink of a glass? Surely he isn't drinking when something serious is kicking off.

'Martin, will you ever tell me what the hell is going on?'

A strange noise comes down the phone and then she realizes.

'What did you do?'

Nothing.

'She's left you, hasn't she?'

Another long pause.

'What do you think?'

The sick feeling grows stronger. Joan would love to ask who the girl is. She wishes now she'd told Siobhan, after she'd found those text messages, to get rid of Martin once and for all.

'Can you at least tell me what flight they're on.'

'I don't know. They were all leaving this evening.' Joan can see him sitting on a bar stool, shrugging his shoulders, taking a swig of an overpriced brandy. Doesn't he care about his own children? The vows he made to his wife?

'Sort this out, Martin. Be a man.'

'Look, Joan, I've got to go. I'm sorry. Sorry.'

'Don't you hang up on me. Martin—'

But he's gone. She tries to call back but the phone has been switched off.

The grandfather clock in the hallway chimes. Joan stands, walks to the window, walks back from the window, sits on the bed by her bag, then walks back to the window. She peeks out of the blinds. The street is quiet, Pat's car long gone. For a second, she is tempted to ring him – anything for a bit of comfort. But no. She knows exactly how he will respond. He'll start minding her and the thought of this irritates. She doesn't want to be coddled. She's a grown woman. She wants to sort things but how can she, when she doesn't even know what exactly is going on?

Directory enquiries give her the details for Dublin airport. She dials the number and after fifteen minutes of wrangling on the phone with customer service, she realizes she's getting nowhere. They won't give her passenger details for flights and she doesn't even know what plane they'll be on. 'It's an emergency,' she keeps on saying, but they keep asking her what the crisis is. What can she say? 'My son-in-law is a cheat. Call out the national guard.'

There are no flights till six a.m. What can she do but go to the airport at five or so and wait? She sips the glass of water on the nightstand, feeling the cool liquid flow out from her chest and stomach. After a few moments, the dryness in her eyes begins to dissipate.

Time to change into something practical. She lifts a pair of jeans and a grey gilet out of the press. Her cocktail dress sits on the handle of the wardrobe door, ready to go to the dry cleaner's and, as she sits back down on the bed, it reminds her of her evening, the new possibilities that had been emerging, which now seem snatched away. Surely, there is no way in heaven or hell that mild-mannered Pat will be able to handle all this chaos?

She leans against the pillows but keeps rearranging them.

No chance of sleep tonight. She checks that her phone's ring is as loud as possible and places it on her lap. This time tomorrow, her house will be full with the shouts of the boys and Siobhan climbing the walls, trying to figure out what to do next. And Trevor. Lord knows how he'll be able to cope with this sort of drama.

What on earth can she even say to Siobhan? A tiny, tiny bit of her wants to shout, 'Stop being melodramatic. Get back to Dubai and talk to your husband, if for no other sake than the boys.' But that's just the part that feels worn out, that's tired of always being 'the strong one'. In reality, she'll never ever say those words.

Bottom line is that her kids are her kids. Her grandkids are her grandkids. It is their job to make mistakes and hers to love them either way. It could be worse – one of them could be hurt or dead even. As long as they are alive, anything can be dealt with. She'll have to stick it out for now and try to keep her head above water.

Head above water. A wrong choice of words. She glances down at her phone, thinking that the next time it rings, her life will be changed for good. Closing her eyes, she says a prayer, not to God, but to her dead husband. 'Jack – I could do with you now. What should I do? What the hell should I do?' Of course, there's no answer but silence.

Gete

The RTA slips out of the driveway and Gete watches it glide up the smooth tarmac road. Ma'am gives a wave from inside and Gete raises her hand.

It vanishes around the corner. Gete turns, feeling the sun's rays on her cheeks. But they don't give much warmth. It's getting cooler in the evenings now winter approaches. What does all this mean? The trouble with the police, and now Ma'am is flying away. She said it was only for a short time – that they'd be back. But why give her the money if so? They must not be coming back soon.

Gete stares at the double garage with the unused balcony on top, the green lawn that looks like grass but is some other kind of plant – like millions of small cacti – the full-grown palm tree by the dark-wood front door, and the bluish windows that keep most of the hard sunlight out. How clean it all looks, unlived in and not quite real.

So different to the Addis Ababa she knew: dirt, beeping cars, people everywhere, broken windows, cracked pavements, men haggling with vendors, prostitutes, drug dealers, roads that were little more than broken stone and clay.

Could she go back and be happy in her old world, now that she has experienced something quieter, calmer . . . richer? Yes, Milo and Rocco make lots of noise but nothing to the bustling crowds in Addis Ababa – a city not big enough to house them all. Or back in the countryside where Baba and the others toiled outside, praying for machinery like the investors in the neighbouring farms, with their square fields and advanced irrigation.

She has grown used to a solid silent roof over her head. She likes the hot water that comes out of the taps. How would it be to live again in the village where rain hammered on the corrugated roofs? Or Addis Ababa with its cramped houses? Would she find herself caught between two worlds, unhappy in either?

She doesn't mind working long hours; she'd worked just as hard back home, spending mornings with Lemuel in the fields. Then, in the afternoon, cooking, carrying water and cleaning with Mama. Her bed, after all those labours, was a thin mat which, no matter how she moved, would cause her back to ache if she stayed in one position too long. It'd all seemed enough then, but would it be now?

Poor Lemuel out in the fields; she is reminded of the pain that formed in the centre of her back, right in the spine, after a day of sowing corn. By comparison, lifting Milo, scolding Rocco, ironing while listening to the radio, hoovering and washing don't seem so bad.

Even last year, when Ma'am had gone home suddenly, and she'd stayed with Rocco and Milo alone, it'd been easy. There'd been an accident with her brother, and Ma'am looked awkward as she gave her instructions of what to do while she was away. 'The money is in the drawer and you have the card if you need it.' Milo had cried for his mama but he'd been soothed with hugs and sweet things. And Ma'am had even given her an extra bonus that month and said she'd be 'lost without her'.

There are voices on the breeze. She turns again. The children playing outside number fifty-one start screaming as the sprinklers come on. Jenny, a maid she has spoken to a couple of times, comes out and shoos them in.

'How are you, my friend?' She waves. She has a happy face.

'I am good,' Gete calls back. Should she say to Jenny what has happened? Maybe Jenny might come sit with her when the children have gone to bed.

No. Jenny might tell her Ma'am and then anything could happen. Some of these ladies seem very nice but are no good. They smile in public but when doors are closed they do terrible things. Poor Zulfa looked very ill during the week. It is frightening. You land in a strange country and you are given a family that might be nice, but might also be bad. It is all a gamble.

Gete steps inside the villa, not wanting to bring more attention to herself. One of Rocco's jumpers is hanging on the balustrade; she picks it up and begins to fold it, thinking she should put it in his chest of drawers.

She looks at the row of bikes beside the stairs. If Ma'am doesn't come back, she could bring them home. Her young cousins would love these. Yet, what roads or pavements could they cycle them on? They were all broken up and busy with traffic. And how could she even bring them in her luggage?

Silence. She looks up at the skylight. Navy sky. No stars, of course. There are none in Dubai. All of the light from the buildings stop them. Back home, a little way up the hills south of their home, she and Lemuel would lie on the grass and he would point out the constellations that he knew. 'Always look for the North Star,' he said. 'You can always find your way home from there.'

She sighs for her young self, the girl of fourteen who knew little of life beyond the village and nothing of the journey that lay before her. Who'd never been on a plane but had only watched them overhead. Who was good at maths, the best in school, but had no choice but to stop studying in Year Eight like all the other girls. How glum she had felt then on her final day. How she had wondered if anything exciting or different would happen in her life.

Here she is now, behind high white walls with electricity in every room. Fridges. Televisions. Computers. Toys. And more toys. How strange, for this night, one night, she will be Ma'am of a Dubai villa. She could, if she wanted, watch television for the rest of the evening in the big room, eat all the sweet food from the top cupboard, and not worry about Ma'am coming home. She might even try some beer, if there is any left. Even Jesus turned water into wine.

Maybe, if she feels very bold, she might go and lie on the silky duvet upstairs. Even for ten minutes. The mattress seems so soft when she changes the sheets, her fingertips sinking into the foam.

She goes to the kitchen and cleans the pots that are left scattered across the countertops. Pasta and peas for the boys. Chicken Kievs, new potatoes and frozen veg for the adults.

'Something to keep us going. You know what food in economy is like,' Ma'am said.

Ma'am's brother ate his dinner in what seemed like three mouthfuls. Ma'am ate the meat and vegetables, leaving the potatoes. 'You don't mind looking after the plates?' Ma'am said, getting up from the table and putting her dish in the sink. 'Trev and I better get back to packing.'

'Yes, Ma'am.'

Milo's sticky little hands. She will miss him. If they don't come back, will he remember her for very long? If she saw him in a year's time, would he step backwards and look for Ma'am's leg, suspicious of this 'strange' lady?

And young Rocco. Time away from Dubai might do him good. Too many presents and toys. Too many computer games. He needs to be outside in fields, playing with other boys, and not given so much attention.

She is to blame. She hadn't the heart to tell them when they were being bad. Ma'am always told her to be firm, but what did that mean? Did that mean hit them, as Baba smacked Lemuel? What else could she do?

The house is clean. It didn't take long; putting toys away was easy without two boys pulling things back out. All the clothes that Ma'am has left behind: sparkly dresses – forty or fifty of them – jeans made of the softest denim, and tops of shimmering silk. She hangs them neatly, wondering if it would be wrong to try one on.

Maybe Ma'am will be back in a few days. Perhaps she will call in a week or two and ask for them to be shipped to Dublin. Maybe she will buy all new things. How little toys and

clothes matter in the end. As Baba said, 'Easier for a camel to
get through the eye of a needle than for a rich man to get
into heaven.'

The washing machine echoes into her room. Gete closes her
laptop, having no luck contacting Aunt Candace. She turns on
her small television; she could go back to the main room, but
she tried sitting on the couch and found herself glancing sideways every few minutes, waiting for the front door to open.

The house is too big when she is alone in it. She tries not
to think about all the windows. So many ways for people to
spy on her. What would happen if a man found a way in?
Who would rescue her? How long before someone would
know if she was dead or gone?

The sound from the television is comforting. It doesn't
have all the channels that the big set in the main room has,
but she is used to these few stations. The death of the Emirate girl is still on the news. Who knows what the truth is
behind such things.

Gete glances sideways, leans over and closes the blind. It
is not safe for women alone. She looks at her bedroom door,
wondering if the key for it is in one of Ma'am's bedside tables.

What if the police come again? Her throat feels tight.
What would she be able to say to them? Would they arrest
her for helping Ma'am to leave? Would they ask her about
Martin? She had heard Ma'am shouting at him on the phone.

Or what if someone arrives, maybe the landlord or a person they owe money to, and she will be the one in trouble?
There are so many terrible stories of young women thrown
into jail when they have done nothing.

She must leave this house tomorrow, before trouble finds her. But where to go? Could she call Danish? He – Gete frowns – has his future wife back home. Of course, she could call the minister, if only she knew his number. Poor Zulfa would be no good. Her Ma'am is very strict and the men in the house are very unkind.

Gete lifts out a purse, shaking all of her money on the bed. She opens Siobhan's envelope. It comes close to sixteen hundred dirhams. The rest of her money has already gone back to Ethiopia, some to pay what she owes to the agency, some to her family, and a tiny amount in savings.

Sixteen hundred dirhams. Back home, a lot. Here, not enough to go anywhere. And how much more money will she owe the agency if she breaks her contract? She would have to go to them, beg them for mercy and to let her go home. What would they do? Put her with another family? A family who could take her phone and laptop away? Who might choose not to pay her?

What can she do, a maid in a land where maids have no say about anything? Reliant on the goodness of others. Where she has to say 'Yes, Ma'am' to everything, even if they are cruel, and hope, just hope, they will pay her.

Gete sits up, eyes wide, feeling queasy. She touches the purse under her pillow. Her money is still there. But her passport. The agency has her passport. She'd lain in bed, wondering if she could sell a few small things from the villa. She could buy a flight home. If the things were abandoned, it wouldn't be stealing, would it?

However, without a passport, there is nothing she can do.

No amount of money could send her home. It'd been taken the day she'd landed in Dubai: by a smart-looking woman with a clipboard.

Fear tightens her chest. Gete stands, turning off the television, slightly wobbly, and opens her bedroom door. The washing machine is finished and the house is deathly silent. Moonlight travels down through the skylight.

Alone. She is very alone. Thousands and thousands of miles from family. Please, loving God, protect her through this time. Give her some hope. A Bible verse comes to mind:

The Lord is my shepherd; I shall not want. He makes me lie down in green pastures. He leads me beside still waters. He restores my soul. He leads me in paths of righteousness for His name's sake. Even though I walk through the valley of the shadow of death, I will fear no evil, for You are with me; Your rod and Your staff, they comfort me.

Walking through the dim sitting room, she recites the Psalm again and again. Outside, the moon glistens on the swimming pool. She imagines falling under the surface, thrashing, gasping for air but her lungs filling with water.

Her hand makes a few attempts to turn on the kitchen light. The brightness makes her jump. What will happen to her? Does she know any maid, taxi driver or builder whose life has changed for the better after being here? When things go wrong, they are always the first to suffer.

Why had she said yes?

Bit by bit things will stop working. The internet. The electricity. The water. Soon, someone will scoop all the toys and furniture into a skip and bury them somewhere out in the desert to rot. Where will that leave her?

★

The glass of water is nearly gone. She could turn on the television, but what is the point when she won't be able to concentrate on the words? Her phone sits on her lap, but no matter how much she looks at it and wills for something to happen, nothing does. Every hour that passes, the chance that Aunt Candace will contact her diminishes.

She's in trouble and there is nothing she or her family can do about it. Until she has her passport, she is at the mercy of others. It is better to simply accept it. Didn't Christ say, *'Happy are the meek, for they will inherit the Kingdom of Heaven.'*

God will keep her safe. She will read her Bible. She will pray in private, even if a new family does not want non-Muslims in the house. Her contract will be up eventually. They can't keep her trapped in Dubai forever.

More prayers. She hopes God forgives her for talking to Him so much in these bad times and not as much when times are better. But what else can she do?

The doorbell. She opens her eyes, uncrossing her palms. How long has she been sitting? Her heart thunders as she tries to think who it could be: the taxi man after coming back, knowing she is alone? Ma'am's husband? The police?

'Who is it?' she calls out. No response. Maybe they can't hear her.

She gets off the couch, her bare feet silent on the hallway tiles. Sliding the bronze cap, she looks through the peephole. It's dark outside and she can't make out the figure. Should she turn on the light, risk exposing herself?

What choice does she have? She flicks the switch and takes another look, recognizing the ginger hair. It's Ma'am's brother and he is alone. Her hand rests on the latch, unsure of what to do.

The bell rings again.

'Gete, are you inside?' His voice is muffled by the wooden door.

'One moment, sir.' She slides back the latch and pushes down the handle. The door swings in. She takes small steps back until she hits the hall table.

'Thanks.' He steps into the hallway. His face is red as if he's out of breath from running. There is a damp triangle in the middle of his T-shirt.

'Is Ma'am OK? Did she forget something?' Gete asks. Thank goodness she didn't take anything. What would he say now if she was wearing one of Ma'am's dresses?

'Siobhan is fine. She's at the airport with the boys.' He glances down at his watch.

'You do not go?' Gete tries to remain calm, more aware by the moment that she is alone in a house with a white man she doesn't really know.

'No. I . . . I didn't want . . .'

Gete stares at him, not sure what he is trying to say. She pushes her thumbnails into her index fingers, trying to distract herself from the sickening feeling. He can't settle, scratching at his nose. Finally, he stands up straight.

'It wasn't right.'

'What you mean, sir?'

He shakes his head.

'Seriously, no need to be sir-ing me. What I mean to say is, it was all wrong.'

'But . . .'

'After how good you were with Milo and Rocco when I had my accident. I know what's right and wrong.' He says the last few words with a certain emotion.

'That is my job, sir.'

He steps forward and she steps back instinctively. The vase on the table wobbles.

'Jesus, Gete.' He shakes his head.

'I am fine, sir. You do not need to worry.'

'And tomorrow?' he asks.

'But . . .' She cannot think of an answer.

'But nothing. In the morning, I'll ring the agency and see what can be done. We all watch out for each other. If you knew my mother . . .' He pauses a moment and sighs. 'Anyway, I'm gonna crash. I'm absolutely wrecked.'

Gete, relieved as he turns away, watches the strange muscled man go up the stairs, two steps at a time. She thinks about calling to him, 'What about Ma'am? Did she know you came back?' but really that was none of her business.

Epilogue

'Milo, get down.' Siobhan pulls his foot, as Milo tries to climb up the side of the television unit to get his dinosaur. Mam must've put it there when she was hoovering.

'You're blocking the telly,' Rocco shouts, his head lifting off Siobhan's shoulder and twisting left and right, trying to see the screen. Milo slips down at his brother's voice and Siobhan smiles, thinking how Milo pays no attention to her but would rob a bank for Rocco.

The sound of a key in the front door echoes in from the hallway.

'He's back,' Siobhan says, looking at the two boys with an excited smile. The sitting room door opens and Trevor walks in with two plastic bags.

'Come here to me, young fella.' Trevor drops the bags, crouches down and opens his arms. Milo runs straight into them and Trevor tickles him, so Milo is squealing and wriggling. 'They didn't have chips so I got cabbage instead.' Trevor continues to tickle him.

'No, you didn't,' Rocco says. 'You're lying.'

'Liar, liar,' Milo roars through the screams and giggles.

'Easy, Trev. He'll be as sick as a dog,' Siobhan calls.

Trevor lets Milo go and Milo begins to look in the bags.

'Did you get ice cream for after?' Rocco asks.

Trevor rolls his eyes but stays grinning. 'Course there's ice cream.' He pauses and pulls out a rolled-up magazine from the top of one of the bags. He tosses it over to Siobhan.

'Look at that.'

Siobhan glances down at the cover.

'Oh my God.' There is the film star, hanging from the side of the Burj Khalifa.

'It's in the cinema next week,' Trevor says.

'Can we go, Mam?' Rocco asks. Rocco still loves anything about Dubai. When they first got back he was always talking about it, till Siobhan told him he'd have to stop living in the past and get settled in here. Trevor had tried to get him into one of the sports clubs in Terenure but he had no interest. However, there are a couple of lads in the estate who Rocco gets on OK with, and he goes over to theirs to play PlayStation after school.

'You can take them, Trev,' Siobhan says. 'I think I need another decade before I can face it.'

Trevor opens the brown bags of takeout, handing Milo his nuggets and chips, Rocco his cheeseburger and fries with extra tomato ketchup, and finally Siobhan gets her battered sausage with chips and loads of vinegar.

'What did you get yourself?' Siobhan asks.

Trevor lifts up a tinfoil packet along with a Coke Zero.

'A burrito? Ah, for fuck sake,' she laughs. 'I bet you didn't even get cheese in it.'

'Macros,' Trev says.

'That bloody course has made you paranoid. You sure you won't have a glass?' A bottle of red wine sits on the coffee table with a half-full glass beside it.

'I'm grand with this.' His long-sleeved T-shirt can barely

hold his biceps. Each weekend he returns home from Limerick and it's like they've grown another inch. At least he isn't half so moody. Only last week, she'd said to Mam, 'Maybe if he'd done the degree straight after school, we might've saved a lot of heartaches,' but Mam replied, 'Could you imagine him five years ago with thirty kids, running around a pitch? Not a hope.'

Siobhan picks through the chips, looking for the small crispy bits. If she only eats them and leaves the fat potato-y ones, she'll cut down on a load of calories. She can't be dealing with skinny Claire in the shop, eating salad all the time and telling everyone about her workouts when they are on break.

Mam couldn't believe it last March when she went out and got her old job back in Vodafone. She'd replied she was hardly going to sit at home moping while Martin sorted things out. Granted, Martin does transfer cash from London but she spends all of it on the boys (and some money for Mam for their keep). She'll be damned before she buys anything she wants with it. No, she'll earn her own money. Fuck him. Mam said no more about her job, but since then she's volunteered to look after Rocco and Milo most Friday evenings.

'Any word from Mam?' Trevor asks, swigging back his Coke, his legs hanging over the arms of the other sofa.

'No texts with "hisses" yet. Pat must've taken her somewhere fancy.'

'Or maybe just back to his.' Trevor pulls a face.

'Would you stop.' She takes a sip of her wine.

'At least he got that tooth fixed. Good man, Milo.'

When he was introduced to Pat, the first thing Milo had said was, 'Where's your tooth? You've got a big hole.' There had been an awkward pause but then Pat laughed and they all joined in. The tooth had been capped within the week and, now that it's actually done, he isn't a bad-looking man.

Mam had declared she'd give up Pat, that it was only a bit of nonsense, when Siobhan and the boys had first returned from Dubai.

'No, you won't . . . Mam . . . listen to me . . . God . . . will you ever listen to me . . . There's enough crap going on right now without you being miserable too. If you like him, see him. We'll all be fine. You keep doing what you were doing.'

Milo is staring at his chips despondently.

'You don't have to eat them all, love. Just eat what you can.' Milo nods, happy to have the decision made for him. 'Trev, will you get him a tissue to wipe his hands. Bring in the roll from the kitchen.'

Trevor nods and leaves the room. The three watch a singer butcher a Celine Dion song. The judges are going to tear the poor girl a new one. Rocco tucks his head into her arm; he can't stomach people making fools of themselves.

'Here, Milo, now wipe your face too, not just your fingers.' Trevor appears and tears off a square of kitchen paper. He hands the roll to Siobhan and glances at the television. 'Jesus, she's brutal.'

'How was your burrito?'

'Grand.'

Siobhan watches Trevor, whose eyes remain glued to the screen. Milo has followed him back to the couch and has plonked himself on top of Trevor's stomach and chest. Maybe it's the second glass of wine, but Siobhan feels her eyes growing wet. Thank God the boys have Trevor. Martin only sees them once a week on Skype.

Claire in the shop said Trevor was gone different. 'He's very serious.' Though Claire was wrong. He is less erratic. She could've killed him for abandoning her and the boys at the airport but now, a year later, she's over it.

She did feel bad that she'd left poor Gete like that, especially when Gete had been so good with Rocco and Milo. Quite often, when she recalls last year, she feels a queasiness in her stomach. She thinks about Mam, about them all 'looking out for each other'; if she hadn't been scared shitless, maybe she'd have done things different.

Who knows what has happened to all their things in Dubai. Probably in landfill. It hurts to think of the villa, the cool air-conditioned atmosphere that greeted her when she opened the front door. It's painful to remember waking in the king-size bed and gazing out at the rising sun. Funny, she thought it'd be the dresses she'd miss, but she's forgotten half of what she once owned. What she misses most is the feeling, the exhilarating sense that anything was possible, that life was getting better for them all.

After she got back, she looked at all the articles from newspapers that were blocked in Dubai, and the YouTube videos of the prisons and the police, if only to remind herself she had done the right thing to leave. What'd really happened to that girl? Would anyone ever really know?

Her phone beeps. It's Martin. *Transferred the money there.*

K. That's enough for him. She sighs and stuffs her phone

back in her cardigan. She glances over at Trevor, who is also on his phone.

'Anyone you fancy?'

'What?'

'Tinder?'

'When would I have the time? I've a bloody anatomy exam Monday. I shouldn't even be watching this.' Trevor gestures at the television. Milo nuzzles in closer to him.

The main judge is relishing his put-downs of the poor young one with her Celine Dion rendition. Celine Dion – every fool knows not to do one of her songs. Still, it's nearly impossible to watch him being so mean.

Siobhan picks up the magazine that Trevor dropped and looks at the cover again. The film star's eyes are sparkling blue, his teeth a gleaming white. Behind, the cylinders of glass and metal rise up. It's still the tallest building in the world. She thinks about the times she drank with Martin at the bar at the very top. Her stomach tightens and she puts the magazine face down, pushing it away with the tips of her fingers to the far end of the sofa.

The limousine smells of beeswax and lilies. The air-conditioning is refreshing on his face compared to the Dubai heat outside. Hanging from one of the hand grips above the door is the star's steamed charcoal jacket, to be put on just before his arrival.

'I wouldn't advise the light grey suit,' the stylist had warned. 'In case your deodorant fails. And no need for a tie. A crisp white shirt will be enough.'

Next to the star, an actress in a red strapless evening dress smiles as she sips a glass of Krug Clos d'Ambonnay – a gift from a member of the royal family.

'It's a beautiful dress,' he says.

'Isn't it wonderful?' She touches her earrings; pearl drops, like tears.

The privacy barrier in the limousine lowers. The driver smiles as he turns his head. 'We must wait here for a few moments. You, the guests of honour, must arrive last.'

The star nods. A smile. Patient as ever. The screen climbs up again. The star leans forward, looking out of the tinted glass. Both sides of the street are lined with barriers. Policemen in green-and-red uniforms direct people and traffic. Huge lights shine from the front of the cinema, searching the sky, like they used to do in old black-and-white movies.

How many premieres is this? Fifty? One hundred? Five hundred? They've all become a blur. Even so, the sense of possibility the film promises makes the skin on his arms tingle. He's seen the posters where he hangs from a windowpane over one hundred floors up, and he can't quite believe that was actually him a little over a year ago.

Some way in front, less important celebrities arrive. A few flashbulbs. Security guards and bollards hold back rows of fans. A television crew stops a young singer; she gushes with excitement.

'Isn't it incredible that he did all the stunts himself?' the interviewer asks.

'I would be petrified.' The young woman laughs, touching the strap of her dress. 'Only yesterday, I was in the bar at the top. It was terrifying.'

The interviewer smiles, turning to greet the other stars arriving. Similar answers to the same question.

'A legend,' a golf champion says.

'I can't wait to watch the movie. I love the whole series,' says a reality television winner. 'What number film is this, three . . . four?'

'Careful, George,' a woman shouts as her son tries to squeeze through the security barrier. 'Gete, have you got his pen?'

'Yes, Ma'am.' Gete pushes backwards, trying to give the little boy as much space as possible. The people behind begin to complain. She smiles at George's enthusiasm. He's a good boy really. No interest in video games but, like all boys, a bit of a temper when he doesn't get his way. No doubt Baba would have a scripture to stop this behaviour.

'Whoever spares the rod hates their children, but the one who loves their children is careful to discipline them.'

All that chaos and fear a year ago. Ma'am had never returned; if her brother hadn't helped, what would've happened? It doesn't bear thinking about.

The email in the New Year:

Dear Gete,

Sorry that we had to leave in such a hurry. I hope you understand. I couldn't risk the safety of the boys. I'm delighted that Rebecca was able to give you work. I emailed her to say thanks but no word. Oh well.

I was furious with Trev when he got back. Abandoning us like that! But you know him. He has his ways. As stubborn as

330

his father. And in a way, I'm glad now that he did what he could. You were always one of the family.

They've charged that Pakistani man with that girl's death. I can't believe it. Martin is in London with his tail between his legs. He swore to me he had nothing to do with it and he doesn't think the Pakistani guy did either. He keeps saying it must've been an accident. 'You know how many people die in building sites out there?' he was saying. I told him to put his money where his mouth is and help the poor fella out with a solicitor or something, that it'd be a start to sorting this mess out. I keep thinking, that could've been us. Makes me sick to the stomach.

Christ, who knows where it'll all end? I'm forever asking Mam what I should do about Martin but she won't say a word. 'I'll support you no matter what,' she says, driving me mad. Don't you wish sometimes that someone would just sort your life?

Well, I better get back to the boys. All I can say is, thank God for family.

Keep in touch. Sio x

Gete didn't bother replying. What was the point?

George tugs on Gete's T-shirt. People surge forward as the limousine door opens. The movie star steps out, followed by a beautiful woman. The crowd roars and screams. Cameras flash. How can he smile and wave through all the chaos?

He walks the red carpet slowly, signing autographs, leaning in for people's selfies. Security guards peel away fingers, asking people to move back. And yet through it all, the smile remains perfect, unchanged, as if he knows a great secret about the world that no one else does.

The crowd squashes against Gete's back.

'Are you OK, George? Here he comes.' Rebecca is giddy like a child as the star approaches. Gete lifts George. Her shoulder niggles with pain, but it doesn't matter. The boy leans out over the barrier with his poster and pen.

'We love you,' Rebecca shouts, deafening Gete. The star takes the poster from George's hand and he whips the pen across the page. Rebecca takes picture after picture on her iPhone.

The poster is handed back. The star ruffles George's hair.

'Handsome,' he says, before his gaze moves to the next group of fans.

George turns around, eyes wide with excitement.

'Handsome, eh?' Rebecca smiles, as if seeing her son for the first time. She goes to touch his hair, but stops, as if trying to hold on to the moment.

Perhaps this is the peak of their lives: living in a sparkling city, richer than ever, spending spare afternoons greeting movie stars. Maybe, this time next year, Rebecca and Mike will return to Frith Hill in Surrey and give up the Dubai dream, while Gete will travel back to Addis Ababa and open up her business, using her slowly increasing savings. Who knows?

The city itself, only two decades old, might vanish just as quickly as it has appeared – a modern-day Atlantis. Anything is possible. Things begin. Things end. Empires come. Empires go. Nothing stays the same. But these are worries for another day. This is now, this is Dubai, and nothing else matters.

Acknowledgements

I'd like to thank:

The Arts Council of Ireland, Dublin City Council, Cork City Council and Culture Ireland for their financial support over the past decade.

Sky Academy and Ideas Tap for their mentorship in 2014.

Friends have been supportive of my work over many years: James H. Murphy, Ann Luttrell, Susan Stairs, Claire Coughlan, Teresa Daly, Orlene Denice McMahon Fournié, John Keane, Sean Carr, Gary Quane, Aidan Quigley, Jennifer Matthews, Noel O'Regan, Eibhear Walshe, Sarah Cassidy, Laura Feeney, Judith McAdam, Katie Singer, Maire Bradshaw, Fidelma Maye, Madeleine D'Arcy, Mary Morrissy, Evelyn Conlon and Maurice A. Lee.

My lecturers and supervisors from University College Dublin: Éilís Ní Dhuibhne, James Ryan, Paul Perry and Frank McGuinness.

My English teachers from Coláiste an Chraoibhín who instilled a deep love of the written word: Deirdre O'Connor and Niamh Breathnach.

My agent, Marianne Gunn O'Connor, for all her advice and encouragement over many years.

My editor and publisher, Fiona Murphy, as well as Sophie

Wilson and the wonderful teams in Transworld and Penguin Random House Ireland.

Friends in Kenmare who have made me feel welcome while I have edited this novel during the pandemic.

My siblings, Kelly, Beverly and Michael.

And John, for all the love.